Praise for *The Water Man's Daughter*

"[*The Water Man's Daughter*] is equal parts mystery, social commentary and political critique. . . . Important. . . . It is apparent that Ruby-Sachs knows, loves and has much to say about South Africa and the injustices she has witnessed there."

– *Winnipeg Free Press*

"[An] impressive debut. . . . Ruby-Sachs portrays her three female characters with deft precision, the subtle chemistry between them forming the basis for the novel's emotional and narrative arc. . . . The novel is a comment on post-Apartheid South Africa – where the murder of a white man still matters more than the murder of a black man – without resorting to didacticism. *The Water Man's Daughter* plays like a classic whodunit, but its true mystery involves how much we really know about others – especially those people we think we know best."

– *Quill & Quire*

"The story, set in post-apartheid South Africa, tears right along. The prose is good – sometimes powerful – and you want to root for the characters. . . . *The Water Man's Daughter* has great energy and shows a ton of promise."

– *NOW* magazine

"'Nomsulwa plays with bullets in the alleyway...' So begins this ambitious tale of murder, intrigue, and business-disguised-as-development set in post-apartheid South Africa. It is a striking image, and the storyline it launches plays all the way through."

– *The Rover*

Emma Ruby-Sachs

THE
WATER MAN'S
DAUGHTER

A Novel

Emblem

MCCLELLAND & STEWART

Emblem trade paperback with flaps edition published 2011
This Emblem edition published 2012

Emblem is an imprint of McClelland & Stewart,
a division of Random House of Canada Limited
Emblem and colophon are registered trademarks of McClelland & Stewart,
a division of Random House of Canada Limited

LIBRARY AND ARCHIVES CANADA CATALOGUING IN PUBLICATION

Ruby-Sachs, Emma
The water man's daughter : a novel / Emma Ruby-Sachs.

ISBN 978-0-7710-4771-8

I. Title.

PS8635.U298W38 2012   C813'.6   C2011-907966-6

We acknowledge the financial support of the Government of Canada through
the Canada Book Fund and that of the Government of Ontario through
the Ontario Media Development Corporation's Ontario Book Initiative. We
further acknowledge the support of the Canada Council for the Arts and the
Ontario Arts Council for our publishing program.

This is a work of fiction. Characters, corporations, institutions, and organiza-
tions are either products of this author's imagination or used fictitiously.

Published simultaneously in the United States of America by
McClelland & Stewart, a division of Random House of Canada Limited,
P.O. Box 1030, Plattsburgh, New York 12901

Library of Congress Control Number: 2011945922

Typeset in Caslon by M&S, Toronto
Printed and bound in Canada

McClelland & Stewart,
a division of Random House of Canada Limited
One Toronto Street
Toronto, Ontario
M5C 2V6
www.mcclelland.com

1   2   3   4   5   16   15   14   13   12

For my parents,
Harriet Sachs and Clayton Ruby

NOMSULWA PLAYS WITH BULLETS IN THE ALLEYWAY, next to her cousin. He is talking to one of his tsotsi friends, boys who strut in packs around the township pretending to be members of gangs they are too young to join. They stand above her, leaning against the uniform brown of the house next door. Their shoes leave scuff marks in the dirt at their feet. The sun, which will eventually creep into every corner, bouncing off the bright corrugated metal walls and roofs, has not yet reached where the boys stand. Nomsulwa can barely keep track of all the gold and silver pieces under the shadows.

"Why do you always have to bring her around?" one friend asks. Nomsulwa's cousin shrugs, but doesn't send her away.

"We can't do anything with her here. Mira, get rid of her."

"I can't," Mira answers. "My mom says I have to take care of her."

Nomsulwa looks up. Mira's mother never tells him to do anything. She is busy working and feeding half the neighbourhood, and Mira pretty much does what he wants. He never listens to Nomsulwa even though she's older than him. She continues playing in the dirt.

The boy next to Mira pulls a gun out of his pants and turns it on Nomsulwa. He cocks the hammer as if to shoot and then relaxes his arm. Nomsulwa watches him as he does this, sees how the head of the gun contains circles surrounded by more circles, huddled around a dark tunnel. She puts out her hand.

"Can I see that?"

The boy looks to Mira.

"It's okay, it's not loaded."

Mira nods and the boy hands the gun over. Nomsulwa feels its weight in her hands. They are small hands and the gun is a big gun. How does the boy point this at anything while keeping it steady? The metal on the handle is thicker than the head. It is silver and bumpy and some parts of the gun are cool even though it is very hot outside.

The boys begin arguing. There is a blast of dust as Mira pushes one of them against the wall and tugs him down into a headlock. Nomsulwa gets up and brings the gun out of the alley into the sunlight. She looks back and sees Mira bent now with his arm pulled behind his back. Across the street there is a dog curled into the curb. His hind legs fall at crooked angles. The bones announce themselves through the skin, a skeleton caked with brown fur. The muscles that may have once padded the dog's behind are gone. Patches near the belly and where the front legs fade into the chest are bare of fur. There is only brown skin, scabbed and seeping.

Nomsulwa cocks the gun just like she saw the boy do. She presses a dark black button above the fat circle where the bullets are kept. The chamber releases and reveals five

2
–

empty holes. She takes one of the bullets she had pocketed from the sandy ground, dusts it off on her pants, puts it in the very top hole, and clicks the chamber back into the middle of the gun. Nomsulwa knows the gun is loaded. She has seen this done before.

The dog lifts his head, eyes huge, mouth dripping. His tongue is pink – a healthy, beautiful pink. It hangs out of his mouth, just dabbling in the water collected in the crevices of the street. Nomsulwa checks on the boys behind her once more and then raises the gun and aims. The chamber clicks softly the first two times she pulls the trigger. The third time there is almost too much resistance against her fingers, and then a loud crack, like a thick balloon popping next to Nomsulwa's ear, sounds out of the gun. Her arm is thrown backwards. The boys run to where she stands.

"Amazing!" the boy who brought the gun exclaims. "That is so cool."

Nomsulwa smiles and looks at Mira, seeking approval.

"What did you do?" he asks.

The dog's body pushes backwards and it turns away from Nomsulwa, looking behind for the source of the noise. Its head sinks slowly, stopping bit by bit as it reaches sand. The tongue hits last, lapping at orange grain instead of brown water. The rib cage opens and closes, then is still.

"I think I broke my arm." Her hand still clutches the grip, but her forearm hangs at a strange angle.

Mira grabs the gun, throws it to the ground, and starts to drag her back into the shadows. A few mamas out on the street have stopped to look at the dog. They glare over at Mira, sucking their teeth. The older boy takes the gun from the sand and begins to run in the opposite direction. He runs fast, scared, but Nomsulwa doesn't see anyone move to follow him.

An old woman buys three cabbage heads from the stand halfway down the block. A toddler pokes the dog with a stick and then shrieks back to his mother. The pain in Nomsulwa's arm is just beginning to set in. Her mother is going to kill her for this.

THE CLINIC IS AT THE OTHER END OF THE SPRAWLING township. It is after midnight by the time Nomsulwa and her mother return home.

"Off to bed." These are the first words Nomsulwa's mother has said to her since Mira pulled her through the door and explained that she had fallen while chasing boys through the alley. It is a welcome overture after the tirade that greeted Mira, dragging the sobbing Nomsulwa to her front door. How could they be so irresponsible? Plus, don't they know that Nomsulwa is too old to still play with boys?

She lays her head down on the pillow her mother has puffed up so it feels like a cloud when she touches it. She squirms and calls out, stopping her mother on her way out the door.

"Mama! Mama, ngicela ungixoxele inganekwana." *I want you to tell me a story.*

"Which story, my girl?" Her mother puts mother hands on Nomsulwa's forehead and kisses her twice, then she readjusts Nomsulwa's arm, out of the covers, so the cast won't go soft in the heat.

"Amanzi." *Water*. It is Nomsulwa's favourite. "Tell me how blue the Rain God's skin is. Tell me how he breathes out the smell of morning dew wherever he goes."

5

It was dry in Africa. The salty sea surrounded the land, mocking it with the folding blue-green of the waves. The people, inching outwards towards the rocky shore, spent days watching the water, praying that it would transform into sweet rain and share itself with the arid earth. They sang beautiful songs, and after the songs they built large fires and killed struggling goats, watching the red blood wet the ground for a moment before disappearing.

The Rain God had ignored the prayers of the people, but he could not ignore the smell of a young woman from deep within the village huts. He searched the ground until he spied a girl who was more beautiful than the rain. She had hair as black and shiny as a wet rock, eyes as gold as a soaked field, lips as brilliant red as a berry, and teeth so white you could reach into her mouth with your tongue and lap them up. The Rain God wanted the girl and so he transformed himself into an enormous bull and travelled to earth on a bolt of lightning.

That night, a shock of light woke the girl from sleep. She walked to the door of her hut and saw, across the field, a gigantic blue bull in a halo of white. As the animal approached, the mist of his breath filled the hut with the wonderful scent of fresh rain. The bull fell to his knees before the girl, his ears back and tail flat to the ground. The girl could see a man's desire behind the bull's eyes. She was frightened and pulled her wrap close around her, but she remembered that any hope of rain must be welcomed with love. So, she took a tuft of his purple hair in her hand and pulled herself onto the bull's great back. The two left the hut, the smell of rain retreating with them, and trotted across the fields that bordered the village. He went with her to the distant mountains where the rain comes from.

As the water holes in the village filled with thanks from the Rain God, the girl's people sang her praises. She had not angered the Rain God, but had given herself freely in the hope of water for all the villagers to share.

"Kwaphela ngenganekwane, lala manje." *It's finished, my baby. Sleep now.*

"Sengilele." *I am sleeping, Mama.*

ONE

NOMSULWA CROUCHES NEXT TO A BENCH LINED WITH men in tan work suits. Her thighs press against her calves and the sweat that gathers between them is uncomfortable. She squints, looking out over the neighbourhood she used to play in as a child. One hand wipes her carefully twisted hair out of her eyes. It is hot for fall, feeling more like the unbearable city summers when the township hides under metal roofs, trying to move as little as possible.

Mothers begrudge each step on their way to the store next to where Nomsulwa waits. Their children whinge and twist, dragged behind or strapped to broad backs. Nomsulwa looks for evidence of heat exhaustion among the crisp white shirts and shorts of the workmen across the street, but they keep moving at a steady pace. The coloured foreman – lighter-skinned than his employees – keeps his hands in his pockets, walking along the line of men, inspecting pulsing black forearms and straining black necks. They shovel like a single machine, and Nomsulwa understands why these men were plucked from township construction jobs and transferred to the big municipal water company. They are the best of the ragtag group that waits by Phiri's central station, hoping the company vans will drive them into Johannesburg for one good day's work and enough money to last their families for the week.

Nomsulwa is not the only one watching them. Her cousin sits on his own corner a block and a half down and across the orange dirt road. She tries not to look at Mira, the way he lags against the bench pretending to watch for passing women and only gently glances in the direction of the workmen. No one must know what they are watching for. Nomsulwa doodles in the sand at her feet, committing to memory where the pipes attach, at what angle they enter the ground, and how many minutes it takes to dig the ditches they are housed in. She counts the parts – fourteen on this street. Fourteen large steel pipes to facilitate Phiri's new water system.

Once the steel is laid the digging begins again, transferring the dirt from its neat piles back into the ground. Periodically, the men use a hose connected to a truck behind them and water the area, persuading the earth to congeal and pack each crevice of the ditch. There are eight layers: dirt, then water, then more dirt, until finally the sand is flat. Some of the men run the hose one last time and the others rest on their heels, mimicking Nomsulwa's pose. Only now can she see their exhaustion, the way the sweat drips through their shirts and down their legs. The logo for the Amanzi water company on the front of each of their uniforms is crumpled, some completely obscured by yellow sand.

The foreman barks an order and the hose abruptly shuts off. There are rivers cascading through the newly laid earth, and, as the men begin to congregate around their truck, children materialize from doorways of the tenant housing complexes nearby and run to the muck. They play in the wet sand, using sticks to create patterns, while the workmen drink water on their break. The children get no more than five minutes before the foreman shoos them away, and a new contraption, wide and flat, is pushed across the wet ground so that the designs disappear and the dug up stretch matches the even height of the rest of its surface.

Nomsulwa checks her watch. It is four o'clock. The road will be dry and hardened before nightfall after all this sun. That will make it more difficult to dig into again.

She stands up. Her knees feel weak from the squatting but she doesn't show it as she saunters from her post. She takes side streets back to her house. The plans are finalized. Today confirmed how many pipes they must remove to ensure that the water system will be delayed until the cold, wet weather makes it almost impossible to lay it in the ground again.

As Nomsulwa makes her way through her township she passes the colourful array of houses stuck together in the downtown core. Here, the materials used in building are mismatched and scrounged from construction sites in Johannesburg: eGoli, the City of Gold, the only place where wood, bricks, and corrugated metal can be purchased by the homeless for a reasonable price. Rarely do all four walls match, and so the street gives the pleasant impression of a collage. Everything is bordered by the yellow-orange sand that covers the streets, coats the gardens in dust, and tracks up the front walks to the houses. Even the sky, obscured by swirling sand kicked up by the fall wind, takes on a yellow sheen.

As Nomsulwa gets closer to her own house in the new quarter of the township, the colours dull and become more uniform. Government-issued brick houses, sold at a profit to more affluent residents, line the streets here, and some of the road is paved. Front yards are more plentiful and a few television satellites jut out from the roofs.

Nomsulwa's house has no dish, but her front yard is landscaped, unlike her neighbours'. She has proudly lined her section of the road with bright blue flowers and a larger second row of shrubs. White rocks, stolen from a lime quarry at night, accent the plants' placement. Every spring, Nomsulwa spends her mornings re-soiling the flowered plot of land, and every fall she takes time in the evenings to plant new bulbs where empty spaces have appeared.

She enters her yard, picking up stray leaves from the stepping stones leading to the front door. This moment of the day is her favourite: the anticipation of the quiet, orderly house, the sun setting on her garden, the home she has made for herself, by herself. Her friends have married or tote children behind them, and she has created a different kind of family within the movement. But the part of her that needs something all her own has this house.

Once inside, Nomsulwa takes off her shoes, and her sock feet make no sound on the linoleum as she moves to the bathroom. She wipes herself down with a wet washcloth, knowing that the bath she can afford twice a week will be best used tomorrow. Then she crosses the hallway at the back of the house and falls into her bed. The layers of quilts, gifts from friends or sewn by her mother, sink with her weight and fold over her thighs and shoulders. She rests her head to the left and holds her wristwatch in front of her face, setting the alarm just in case. She can feel the sun's heat seeping from her skin into the cool covers. A wind that rises with the late afternoon blows over her, moving the hairs around her face and brushing her lips dry so they feel stuck together. With purpose filling her up, she feels ageless. Not twenty-six but ancient, part of a thousand generations of women who have fought for their community. They have the wisdom of having something to protect. With all this feeling welling up in her, she lets her body rest to prepare for the work it must do tonight.

A bottle cracks outside and to Nomsulwa it sounds like footsteps. She opens her eyes and checks her watch. The alarm is set to sound in fifteen minutes. She sits up carefully, silently walks to the screen covered with metal bars, and peers through the darkness. The lit windows that illuminate like highway beacons in the evening are all off now. Doors that were open and busy with women and children relaxing at the end of the day are locked. Nomsulwa half expects to hear a knock at her door, for uniformed men to appear out of the black night and bring her in to the station. She imagines the arrest so vividly, the outside acting like a projection screen for her fears. It is as if the empty house is strapping her hands behind her back and pushing her down the front walk.

Nomsulwa leaves, but only after she has made sure that the street is, in fact, deserted. The creak of a door across the street startles her for a second, the panic returning, but then she sees Mama Nominki, her husband and youngest daughter behind her. They nod at each other and walk in the same direction, being careful to keep a block's distance between them. Nomsulwa leads, sure of the location. She tries not to look back too often. It is a futile effort to seem inconspicuous. No one but the men of the township venture out after dark, especially on a Sunday. Even in emergencies, families are bustled into locked cars away from the gangs that roam the streets.

This would be a dangerous adventure if Mira hadn't made a deal with Kholizwe for protection from the Numbers gang for the night. They'll have to give up the price of one pipe in exchange, allow the runners to sell it on the black market, but it means all the families will have safe passage to and from the dig site. Mira played on the Numbers' hatred for the police and their sympathies for the Phiri Community Forum. He reminded Kholizwe how they had reconnected his girlfriend's electricity box for free when the company switched it off.

"Do it again, then. She doesn't have water, either," he told him.

But the water boxes are more sophisticated, harder to open and rewire. Some are even built with anti-tamper devices that send out an alarm the minute the casing breaks. Digging the pipes up is the only way to ensure that the new pay system is not implemented throughout the township. As long as some neighbourhoods remain on the unlimited government-funded water supply, a relic of the Apartheid era, members of the PCF can transport clean water to those who have been shut off for the month.

Nomsulwa approaches the corner where she and Mira spent the afternoon and sees a small collection of people milling about. It looks so different at night: the sand settles, changes colour to reflect the evening, stops covering everything. The sky is no longer blue but deep black, and the lights from the city wash out any stars. Sounds separate themselves, each one distinct – a kicked tin, a sigh from an old man refusing to give in to stupor and head home.

Nomsulwa is one of the few women who own the night. She never scurried in when the sun went down like other girls, but stayed out, drank with the boys, ran with the boys, broke the same rules they broke and received the same scornful looks they received. Because of that, she has learned to love the township after everyone goes to sleep, when the drunks and the tsotsis take over. The rules change, but there is an order to the darkness that she appreciates. Though she is not a man and certainly not one of the

13
–

women who wear nothing and hang off their arms, she belongs more to this version of her community than to the sunny, bustling world full of families and old women tutting their disapproval.

When Nomsulwa arrives at the site where the pipes are buried, Mira quickly appears and walks towards her. He has a big smile on his face and his skinny body wriggles with excitement.

"Sesilungile!" *We're ready!*

"The Numbers are here?"

"They are stationed at the perimeter."

"The families?"

"Most of them."

"Your girlfriend?"

"She's at home, taking care of the kid. And she's not my girlfriend."

"You're right. Can a married woman even be a girlfriend?"

Mira feigns anger at her jibe. Nomsulwa ignores him.

"Okay, let's begin, then. Set them up in a line. Make sure the shovels are evenly distributed. Keep the children near their mothers."

The two of them split up and begin talking in hushed voices to the people in front of them. Nomsulwa maps the line of the pipes with a stick, making sure to point out the places where the pipes attach.

"That is where we must dig first."

She chooses every other pipe to begin with, making sure enough damage is done even if the job takes longer than planned. She is calm now, as she knew she would be, surrounded by people who need her direction. A few families have brought flashlights and she motions for them to be turned off. The largest one she takes for herself, to be sure that there is one light at hand if needed. Finally, Nomsulwa positions herself next to Mira in the centre of the line.

They have managed to get all of the volunteers standing in a perfect row, always moving, part of the same snake-like beast. The mothers and daughters check over their shoulders constantly, scooping hard earth with no sound, slipping the dirt into the piles beside them with the utmost care. The men and boys are more comfortable.

Mira digs into the ground and then lifts. He grunts, half in jest, with the weight of the shovel's load. Then he elbows the man next to him and they begin to laugh.

"Mira, shhh!" Nomsulwa whacks his ear lightly.

"Ow!"

She whacks him again. "Thula thula bhuti. Amaphoyisa." *Quiet, the police.*

He grimaces a little at her, but quiets down.

The earth gets heavier as they break the first layer. It is full of rocks and debris and the shovelling slows. Every movement is a strain and, while the ditch begins to grow, enthusiasm for the dig wanes. Nomsulwa can sense this, but can't think of how to help. She is scared they won't make it in time for morning. Though she would never tell Mira, she also fears that they have the wrong spot, that the pipes were moved, that the water men knew the dig was coming. These doubts are Nomsulwa's secret, and they become heavier with every heave of the shovel. She pretends complete confidence and smiles at the women who stand back, taking a minute's break. She slaps Mira on the shoulder.

Headlights turn the corner to the left of the trench. The group freezes. Women cover their shovels with their dresses. Kids make little cries of alarm. Nomsulwa's heart surges with adrenaline. How could the Numbers have let the car through without issuing a warning? The black Honda slows down near the group. Its wheels are lined with red rust, the tires seem deflated under the weight of the body. A hand is casually hanging out of the window, barely visible behind the headlights. It holds a rolled cigarette. The car stops in front of Mira and Nomsulwa. Alcohol and kwaito beats breathe out of the interior as the trio of boys inside whisper collectively, "Amandla." *Power*.

"Awethu." *To the People*, Nomsulwa returns.

The car rolls slowly, offering "Amandla" to each worker as it passes. The diggers respond, then return to their shovels. A boy at the end of the trench holds up his fist, small and lost in the night. He watches as the car drives away.

Nomsulwa takes a turn digging again and lets the physical labour quiet her. Women turn and scoop the ground, turn and scoop. Men smile to themselves. Children scrape with their fingers.

Nomsulwa's shovel touches metal and the ring reverberates

down the line. There is a small whoop from the group and everyone renews their efforts.

The girl next to Nomsulwa crouches immediately and digs faster with her hands. Nomsulwa uses the edge of her shovel to scrape away the dirt that surrounds the pipe. She can see where the two pieces are screwed into each other. The pipe is new, glistening like silver as it had on the truck that morning. Just one pipe would bring over 2,500 rand in the Saturday market, but Nomsulwa has made it clear to everyone that they must leave the bounty in the borrowed dark blue pickup, parked earlier that day one block from the site. She isn't going to let greed motivate her neighbours. The promise of a rich day on the black market would have brought more people out tonight, for sure – people who didn't care enough about their wives' dry taps or who couldn't wait for more pennies to chalk up credit on their water meters. They would have been loud, excited by each pipe's discovery. There would have been fights. No, it wasn't worth it. Better to stick to a smaller crowd, a more dedicated community.

Mira comes up behind her and tickles her sides. She jumps.

"What are you doing!" she hisses.

"Sorry. Where are we moving this stuff when we finish?"

"To the shed behind my mother's house. The chickens will cover it in shit and sawdust. No one will find it there."

"Letting good steel rot in a chicken coop?"

"Leave it, Mira. We decided it was better than selling. It's too risky to wander into the market with a barrowful of pipe."

17

"Understood, boss." Mira's smile seems genuine and lets her breathe easier than she has all night. "We'll leave it there, then. But after a while, we should sell it. The money can be divided among the community."

Nomsulwa half nods to appease Mira and turns away from him to dig. She is happy, she thinks, maybe for the first time in weeks. Here, with her family of neighbours, they are going to bring the water back.

She begins to sing quietly, hoping the traditional song will encourage their tired backs:

Uzothwal' umgqomo, uyokh' amanzi
uzungabanak' abantu, uziphathe kahle, oh ngane yami
ngane yami, ngane yami, ngane yami
oh, ngane yami!

You will carry a drum, my child, to collect water, my child
ignore what people say, my child, you must behave well,
*   oh my child*
my child, my child, my child,
oh, my child

Mothers join in with her, each carefully controlling her voice, leaving a chorus so soft it might be only the memory of a song.

Nomsulwa breaks off as another car turns the corner. The headlights obscure the colour of the vehicle and light up the trench. The group freezes again. Nomsulwa is less worried, trusting now that the Numbers are being careful in their watch. Then she sees the South African Police Service insignia. She stands motionless as the car slowly passes the small groups one by one, moving only inches each second, as if savouring the power it has over the diggers. Nomsulwa wants to yell, "Run!" She mouths the words, turns her body. "RUN." But no sound comes out.

Mira drops his shovel and drags the child nearest to him back from the trench into the shadow of the house behind. Nomsulwa remains fixed next to the trench as the car stops in front of her. The lone woman inside doesn't open her door, she doesn't step out, gun in hand. She doesn't call on her radio for backup. Instead, the window rolls down and Zembe Afrika takes off her police cap and runs her fingers over her tightly tied hair.

"Amandla," Zembe whispers to Nomsulwa. It sounds so beautiful, the words coming from this woman's mouth, that Nomsulwa pauses, her mind blank. It takes a second for her to reconnect with the car in front of her, the officer leaning out.

"Awethu," Nomsulwa returns. She raises her fist and leaves her hand clutched long after the police car has moved away and her comrades have begun to chatter among themselves.

"Who was it? What did you say? How did you – ?" Mira rushes to her side.

"It was Mama Afrika."

"What did she say to you?"

"She said, 'Amandla.'"

Mira lets out a big barrel laugh. He slaps her on the back hard enough to make her stumble and then helps her get her footing again, apologizing and laughing still.

Nomsulwa chastises the young girl next to her, "Keep working!"

Her neighbours unveil their shovels and finish digging up the water pipes.

THE NEXT MORNING NOMSULWA FEELS LIKE SHE
has a hangover. Her muscles ache and grind as she rolls
out of bed and touches the floor with her toes. The air is
cold enough that she can actually feel it fill her lungs. She
stretches upwards and tries to quiet her body, but she
knows she will not be able to relax until they get the pipes
away, up to the village where her mother lives. Although
the truck with its load of thirteen pipes is well hidden, as
long as the steel is in the township she must worry about
the police recovering it, her comrades selling it, and the
Numbers stealing more than their allotted payment.

A grunt comes from the living room. She steps out of
the bedroom and walks towards the couch. Mira has one eye
open and is in the process of cursing the sun, now illuminat-
ing his makeshift bed with early white light. Nomsulwa
acknowledges his complaints as she moves past him to the
counter where the kettle and stove are. She begins to boil
water to warm up the frigid stream that runs into her bathtub. She puts a small amount in a bright-red electric kettle
and then transfers it to a huge steel pot half full with cold
water and sitting on two stove burners.

"You going to wash today?" she asks Mira. He shakes his head, covering his eyes with hand. "You always say no. But you're covered in dust from last night and you stink. Wash. The water will still be warm when I'm done." He shakes his head again and whines at the same time. His squirming makes him look even more like an overgrown child than usual.

Nomsulwa transfers more boiling water into the pot and then walks into her bathroom and fills the bath with a few inches of water. She returns to the kitchen and waits for the third kettle to sound. They will hold the meeting for the PCF today as usual. Their pattern can't change just because so many of the members will be exhausted and as dirty and aching as Nomsulwa and Mira. Any deviation and they could tip off the police. Not that it won't be obvious who took the pipes. Absent some large plot by a gang to steal them for profit, their group is the only one with the organization and the bodies to pull it off. And Mama Afrika could turn them in at any moment. Still, behaving normally will make it easier to deny the charge if it comes.

NOMSULWA AND MIRA WALK THE TEN BLOCKS TO THE community centre. Although it is early on this weekday morning, the township is busy. Women and old men have taken over the streets. They sit on their front stoops in twos and threes. Some of them wave a friendly hello to the pair as they pass. Nomsulwa keeps expecting to see the police appear from behind a corner, ready to arrest. She can't shake the uneasy feeling.

The creaking community centre sits in the middle of a concrete pool. From the outside it looks empty. A scatter of shopping bags and food wrappers dance in front of the door. A young man steps out, leans against the brick wall, and lights his cigarette. He inhales. A bag catches on his running shoe. He exhales, ignoring the plastic. A cheer sounds from the inside. The members have beaten them to the meeting.

The large room is full of women who create a moving mass of red. Each one wears a PCF T-shirt. The older women have wrapped their heads in brightly coloured scarves with geometric patterns that fold into their necks. The younger girls swim in the huge T-shirts; their small shoulders and short hair poke up between their mothers. The room they sit in dwarfs them, but that doesn't mean there aren't enough people there. There are over a hundred women gathered, talking and singing, waiting for the meeting to start.

Nomsulwa begins yelling as she runs forward and up the stairs, "Phansi ngoAmanzi Phansi!" *Down with Amanzi down!* The people on the floor in front of the raised stage call back to her, repeating her cry. Mira is right behind her, and he leans first into the microphone, "Molweni, ninjani?" *Hello all, how are you?* The traditional greeting. Mira waits for silence and then opens his speech.

"Last time we walked into downtown eGoli and demanded the water we were promised, we stopped traffic for an hour. This time, let's shut down Rissik Street for the whole day!" They all cheer and wait for him to continue.

"First, our government sold off the public electricity company and we were left with meter boxes and no coins to put
in them. Now they have done the same with our water. Our
Constitution guarantees us access to water, they promised
that the new South Africa would take care of us. But we had
more water, *more* electricity under Apartheid."

The PCF started small, as a collection of teenagers who
learned how to fiddle with the electricity boxes in the poorest
neighbourhoods. When the company cut off those families
who couldn't pay, the community called in the "electricians"
to reconnect their electricity. They marched into the neighbourhoods in the daytime, under the noses of the company-
controlled police and under the protection of the community.
Now they hold meetings in massive halls. They bus in women
from over ten different sections of Soweto. They have white
women from America come to study them. They march
down the streets of the business district, stopping traffic,
demanding access to electricity. Water is new for the PCF.
When the women of Soweto were cut off from their taps,
they didn't have anywhere else to turn. The new meters,
tightly monitored and equipped with brand new anti-tamper
devices, are hard to reconnect. But Nomsulwa's women are
organized, and there are a lot of them – if technicians can't
do it, they will reconnect the water through their protest.

"We will meet at eleven here, and there will be pick-up
and drop-off points in Chaiwelo, Mapetla, and Protea South,"
Nomsulwa explains. "It will take us an hour to get into the
city centre and then we will congregate for the march. The

route has been sent to the police, but we must be ready for everything. Once we make it down Rissik Street we will end on the steps of the city legislature. Mira and I will then enter the lobby and demand an audience with Mayor Masondo."

Cheers rise again. They are all excited about raising the stakes. Some women will bring bandanas soaked in vinegar to combat the tear gas, but most will brave it with nothing. Despite the vicious stinging in their eyes, they will continue forward. Some women will bring chairs to sit on, but most will endure the hot sun for hours, sitting and standing on command with the crowd. They will stand even though their legs are pressing inwards from too much weight for too many years.

"Bring your kids," Nomsulwa tells the women, but they know to do that already. Kids form the front lines, right behind the banner. The police are less likely to use the water cannons and the gas if the TV cameras are trained on the youngest marchers.

Nomsulwa yells, "Fire the Mayor! Fire the Councillor!"

The women answer back at her, repeating the sentence.

She calls again, "Viva PCF viva!"

There is a low rumble as Nomsulwa waves her arms and leads the group in a chant of "Shame! Shame!" Mira pauses for it to build, then, when it is at its loudest, he yells over the voices, "We will demand what the ANC promised us!"

The cries are joyful again and turn quickly into a song led by an old woman in the front row, standing with her granddaughter. Their voices warble and are disjointed at first. Then they find the harmony and the melody comes through strong and supported. Nomsulwa sings too, enjoying the sound of so many voices. Filling her lungs with grand air, the people's air, the air you only get in churches or at funerals.

"MAMA, WE'RE ARRIVING SOON. IT'S A LARGE TRUCK. . . . No, not more than four men. . . . They won't notice. They won't. Sesizofika lapho." *We'll be there soon.* Nomsulwa clicks her cellphone closed before her mother has a chance to protest further.

The pickup truck moans along the dirt path, and Nomsulwa can hear the pipes thunk hollowly against one another, although they tied them down as tightly as possible. They are driving along the edge of the shantytown. The shacks creak and move with the wind that has risen up just as the cover of the township buildings falls away and there is nothing but flat field on the horizon. Nomsulwa gives over to the bumps in the road. Her body jolts up, to the left, she flops nearly into her cousin's lap. She doesn't have the strength to hold herself upright anymore. Her eyes are closing even though she is pinching her palm to stay awake. Jolt to the left . . . jolt to the right . . . flop forward . . .

WHEN NOMSULWA WAKES UP, THE MEN ARE ALREADY out of the truck. There is nothing around. Crickets and cicadas break the silence of empty landscape.

"Mira!" Nomsulwa whispers hard. "Where are we?"

"Shhh, sisi. This is as good a place as any. We'll bury the steel. By the time we pick it up again, everyone will have forgotten what happened."

"No!" Nomsulwa yells this out loud. Her voice dies close to her, despite the volume, finding nothing to bounce off of. The other men stop unloading the truck and step behind Mira. He is buckling under their pressure, she thinks, like he so often does. "We are taking the steel to my mother's house. We will not sell it, not now, not for a long time. It's too dangerous."

"Voetsek!" One of the men swears at the ground, but Nomsulwa knows it is aimed at her.

"Do you have something to say, bhuti?" she challenges him.

"I do." Mira steps forward. "We do this work for you. We load this steel. We are starving. We need these pipes close, to be able to sell them fast. . . . The pipes are staying here."

"You'll use that money to buy cigarettes and Black Label. Mira . . ." Nomsulwa tries to hide her dismay about Mira giving in to his friends. "Listen to what you are asking. You can't risk it. I'm trying to protect you."

The shortest man steps forward. "We don't need you to protect us!"

"This place is the first field outside of the township. It will be the most likely place for us to hide it, the easiest spot. It's also," Nomsulwa turns to the quietest of the three men, "where you, Duma, were caught with the copper piping from the Premier's house just three months ago. You really think this is the best spot for us?"

"If we bury it, they will never find it."

"They will discover the newly turned earth immediately." Nomsulwa doesn't wait for his response. "If you are stupid enough to leave the steel here, I will turn us all in to the police."

Mira stands inches away from Nomsulwa. He looks down his slender nose at the top of her head. "You can't do that. For yourself, too. We can't involve the police."

28

Nomsulwa takes Mira by the arm and drags him away from the group. "Mira! What are you doing? Showing off in front of those tsotsis! Lalela mina! Load the steel back onto the truck. Get into the front and start driving the rest of the way to my mother's."

"We should sell it now. Get it off our hands."

"Mira. You're my family. We built this movement together. You want to see it fall apart because you and your buddies can't be patient for a few weeks?"

"As long as we have these pipes we're in danger."

"You think I want to risk being caught? Now?!" For a second Nomsulwa lets the panic rise in her voice, imagines the police. "We have to be extra careful. The police will have informers all over the black market and we'll be finished."

Mira lets the words sink in. Away from his friends he seems more reasonable, finally listening rather than arguing. "Okay, but only a few weeks? You promise?"

"Ngiyakuthembisa." *I promise.*

Mira walks back towards the truck and mutters to the group, "Over thirty thousand bucks. Can you believe it?"

The men grunt their frustration under the weight. When the pipes are reloaded onto the truck all five pile back into the front seat.

"It will be nighttime in an hour and a half at best. We won't get home before dinner at this rate. Look what you've done with your antics." Nomsulwa's nerves have quieted down enough that she can afford to chide the men in the truck with her again.

Mira gazes glumly out at the darkening sky. Nomsulwa punches his arm in a friendly gesture and he flinches away. The truck lurches. She hears crickets sing, they serenade the group's arrival into her mother's township. Nomsulwa's mother is already making tea in the kitchen for the visitors when Nomsulwa and her crew arrive. She shushes them to the back shed. With an uneasy wave through the open doorway to her daughter, she turns up church music from the radio to drown out the squawk of the chickens as they are moved aside for the bounty.

THREE

THE HIGHWAYS ARE WIDE AND TRAFFIC PEPPERS THE lanes, leaving too much empty space. The sun is rising, maybe more brilliant and orange than back home, but Peter can't tell. He takes in the shadows fleeing past. Beyond the transparent reflection of his angled nose and now hapless mop of hair, he can see rows of boxes pile onto one another just behind the line where the scraggly grass separating highway from ditch ends. Between the boxes, little lights flicker like ghosts, following them as they drive. The plush limousine tops a hill and Peter gets a quick look beyond the sentinel layer of structures. Shacks, paint chipped and sides falling, colours fading into the dusky morning, extend back from the highway in a massive wave. He sees a meadow of metal roofs and walls, slanting in unpredictable patterns. Smoke rises from spaces between the homes and mingles into a shallow cloud.

Africa.

"We will be at the hotel in less than an hour," the driver says in a low voice with a thick accent. He wears an ornate uniform that looks as though it was plucked from the back of a British colonial soldier. Peter feels too tired to respond.

He rubs his arms to get the wet chill of an African fall morning from his skin.

Eighteen hours ago, he was in the pleasant warmth of Toronto in the early summer. The magnolia tree outside his house was still hanging on to its last flowers, and their smell mixed with that of the breakfast his daughter was preparing before rushing off to class. He was in a neatly pressed suit, telling jokes as Claire bustled about the kitchen. His long legs didn't ache from the cramp and pressure of tiny airplane seats.

Eighteen hours ago, he wasn't a little hungover from the champagne and Tylenol PM taken at the beginning of the flight. He wasn't about to lug a large suitcase into yet another foreign hotel, tipping every black boy who ushered him through the maze of desks and identical doors. He wasn't about to speedily unpack clothes stained with the smell of airport before skimming the papers for the day's meetings.

There was a time when a trip to Johannesburg would have been a thrill – a chance to prove his stuff to the company management, but, more importantly, a chance to effect some real change. That was what they'd called it then: *real change*. Then, it was as if the permanent structures the taxi whizzed by, the large city that sprang up around them, and the row of fancy hotels they stopped before, were simple children's toys. Peter could have picked up the pieces, changed the hats on the players, and created a little utopia all of his own. It certainly wasn't the complex mess he sees now. *This is a country*, Peter thinks to himself as he exits

31
–

the car and hands ten rand to the doorman, *impervious to change.*

He has to be in the conference room in twenty minutes. There is no time for a hot shower before the day begins. The hotel is freezing, fans going in every room despite the cool morning air outside. He pulls a soft blue sweater over his dress shirt and a navy sports coat around his shoulders. The day will heat up, but at this moment it seems as though Peter never will. He breathes in deep and heads back out to the elevators.

The township councillor is bringing a delegation of community representatives who are willing to work with his company's subsidiary, Amanzi, in controlling local resistance to the water systems. Peter doesn't feel at all ready for a confrontation full of half-English sentences and misunderstandings. He knows from too many meetings in conference rooms like the one he is about to enter that local leadership is weak and often corrupt. The people hate this councillor as much as the company does. He cups his hands over his eyes and closes them. Little light trains play in front of his eyelids. For a moment he is back at home in the kitchen with his daughter while she tries to finish her reading for class. His wife is there too, rubbing his shoulders before ushering him out the door. Peter thinks once more of Claire laughing, feeling the calm it brings. Five more days and he will be on a plane back to Toronto and his family in his clean house that is always just the right temperature.

He walks very slowly down the last flight of stairs to the meeting. The man who must be the senior city councillor is sitting at the head of the table already. His suit is patched and has a little ring of dust around the cuffs of the jacket and pants. He has a beard, curled close to his skin, and small eyes set deep in his huge bald head.

"Mr. Matshikwe." He holds thick fingers out to Peter.

"Peter Matthews." Peter shakes his hand and sits down. He does not try to repeat the man's name, stopped trying years ago. African names are impossible. The table is almost full, men tucked into corner seats, all wearing mismatched suits with dust rings. Mr. M., his name shortened in Peter's head immediately, is the only one with a beard.

Alvin Dadoo is smiling widely. Peter is glad to see a familiar face, even if Alvin's polite and accommodating nature tests Peter's patience. Alvin doesn't mean to be a nuisance. His obsequious demeanour covers a backbone Peter respects. The two men have been close at times, even though it is a closeness born of too many harrowing days spent tracking their way through the parts of South Africa any sensible executive avoids. Alvin isn't sensible, and neither is Peter. That is why they are both so good at their jobs. But at the end of the day, Alvin is a babysitter, and so he must smile and nod and pretend agreement when men like Peter are around. More often than not, Peter is gripped with the urge to shake the pleasantries out of the small Indian man now standing next to him, to have just one real conversation.

The meeting begins slowly, constant translation whispers in the background as the black men huddle around one another. Peter waits for Alvin to make the introductory remarks.

"Gentlemen, as you know, we are here today to discuss the unfortunate recent incidents of sabotage of our water distribution system. Despite our efforts to disseminate accurate information, we have yet to convey to the local population the necessity for our services. In other words, they still aren't pleased about having to pay for water services, and, despite the improvements we have brought to the system, many hold on to a misplaced nostalgia for the substandard water service we had under Apartheid. Efforts to convince local leadership otherwise have failed." Alvin pauses and looks directly at the councillor. For just a second, annoyance peeks through Alvin's formal exterior. He explains how even this morning they discovered that Phiri's most recent infrastructure upgrade was undone last night by what must have been a crew of villagers armed with old shovels and flashlights. No police presence was requested to protect the asset.

"They were very busy, sir, the police," Mr. M. interrupts. "There are only ten officers for the entire area, including the informal settlement. And they have only two cars."

"I understand that, Mr. Matshikwe," Alvin snaps back, "but their negligence cost our office an extra 60,000 rand. Perhaps police presence through the night would have been a better investment?"

Peter sees Mr. M. open his mouth to retort. His neighbour

touches his arm, a gesture to calm him down, and so Mr. M. sulks instead. He knits hit forehead and glares at Alvin.

Peter is used to this kind of tension at meetings and, as the regional director, it is his job to sweep in and resolve the impasses when negotiations with local politicians have broken down. He prepares to be authoritative.

"And why," Peter interjects, his voice cold and quiet, "would you have taken it upon yourself to decide when it is appropriate to guard our company's investment? This is not a job to be completed at your convenience. I expect you to have someone looking after the steel twenty-four seven."

Mr. M. shakes his head. "You don't understand, Mr. Matthews. No officer would agree to be stationed in the streets all night. It is too dangerous."

Alvin sighs, exasperated. Peter stands up.

"I understand." Peter sees Alvin start to interject and motions for him to be quiet. "I understand that your people understand money. So pay them more. Give them more guns. They're worried about dying in the street? Make it something they can't refuse. With the amount of company money you've squeezed out of us already –" Peter ends abruptly. He moves to silence Alvin again, but his outburst has stunned more than just the councillor and Alvin has moved to the farthest corner of his chair. Peter ignores the reaction. Apparently, Alvin hasn't made it clear to the councillors just what they are dealing with. He knows as well as Peter that this project is vital to the company's international expansion. The whole world is watching to see how South Africa's water experiment works out. The entire continent's water system depends on this project. Peter is not going to let it fall apart here.

"What would it take to convince the people that the work we're doing is to their benefit?" He tries another tactic, tries to soften his tone.

"Perhaps another ad campaign, this time only in the township, with the young male demographic in mind?" Mr. M. offers a quiet suggestion.

Peter responds quickly. "God no, we have to get at the women if we want to keep those people in line." This is something Alvin has missed. Peter reviewed their strategy to date and found myriad briefing papers on local hiring practices and school visits. All money spent on men and children. But the Phiri Community Forum – their chief opposition, if you could call it that – is mostly made up of women. Their leader is a woman too, if he remembers the reports correctly.

Mr. M. leans forward. He uses his arms for emphasis, obviously frustrated with the finer points he is sure Peter is missing about the situation in *his* township. "The women will be controlled by their men."

"Oh, really?" Peter leans in as well. "You think the men have done a good job so far controlling their women, keeping them away from protest meetings and stopping them tampering with our meter boxes?"

"The men have not had the proper incentives to be completely on our side. We are working on them, getting them to understand that the women must not be allowed to undo all of the township's progress." Mr. M. looks to his cohorts; they listen to the translation behind them and then nod their agreement at Peter.

Peter wants to believe that the women can be controlled. He can't really imagine how the women of the township manage to organize the undoing of every pipe system they install. On his last visit, Alvin took him into the community that would become the central location of the company's service system pilot project, and they found themselves at the mercy of just one of these insurgents.

They were doing background research on community repayment, trying to understand how debts could grow so large in otherwise stable areas of the township. Alvin left Peter alone in a house with a huge woman rustling in the background in search of the water meter printout that detailed her usage for the last month. The living room stank of warm milk and rotting vegetables and the windows covered with wrought-iron bars and thick glass let in little light and no air. He was desperate for escape from the whole township by the time Alvin returned to announce that the company car's tires had been slashed and it would be hours until a replacement could arrive to transport them back to the hotel.

Hours of sickly sweet tea and the smell. By the end of the day he felt as inhuman as the people in that godforsaken shantytown: part dust, part liquor on the breath, part shiny skin slick with sweat.

The woman never did find her water bill. It was dark by the time they left her house and Alvin urged Peter to crouch into the seat of the car to hide his white face as they slipped past the shebeens just lighting up for the night. Peter peeked up once to watch two young boys scuffle in front of a building advertising Black Label beer. They swung off-balance punches, and one of them threw up on the side of the street. Alvin pushed Peter's head down with surprising strength.

"Shit, man, you want to get us both killed?"

And yet, these people are single-handedly destroying the company's flagship project. If Phiri is not up and running before the African winter, Peter will be held personally responsible.

THE MEETING DRAGS THROUGH THE LAST LIGHT OF THE day and dinner is served in the boardroom. The food is awful, grey pork sunk in gravy. The fresh vegetables promised on the menu are creamed spinach and squash. Peter realizes he is starving and eats quickly as the presentations continue. There is much discussion of profit margins, of plans to increase the charges per litre for the township residents in order to offset the increased costs of civil disobedience in the area. By the end of the evening, even the wallpaper in the room seems to sag from exhaustion.

"No way." Peter is standing. "There is no budget for that kind of payout."

Mr. M. remains calm, matched only by Alvin, as the rest of the room squirms uncomfortably.

"Why should we pay more to those officials who already support the plan, giving you money with the hope that you will protect our pipes? You have sat by while a bunch of girls with shovels undid months of work. And now you expect me to believe that you are capable of that kind of mobilization?" Peter sits, looks at Alvin, and then glares at Mr. M. He sees the project slipping away, worries that he will have to recommend abandoning Phiri and can only imagine the kind of damage that will do to the company's reputation, to the country's welfare.

Mr. M. is thoughtful. "We know who is in charge of the vandalism. Perhaps . . . er . . . neutralizing those few individuals will end the trouble. The money is necessary to permit their removal without community reprisal."

The room goes quiet. The black men stay very still. Mr. M. continues, "I was told, earlier, by your office, that this fee was secured."

"My office?" Peter, incredulous, leans back. "My office promised you the money? Well, as of today, I am the office. And payouts to you are not likely under my watch. Certainly not for some half-thought-through scheme to 'neutralize' people with significant popular support. Not interested."

Mr. M. looks ready to pounce, insult now compounding disappointment.

"It's been a long day." Alvin stands, putting a hand on Peter's shoulder. "We will think this over and return with an answer at the end of the week. Until then, thank you for your time, gentlemen." The translation takes a few moments and then the black men rise and get their coats. Peter is almost out the door when Alvin stops him.

"Where are you going?" Alvin looks defeated, hunched and tired.

"To my room, it's late."

"We are moving on to a local bar. You are expected to join us."

"Tell them I'm going to bed." Peter begins to walk again. He can't do this tonight, pretend niceties when he is so frustrated and tired. He needs to sleep. Tomorrow will be better, he will be better and more himself.

"It will cause a lot of trouble. After today's meeting, declining their hospitality might cause irreparable damage. Come out for a drink and I'll escort you back to the hotel."

"Really?" Peter pleads. Alvin only looks at him expectantly, understanding that this is all it takes to get Peter to turn around fully and follow him out the door. It's cold outside. Peter is exhausted. He hates Mr. M. and his fat bald head. He hates the greedy eyes of the men who accompany them as they march down the hill from the hotel onto a main street. They pile into a minibus waiting on the sidewalk. Once the door closes, the bus weaves through a nice neighbourhood with big houses and high fences, rides the empty highway for a few minutes, and ends up at the top of a busy street, filled with bars. People walk from door to door, black outfits shining under the streetlights. Peter is led out of the minibus and Alvin walks him to the front of a large club, dimly lit and full of people.

The crowd inside is young and dressed for a night out. Peter feels old and his suit is constricting. He begins to sweat from the heat of so many people. Black women in tight tops lean on the shoulders of white men in business suits. An Indian woman takes their coats at the door and Alvin slips her a hundred-rand bill for security. The bartenders are gorgeous blondes, Afrikaans accents slipping into the ears of customers as they deliver beers across the counter. Peter stares for a moment before Alvin nudges his side.

"They're having Black Labels, I'm having a Windhoek. What do you want?"

"Jack and Coke, heavy on the Jack." Peter knows there will be no ride from Alvin anytime soon. He commits completely to a night out.

THE BLACK MEN LAUGH LOUDLY AS ANOTHER ROUND of drinks is served. A couple of them have met up with women they seem to know. Those men are dancing behind the table, rubbing against their friends in a circular motion as the beat pounds into Peter's head. Peter stares at the woman who serves him another Jack. He gave up on the Coke two rounds ago. She is long, stomach flat and exposed between her white shirt and jeans. He reaches out to touch her and then sees her stiffen in alarm. He redirects his hand to the top of his hair and pats down curling strands that have fallen out of place. The meeting has disappeared from his mind, but his annoyance is still there, bolstered by the alcohol. He feels a strange mix of anger and frustration and the thrill of slowly losing control. Drunk. Peter feels drunk.

Alvin is talking in a corner with the woman from the coat check. His head falls close to the woman's breasts and then jerks back up to her face. She is smiling, nursing the drink he bought for her, checking on the front every few minutes. Mr. M. is gone, disappeared into the back room with a girl too young to wear skirts that short. The man next to Peter falls over in his mirth and takes a long moment to sit back up again. The waitress brushes her chest against Peter's collar. The song changes. Peter feels alone, merely a witness to the world around him. Just then, he is dragged up by one of the dancing men and shoved towards the middle of a sweaty circle. The isolation ends as he focuses in on the hips of the girl in front of him. He vaguely remembers being introduced to her by one of the men from the meeting. He doesn't remember her name. She is small and slight, with bare shoulders. Too young in her tight red miniskirt, but it's just a dance. She sways, standing far away at first and then, after she catches him looking at her, inching closer. Soon she is dancing right next to him, brushing against his body and then moving away, again, looking at the floor. *She is teasing me*, Peter thinks, and then perhaps he says it out loud because the girl smiles and wiggles closer.

They are in the middle of the room. Now the girl, all limbs and chest, is pressed against him, guiding him in time to the music. She is smiling, laughing almost. She looks as though she is having fun. Peter is not having fun, but he is dancing, desperate to keep his body touching hers. He becomes hard slowly, fighting the alcohol the whole time. She bumps against him and he can feel his penis swell in reaction. He is too drunk to feel embarrassed. *A game*, Peter thinks, and then perhaps he says it out loud because the girl wraps her arms around his neck and begins to press up and down his thigh.

Peter thinks that the girl is very beautiful. She is young, but not younger than the one Mr. M. disappeared with. Peter could think about what that means, if his head wasn't so fuzzy. He hugs her tight and smells beer on her skin. Her thighs are still moving from side to side while her body rubs up and down. It is magic, all this moving at once. The magic makes him want to see her naked. Her skin is very black. Peter wonders if her breasts are as dark as her arms and chest. He wants to touch her stomach, to lick her thighs. He thinks about hips swaying and rubbing and breasts pitch-black and full. He holds tighter to the girl's waist, pushing and rubbing harder. She breathes in his ear, spots of saliva tickling him.

"Come with me." Peter motions to the door and then tugs the girl from the dance floor.

THE MINIBUS DOOR SLAMS SHUT BEHIND PETER. The driver is passed out in the front seat. He presses into her and kisses her hard. She tastes sour, like the milk these people leave on their counters overnight, waiting for it to curdle. She kisses back, then puts space between them. "It's four hundred," she says, all of a sudden matter-of-fact. She seems inexperienced, not aware of the way to coax bills out of drunk men's pockets. *Could this be her first time?* Peter thinks, and this arouses him more, the excitement filling his body, every inch of skin in the same state of fevered expectation.

Peter digs into his pants and realizes that he didn't even go back to his room for cash and has been relying on Alvin for the night's expenses. He panics for a moment. The girl leans in to kiss him and moves back again, making an impatient motion with her hand. He follows her, breathing as he kisses, allowing no pause. His teeth catch her lip. There is blood. Peter keeps moving against her. He stumbles, knocks his head on the roof of the van, and falls forward. The girl is sobbing now. Peter holds his free hand over her mouth, pins the girl underneath him, crushes her with his weight. "Be quiet," he whispers. He shifts his leg to reach his belt. He opens his pants and guides his penis out. The girl tries to wriggle away and Peter pins her down. He looks into her eyes, big, not blinking, terrified. He looks at his hand, pressing on a tiny face. He stops, noticing his penis has gone soft in his hand. What has he done?

He collapses next to her and clutches her with one arm as he zips his pants up. He feels inhuman, too dizzy. He cannot think now. He leaves the minibus, shutting the girl in with the unconscious driver, and stumbles back into the bar.

THE YOUNG GIRL IS MORE BEAUTIFUL THAN THE RAIN. She has hair as black and shiny as a wet rock, eyes as gold as a soaked field, lips as brilliant red as a berry, and teeth so white you could reach into her mouth with your tongue and lap them up. The young girl rolls over, runs out of the minibus and into the arms of a man waiting on the corner. Mouth cut, black hair pulled sideways, rain seeping out of every fold of her skin.

FOUR

46
–
Zembe Afrika looks imposing even when she is bustling about her cluttered kitchen. Her big frame moves with a deft certainty as she gets a mug down from the cupboard overhead. Her nightgown is boxy and made of cloth so heavy that it stays in place when she moves. During her morning routine, Zembe gives no indication that she is dreading her meeting with the Soweto Police Service Regional Director. She doesn't allow any hesitation or uncertainty.

She had received the call yesterday, not long after the pipes had been completely dug up from the main street in Phiri's residential neighbourhood. Her boss had not sounded happy about being awake at six in the morning on a Tuesday. Zembe had been up already, boiling water for tea and deciding which skirt and jacket to wear to the office that day. She had unwrapped her hair and pressed the few wayward pieces back into the bun. She had been ready to pretend nothing had happened.

It surprised her that the provincial office was so involved in the disappearance of township property. Sipho's voice on the other end of the phone had been deeper than usual. He had demanded to see her the next day in his office and said she'd better have something to report. Zembe complied, clearing her schedule for this morning, making sure her rounds of the informal settlement were covered by one of the nine other officers, bringing her own vehicle to work so that the two functioning police buggies would be free for the duration of her absence.

As she is the chief officer for the Phiri police station, the responsibility for the lost pipes rests squarely on her shoulders. Their recovery would lead to a significant boost in her career, one that might catapult her past the glass ceiling that exists above the regional stations. Failing to find the steel will guarantee the end of Zembe's advancement. Zembe has already resigned herself to this latter result, knew she was accepting it when she drove past the men and women with shovels in their hands – the women she talks to every day in the township market or at the community centre on Saturdays – and chose not to get out of the police car. She has also made a decision not to regret her actions. Zembe is a rational woman, and rational women can see that those pipes are strangling the life out of Phiri.

As on every morning, Zembe stops for a few moments in her church. It is in the corner of Phiri proper, a white building with a steeple that reaches higher than the two-storey flats next to it. It took her congregation twenty-five years to raise the money for the building, and Zembe remembers going door to door, looking for support with her father after classes at the police academy were done for the day. When the sun shines down on the white siding it glints, not harshly as it does off the corrugated metal shacks, but diffused, like winking, a sun that flashes a slight recognition. Zembe is prouder of her church than she is of the detached brick house she bought for herself four years ago, prouder than she is of the Policewoman of the Year award she won in 2000. This building is the product of her family, her generation and the generation before hers.

When she walks in the church's vaulted front door she becomes someone other than the police officer in charge of their township. She is Mama Afrika, daughter of Khaye Afrika, lifelong devotee of the Nazareth Baptist Church.

Today, it is quiet and Zembe needs only to nod at the pastor, who is reading in the near corner of the huge room. The weekday worshippers, those without jobs, are not here yet. They are still clearing away breakfast, getting their kids out the door for school. The morning trickle will not begin for another hour at least.

She sits in her seat, not kneeling on the rough floor, clasps her hands together, and begins to pray. She describes the anxiety in her stomach, the guilt she feels when she thinks of the lies she will have to tell Sipho, the man who has guided her career, kept her at the top of the service's appointment list. Her God removes the knot in her stomach, absolving her as she presents each worry.

Zembe lets herself need Him in a way that she avoids with everyone else. She comes to church early every morning to pray alone, to garner His attention without any other distractions. She does not try to spread the word of God like the other church members, preferring His word be kept for her. The people dragged into the station – tattered clothes, scraped knees from trying to run, bloody noses from the push to the ground – Zembe doesn't share the teachings with these people. She doesn't hand out church pamphlets in the station's holding cell. She thinks of the blank eyes, as one sniffling young man blends into another, until Zembe can't help but see as criminal all the boys in the township. She sees the guns they might buy next week, the drugs they will inhale tomorrow night. Even the rolling babies who play in the sawdust on the floor of the Phiri community centre are precursors to these hardened men. She starts to believe that God is the only good man. God and her father.

Zembe finishes just as the first congregants arrive for morning prayer. She smiles at the women as she leaves, and then begins assembling a checklist in her head of the day's tasks.

THE SOWETO REGIONAL DIRECTOR'S OFFICE IS IN Johannesburg's downtown, a full hour's commute from where Zembe works and lives. The South African Police Service building is made of cream-coloured concrete with rows of black windows that stripe the exterior. It is magnificently tall and overshadows the smaller commercial buildings just outside of the central business district. Sipho's secretary is perched at the mouth of the elevator bank on the thirty-fourth floor. She recognizes Zembe immediately and smiles.

"They are waiting for you."

"They?"

"You thought the national office wouldn't be in on this?"

"Hmm," is all the response Zembe can manage. She surreptitiously straightens her suit and brushes dust from the township road off her stockinged calves. She marches past the desk into the large office.

The usually bored face of Zembe's boss is wrinkled into a frown. He is sitting with two white men and a coloured man whom Zembe recognizes from teleconferences but has never met in person.

"Commissioner Woolmer, very pleased to meet you." Zembe approaches him first, then officiously shakes the hands of the white men. She nods at Sipho and sits down.

"Ms. Afrika, we are just discussing the fast rate of disappearance of steel in the township."

"Yes, I. . . ."

The white man with brown hair to Zembe's left cuts her off. "Ms. Afrika, do you have any leads on this?"

Zembe opens her mouth to speak, but Commissioner Woolmer jumps in again. "Do you know who might be responsible for the theft? Because if you do, we can authorize you to pick them up. All of them. We need to get on this fast, and protocol shouldn't hinder your investigation."

Zembe nods, stifling a snort. Woolmer has some township experience. He should know that the word "protocol" has little currency with her officers.

Sipho seems agitated. He fiddles with his tie, stares around at the white walls broken by huge windows, at the framed photos that clutter the surface of every filing cabinet and the big, dark, wooden desk they are now gathered around . . . everywhere but at Zembe.

"Sir, I have no suspects at this time. I have informants in the black market who have been alerted regarding the pipes. I have officers randomly searching houses in the informal settlement where the anti-company sentiment is the strongest. But it is my opinion that this theft was motivated solely by financial concerns." Zembe chooses her words carefully. "That will make the perpetrators much harder to find."

Woolmer massages his forehead. The white men look scornful.

Zembe stares straight at Sipho, waiting for him to speak. He looks around at the table and then begins, "Ms. Afrika, is that your report?"

"It is, sir."

"You have nothing else to tell us?"

"Not yet, but give me some time and I'll have more for you."

"Thank you, then. Will you wait in the lobby for the moment? I have a few more things I'd like to discuss when this meeting is finished."

He's punishing me, Zembe thinks, but she stands and shakes the hands of each of the men.

As soon as she sits next to the secretary's desk, the enormity of her lie settles in. This is going to be harder to pull off than she had originally thought.

———

It takes another forty-five minutes for the men to leave Sipho's office. Woolmer nods at Zembe when he walks to the elevator, but the white men pass without a glance. They seem more agitated than when Zembe left them. That means Sipho's mood will have gotten worse as well.

Sipho stands at the door of his office. He smiles warmly at his secretary, and then the smile ends and he waves Zembe inside. He begins berating her before she passes the door. "What was that bullshit you fed Woolmer? You know as well as I do that the PCF is responsible for the missing pipes."

"I have no evidence of that. None. You wanted me to tell Woolmer something we couldn't prove? He would have made me arrest the whole organization on a hunch from a guy who sits in a city office all day."

"I may be in the city, but I'm not an idiot."

"Are you calling me an idiot?"

Sipho takes a breath. He sits down. His skin gleams from sweating through the morning. The air conditioning is blasting and the sweat hasn't dried. Zembe wonders how much stress it takes to cause that kind of perspiration. "Look, sis, we need this. Both of us. Just get me something to tell them. I don't care what it is."

Zembe's phone buzzes in her pocket. She ignores it and lets it go through to voicemail. "I'm going to try. But there's not a lot to go on."

"You've made arrests on less."

The phone rings again. Zembe quickly checks the screen. It's the station. Both calls. She holds up a finger – "Maybe this is about the pipes?" – and then answers.

While the voice on the other end of the line speaks, Sipho taps his fingers with increasing speed. Zembe can see her boss's anger rising, and it almost distracts her from the young officer's report. When she hangs up, her face is starting to sweat, too.

"They found a body in the lok'shini of Phiri, right in the centre of downtown." Sipho starts to interrupt, but Zembe continues. "A white man."

He closes his mouth. Pauses.

"Go back there. I'll call the national office. Don't touch anything until reinforcements arrive, and whatever you do, keep your incompetent officers away from the scene."

Zembe wants to remind him that he gave her those incompetents, asked her to make a team out of them, teach them how to interrogate, make arrests, and process scenes. But he is right. There will be too much scrutiny on this.

She is already calling the station back when she gets out the front door. She drives with one hand, steering with her knee and shifting violently up to cruising speed while giving orders into the phone. Troubling as this body is, part of her is grateful for something to distract Sipho from the missing pipes.

WHEN ZEMBE ARRIVES AT THE SCENE, ONE OF HER junior officers gives her the report.

53
–

"We were doing rounds when we found the body. It was dropped in this yard. Looks like the 28s."

Zembe turns. "The 28s? Why do you suspect them?"

The 28 gang is part of a network of numbered gangs that thrive in South Africa's prisons. The Numbers run the inside, dictating who eats, where each prisoner sleeps, who lives and who dies. The Numbers' network also operates on the outside. Boys join for protection and to make extra money in the drug market. The 28s are perhaps best known for their practice of removing and – rumour has it – eating the hearts of their victims. They are the toughest Numbers, the best organized, and the hardest to control. Zembe has not seen a 28 killing in Phiri for over three years.

The officer leads Zembe to the secluded spot where they found the body. The white man is arranged carefully. His arms are neatly stretched to either side, his legs slightly parted but positioned straight down from his body. He is wearing a business suit, now torn and covered in dirt from the road, and the top of the shirt is open. His chest underneath is bursting. The flesh is split apart, revealing coagulated mounds of blood and tissue.

An officer in plain clothes is leaning over the body. He stands up as Zembe approaches.

"Good morning, Zembe."

"What can you tell me?" Her voice is hard.

"You're not going to like it."

"Out with it. Please. We've got to get this site contained."

"The heart is missing. Cut out. Probably by a rough-edged knife."

Zembe starts to worry. A 28 killing is bad enough, but with a white man as the victim? She cannot imagine worse.

The man's wallet hangs out of the jacket pocket. Zembe takes a piece of cloth from her bag and uses it to open the leather. Inside are four or five credit cards and a green I.D. card with holograms shimmering over the lettering. He is not from here.

She steps away from the body. The skin looks plastic, shiny, and too white. His eyes are blue, one closed, the other open. She takes a deep breath and turns to see that detective services have already sent down two uniformed officers. The older one informs Zembe that the national office has also requested that provincial crime intelligence pull men onto the case. White deaths cause trouble, forcing government attention onto her district, a place they are otherwise content to ignore. The national officers will ask her why there weren't more police patrolling the streets. They will demand to know how a white businessman managed to get into the township without Zembe's knowledge. She will point to her aging buggies. She will complain about gas allowances and sprawling shantytowns that expand her district but justify no extra funding for law enforcement. But she knows her answers won't satisfy them. And they will be looking for someone to blame.

IT TAKES ALL DAY FOR THE CORONER AND IMPORTED officers to finish at the scene. The sun intensifies and then wanes, slipping below the horizon. The small side yard changes colour, from yellow to deep orange to a delicate purple reflection of the evening sky. By eight, Zembe is exhausted. The morning meeting feels like a lifetime ago. The energy it takes to investigate a scene, keep the stomach still while they prod and shift and finally remove the body, train the eyes on another small square of sand, surprises Zembe every time. By the time they are ready to seal the scene for the day Zembe still knows very little: the dead man is Peter Matthews, fifty-two years old, from Toronto, Canada. Here on business with Amanzi's parent company. A water man. Zembe warns her officers to keep this to themselves and then threatens with only one last dark look that lets them know she is serious.

It is imperative the rest of the township know nothing about the return of the 28s or the attack on a water company official. Gang killings are fodder for news crews. A foreigner will ensure even more attention.

The national team finishes, too quickly for Zembe's taste, and she is forced to dismiss her own officers. Men scuttle about, double-checking labels and closing evidence kits before getting into their white sedans. Zembe is the last person to leave. She takes a moment to survey the scene as darkness falls, the way the 28s would have seen it. Hidden from the street, but surrounded by sleeping households, it is a risky place to leave a body.

Zembe takes the long route home. She enjoys the rhythm of the car on the drive and the way she can feel the township settle in around her. When she turns into her own driveway all the doors on her street are closed. She steers her car into the parking pad behind her house and double-checks the gas level. Years patrolling the highways have taught her that keeping the bare minimum of gas in the tank is the best protection against car theft. Anyone who managed to break into her car wouldn't get far on the half-litre she leaves.

The front windows of her house are dark, but a yellow light illuminates the front walk and the keyholes in both locks. Once inside, Zembe bolts the door, drops her purse, and walks directly to the bedroom. She changes into her nightgown, folded neatly that morning, and kneels next to the bed.

In the dark house it is easy to slip into prayer. The day washes away. She forgets the cool metal weight of the gun on her hip, the constriction of the suit jacket, and the dust in her eyes. When she prays it is a chance to digest the day and then interpret it according to His word. She tells Him about the dead water man's blue eye and missing heart. Then she climbs onto the mattress, sets her clock, and falls asleep. She doesn't have nightmares. In the morning, when the sun wakes her minutes before the alarm sounds, she will thank Him for that.

THE SCENE REPORT, READY TWO DAYS LATER, GIVES
Zembe little to work with. There are three flagged pictures.
The first is a close frame of the left gouge mark in the chest.
Flesh splits in jagged strands. The skin is blue under the
white light of the coroner's lab. A note is scrawled over
the red flag: "Serrated edge knife, no larger than 4.5 cm in
width." Zembe makes a rough estimate with her fingers
in front of the magnified cut. It would have taken serious
force to cut through the thick chest muscle to access the
ribcage. She starts the profile in her head.

The second picture is of the back of the head. At the base
of the skull there looks to be a soft impression. The notes to
the side identify cause of death as a cracked skull. Injuring
a grown man this seriously would have taken strength or a
surprise attack that incapacitated him for longer than a few
seconds. Black marker arrows point to a few places on the
skin. Zembe peers closer, holding the frame up to the single
light on her desk. She can't see anything.

Outside the office, she hears the sound of a group of
officers in for their morning break. Tosh, her newest and

most promising recruit, laughs his high-pitched laugh as he walks past the door.

"Tosh," Zembe bellows. "Get in here. I need your help with something."

Tosh looks uncertain, always nervous. His fingers shake when he reaches for the photo, his lips stay pursed long after he's done scrutinizing.

"I can't see what's flagged. These glasses are no good."

"They're hairs, ma'am."

"Pardon?" Zembe takes the photo again. She sees nothing, no black at all cutting across the white skin.

"Right there." Tosh motions to one of the arrows. "Small black circles. My hair does that. Drives my mother crazy, says she's always picking little rings out of her clothes."

Zembe looks at Tosh's hair. It's long enough to add a centimetre or two to his height. The hair is soft, but tight to the head, rolled into thin coils sticking out in all directions.

"Is there a skin tag on them?"

"A what?"

"Do these hairs come straight from the scalp?" Zembe hands Tosh her glasses, he holds them like a magnifying glass.

"Oh, no, they're just pieces that break from the end." Tosh looks sad to disappoint.

"So, no good to us, then," Zembe says more to herself than to him. "Thanks, officer. That's all."

Tosh's lips, which had almost relaxed, scrunch back up upon his dismissal. He thinks he's done something wrong.

But Zembe doesn't take the time to make him feel better, she's already concentrating again on the photo. She picks out the other ten hair rings on the victim's body.

The third photo is of a piece of paper. "Found ten inches from right side of body, half buried in the sand," the note says in the coroner's scrawl. It is a receipt. The top has a faint sun-shaped logo and the words "Central Sun" printed in cursive. There is a bill for one drink: a beer. The space for the room number at the bottom is blank.

Zembe puts down the file and straightens the papers on her desk, then she walks out to the front foyer.

"I'm going downtown. I'll have my phone on me."

The young woman in uniform looks concerned. "Shall I forward your calls there?" She must be nervous about so much attention from senior officers.

"Give them Sipho's number if they insist on speaking to someone."

ZEMBE ARRIVES AT THE WATER COMPANY'S MAIN office by noon and walks briskly into the marble atrium of the building. There are two security guards in white uniforms stationed on either side of the front desk. It is a small room, and the four big men press into one another, rocking slowly, vying for space. The woman between them is skinny, her light complexion fading into bleached orange hair. She watches Zembe while talking into the phone. She is laughing when Alvin Dadoo steps out from the opening elevator doors.

"Officer." He gestures to the elevator, a big smile crossing his face that then disappears too quickly.

Zembe enters the elevator. She feels imposing as her hips crowd the stocky man next to her. They don't speak until they are through his front office and behind a closed door.

"Thank you for taking the time to see me, Mr. Dadoo," Zembe says as they take seats in his large, cool office, masking her township accent as best as she can.

"Not a problem. Thank you for making the trip here. Very sad thing, very sad indeed. I was a friend of his, you know. We weren't just business partners. I mean, we were partners and friends."

"I am sorry for your loss."

"It's the company's loss, really."

"Did Mr. Matthews come here often?"

"This was his fifth visit to Johannesburg on this project. I can't speak of his travels before."

"Is there reason to believe he travelled here before his employment with your company?"

"No . . . I am just not privy to his conduct before that time."

Zembe looks around the office while Dadoo sails through his answers. It is a classic executive's office. The wood is all real, no peeling finishes, and the windows are huge, overpowering the walls. It is as if the small room is hanging in the sky.

"The project Mr. Matthews was supervising, it was the water privatization in the city?"

Dadoo grimaces at Zembe's choice of words. He shifts his chair and taps on the bare surface of his desk. "Public-private partnership. He was here to report on our progress to the North American parent company. He would arrive, spend a week checking reports and meeting with key figures in the company, and then return to Toronto and summarize his findings."

"What were his findings from this trip?"

"I'm not sure what you mean."

"How is the public-private partnership working out?"

"He was reporting on normal progress. That is, he would have been, if . . ." Dadoo's eyes meet Zembe's when he says this. They are unwavering, false in their certainty. Zembe doesn't let him have a moment.

"Mr. Dadoo, part of my job is to find out if Mr. Matthews might have done something, said something, to create animosity among the people he worked with. We both know the water privatization is causing trouble in the townships. I've read the reports about water workers being attacked during meter installation. The police have been briefed more than once about the slashing of Amanzi truck tires and the makeshift roadblocks to as yet unserviced areas of the township. I need to know what he was reporting on, exactly."

"I thought this was a gang killing." Dadoo can't help but let a smug smile play for just a second on his lips before allowing his face to relax into a serious expression.

Zembe is caught off guard. She sits back in her chair.

"We take very good care of our partners, Ms. Afrika," Dadoo continues. "We have made it our business to know every detail of this investigation."

"We are looking at a particular gang that has been known to operate in Phiri. My office is in the process of tracking down the senior members of that organization."

"I trust that process will not take too long."

Zembe wonders how she was pushed to the defensive so quickly. She ignores Dadoo's question and changes the subject. "Walk me through Mr. Matthews's day here."

"The hotel can provide you with better details than I can."

"The national office is in charge of the hotel room and surrounding area. They will issue a report on their findings within a few days, but I want to hear your version."

"We had a meeting with some of our partners here on the ground. We used the conference room in his hotel. The meeting went very late, but I know that Mr. Matthews was at the hotel when I left."

"We found a receipt for a beer at the hotel lobby bar on his body. It was issued at 11:53."

"Beer?"

"Yes."

"Mr. Matthews never drank beer. He only had Jack Daniels. Occasionally with Coke. At least as far as I have ever seen."

Zembe makes a mental note to re-examine the receipt. "Did he have any friends here, any other acquaintances? Anyone he might have called to join him after you left?"

"Mr. Matthews knew no one but me. And maybe a few of our employees. I will be happy to provide you with a list."

"Thank you." Zembe moves to get out of her seat.

"Feel free to call my office if you need any further assistance, Detective Afrika. And do keep us updated on the gang investigation."

As if I need to, Zembe thinks as she nods, and leaves.

BACK AT THE STATION, ZEMBE CALLS SIPHO AND scolds him for leaking information to the water company.

"It wasn't me," he insists.

Zembe, undeterred by his profession of innocence, continues. "Now he is waiting for gang investigation results. This ties my hands, Sipho, I have no freedom to pursue other leads."

"Do you have other leads?"

Zembe thinks about the receipt, a beer Matthews didn't drink, and decides to keep it to herself, for now.

"No."

"Then it's going to be a gang investigation. Either way, start at the top and work your way down."

"You mean track down Kholizwe? It's not easy to find that man even when we know he is in the vicinity."

"You worried you're not up to the job?" Sipho asks.

"No. I was going to start on the other end of the spectrum, work my way up the chain of command."

"Try for Kholizwe," he says. "He is always around when things like this happen."

"Things like this? When was the last time a foreign businessman was murdered in a township? There is nothing like this."

"I trust you, Afrika. Keep me updated." He hangs up.

She would love to keep Sipho updated, but wonders how to run a murder investigation while dealing with the barrage of petty crimes she handles every day. If only she could hole up in her office and study the file until the workday finished. Instead, she takes out a buggy, miraculously available and waiting in the office lot, and begins her rounds. She covers the lok'shini only, focusing on the centre of the township and leaving the violent and cluttered outlying areas to teams of two younger officers. She used to avoid doing rounds altogether, but then started hearing complaints from shopkeepers about a lack of police presence in the downtown leading to increased robberies. It seems the relatively quiet centre of Phiri was a convenient place for junior officers to skip when making it through the informal settlement took too long. Now, Zembe takes a downtown route every other day, and covers all lok'shini robberies herself, proving that a desk job in the township is anything but.

Zembe's first stop is the café outside of the community centre. Ice cream, ginger beer, and Coke are the only things on the menu, but it's still a popular spot. Behind the bar today is a girl, no more than fifteen. She pours ginger beer out of the bottle into a paper cup and hands it to Zembe. Zembe scans the crowd. At the far end, Nomsulwa

Sithu sits chatting with her tall cousin. Nomsulwa catches sight of Zembe and she and her cousin stand up and try to slip inconspicuously out the back gate. Before she is out of earshot, Zembe calls out. Nomsulwa stops, her cousin continues past her almost at a run. Zembe motions for Nomsulwa to meet her outside and then leaves, ginger beer in hand, with a nod of thanks to the girl behind the counter.

"What's up?" Nomsulwa asks the question when she is still a good ten feet from the door of Zembe's car. Her body is tall and thick, strong but with the curves of a woman, it casts a long shadow. She makes no move to come closer.

"Avoiding me, sisi?"

"I wasn't." Nomsulwa scoffs.

"You always run out the back way when you are finished?" Nomsulwa doesn't answer. "Well, you don't have to worry, something else has made your pipes seem like a bar fight in comparison."

Nomsulwa looks up, taking a few steps forward. "What has?"

"Look at you taking an interest in police work. And I thought you were only good for breaking laws. Never mind what has happened. Has your cousin said anything about Kholizwe being back in town?"

Nomsulwa frowns. "Why?"

"If he is, my guess is that Mira knows about it."

Nomsulwa moves the sand with her shoe, swiping back and forth in a surprisingly graceful movement. It clashes with her hunched shoulders and baggy pants. She runs a hand through her twists, flopping them slightly in the other direction.

"Who says he's in Phiri?"

"Look, you didn't hear it from me, but the police are looking into a murder. A white man, a foreigner. I can't move forward on it if I don't know the lay of the land around here and Kholizwe always seems to be the missing piece. Mira's the best connection I've got. And if I remember correctly, you owe me a favour or two." Zembe hopes that divulging this minimal information is the right move, hopes it will convince Nomsulwa to poke around. She is a girl in with the wrong crowd, but she has a moral compass that Zembe respects. She always has. "Could you just get your cousin to call my office tomorrow?"

"Where was the man killed?" Nomsulwa is not exactly volunteering her services.

"Stop asking questions about investigations you have nothing to do with. Just be glad I'm not arresting you. Find me Kholizwe and I promise to leave Mira out of it."

"Mira had nothing to do with any murder!" Nomsulwa really is ready to run now. Zembe needs her to calm down, be convinced that cooperation is the best – the only – path to take, given their recent midnight escapades.

"Find me Kholizwe, and you won't have to worry."

AS THE NEXT WEEK BEGINS, ZEMBE DECIDES TO approach the gang investigation with more vehemence. The national office turned up nothing in Matthews's room and there were no hits on any of the hotel employees. No one reported anyone suspicious entering or exiting Matthews's floor. It seems the entire hotel was populated only by the most respectable visitors in the short time the water man stayed there. The receipt for the beer is tossed under the thick report. Zembe plans to follow it up, but with no correlating leads it is unlikely that she'll be able to discover anything new.

There is no easy way to access the gang systems in the townships. In prison they are in your face: people wear their colours in small ways, a rip in the shirt, a pant leg rolled up, but their declaration of membership is brazen. Out here, the signs are harder to pick up. The whole world knows who to watch out for, but no one is willing to let the police in on the secret.

She decides to make her way to the edge of the informal settlement on her own. She has a hunch that knocking on a few doors might elicit more information than following the elusive thread of the 28 gang and their leader, Kholizwe. She suspects from Nomsulwa's reaction that the man is in town. But that doesn't mean he'll be easy to find.

She checks in with the front desk of the station. "I am leaving. Are there any messages before I go?"

"Yes, one, robbery at the petrol station in Phiri, the taxi drivers are requesting senior attention."

Zembe nods. The minibus drivers regularly throw their weight around to get the word out that they're looking for someone in their bad books, but they don't need police to help with a robbery investigation. They do more police work themselves in a week than Zembe's team has managed in months. Through a system of payoffs and violence, they have created a sub-legal order of their own. Many police units treat the drivers themselves as a gang problem. They point out that the drivers specialize in beatings, brutal ones, for those who trespass on their turf. People who go to them with complaints will often see the culprit they identified bruised and beaten the next day. But they are an arm of the law in her township, whether she acknowledges it or not. And, like it or not, this is a good chance for Zembe to barter for her own investigation. The drivers know the most about what goes on after dark in the township. She will stop at the petrol station first.

ZEMBE DRIVES UP TO A THREE-WAY STOP AND TURNS around a bright red post holding up the far edge of a white canopy. The concrete around the petrol station is cracked and lines sneak in and out of potholes, run under the two pumps, and continue towards the small store at the far end of the lot. Everything is red and white except for a green BP sign hung above the road. There is yellow tape strung across the door of the store, probably stolen from a construction site in the city. The air smells of gasoline. It looks like a crime scene from an American movie.

She parks her car next to the store and ducks under the yellow tape. Inside, four men are arguing in loud voices. The smell of gasoline intensifies. The fattest man, flesh sagging from his small frame, slams down a bottle of Diet Coke and then turns and grins at Zembe.

"Mama Afrika."

"Sanibona, ninjani?"

"Siyaphila. Ulate."

"Late? I didn't realize you were paying my salary," Zembe retorts.

The fat man stands up. His head is too small for the rest of his body and it makes him look more like a cartoon character than a powerful member of the township community.

"Some bloody tsotsi from Diepkloof came in here last night while my cousin was working. Cleaned out over two thousand rand."

"I assume you can identify the culprit?"

"Of course. My cousin saw him coming a mile away. He's been asking for trouble for a while now."

"I see. Then perhaps you don't need my help?"

"Aren't you going to send it out on the radio, tell your buddies in Diepkloof about our man?"

"I might."

"I think you should."

The three other men have stopped talking, they sip their glass-bottled sodas in unison and watch Zembe. The fat man has his thumbs hooked into his jean pockets. He doesn't look at Zembe while he speaks to her – he's using the other three as his eyes.

"I need a favour," she says.

"We don't give favours to police."

"I don't send wires out for suspects without evidence. That means a search, shutting down the petrol station for at least a day, maybe more. Seizing the contents inside, asking witnesses to come down to the police station, answer questions."

"Fine, we won't need your radio. We have our own way of communicating with Diepkloof. But I don't want to think about what might happen to the dumb tsotsi who did this."

"You don't know where the culprit is. If you could find him you wouldn't be talking to me in the first place." Zembe crosses the dirty floor. She steps on a peanut shell and it cracks under her black shoes. She considers for a moment just who this burglar might be: a student at the university who doesn't often hang around the township? A visitor from another district? Another driver, travelling through? She stands close enough to the man that her face will at least register in his peripheral vision. "I need information about the 28s. We're looking into them for a bigger crime, something you don't want to be involved in. Let me know how I can get to them, just one of the members, and I'll send out your hit on the radio, make sure your guy hears about it, too."

"The dead ghost?"

Zembe grimaces. It would be only a matter of time before more of the details leaked to the rest of the township. "Yes. We're looking for his killer."

The fat man sits down. The three behind him stop sipping and look away from Zembe, in unison still. The walls of the store, already close and buckling, feel as if they are pressing in. The fat man's face goes slack.

"I can't help you." The man sits down.

"Then no radio, no report."

"The 28s don't operate here much, and when they do, it's mostly through their runners. We don't deal with them. We don't even know who they are. The drivers don't mess with the Numbers. No one does."

"You won't help me?"

"It's not possible, Mama Afrika. Not possible."

Zembe turns away and steps on another crunching shell. The three background players resume their banter, but in whispers. The fat man follows Zembe out of the building.

"Will you send out the report?" he asks.

"Why should I?"

"It has helped in the past to have us on your side."

"I need something more from you than pesky phone calls if we are going to cooperate."

"Ask me something I can deliver on next time."

"Yes, well, I'll look forward to that."

On Thursday, Zembe hears from Dadoo again. The water company's secretary asks her to hold and then his voice crackles through the old phone's earpiece.

"You were supposed to update me, but I've heard nothing."

Zembe responds too quickly. "There's nothing you need to know."

"I trust that any updates will be faxed directly to my office."

"Of course."

"There is something I would like to speak to you about. I called the national supervisor, a Mr. Sipho Thizwe, about this, but he hasn't returned my call."

"Yes?"

"Mr. Matthews has a daughter. She is insisting on travelling to Johannesburg."

"Coming here?"

"I'm sure she won't be a significant inconvenience, but as you can imagine, we don't have the time or manpower to deal with her vacation on top of the fallout from this . . . er . . . incident."

Zembe has half a mind to ask him why she should care about a girl's pilgrimage to see the place where her father died.

After a brief pause, Dadoo continues, "It would be a great help, to me and the company, if your office could supervise her trip."

"Pardon me?"

"I have already booked the hotel. All that is needed is an escort and a schedule of events. Some of those I can handle, like a tour of the company and the sites where Mr. Matthews worked, but we must make her feel as comfortable as possible while she is here. The project is already suffering from too much bad press. An unhappy family member would not help matters."

"Mr. Dadoo, you can't seriously expect my township station to play tour guide for some white kid?"

"That is precisely what I am asking."

"Can't be done. Sorry."

"That is disappointing. I will have to call the SAPS national director and tell him of our quandary. He is a member of our board, you see, so the girl's happiness directly affects his own financial well-being."

Zembe pauses, takes a deep breath. "Fax me her itinerary. I'll figure something out."

"That is most kind of you, Ms. Afrika."

She hangs up and takes a moment to think about how Dadoo has manipulated her. On top of the difficulties of this investigation, she now has to find a tour guide. Someone she can trust to keep the kid out of the way.

There is a small knock at the door and before she can answer Tosh sticks his head in.

"This fax just came for you."

That was fast. Dadoo must have been desperate to get the girl off his hands.

"And Commissioner Thizwe called again. He seems agitated."

Zembe takes the fax from Tosh's slim hands and glances at the grey type. She finds information about the girl and her arrival date; there is no time to get money together to hire someone. No money either, but that is beside the point. She needs someone she can control, who will do exactly what she says. She moves quickly to her desk and picks up her bag.

"I've got an errand to run. If Sipho calls, tell him his friends at the water company have priority and I'll get back to him when I get a chance."

Tosh protests, but she is already out the door and on the way to her car.

ZEMBE FINDS NOMSULWA PERCHED ON THE FRONT 75 steps of the community centre. Her light skin looks fire-black from far away, and shadows from a cap she's fingering fall across her face, making it darker still. She looks tough – is tough, Zembe corrects herself, a girl who ran with the boys' gangs for most of her childhood. And now a woman who stands up to powerful politicians on a regular basis. But there is a soft side to her too, an instinct to mother that brings many young children off the streets and into the offices of her organization to help paint banners or make phone calls. That side makes Zembe feel better about her decision to trust Nomsulwa with the Matthews girl. Despite her reluctance to help in the search for Kholizwe, she will agree because she owes Zembe. But she will do a good job because she cares too much not to.

"How is your mother? Feeling better?" Zembe is genuinely concerned. Mama Sithu has been failing quickly over the past few years and the change in her has been surprising for all her friends, especially for ones like Zembe who do not get the time to visit often.

"A little. Her emphysema acts up less in the cooler months," Nomsulwa answers matter-of-factly. Zembe wonders why Nomsulwa refuses to acknowledge their past, never mentions the many nights she spent with her family, the time her mother would have considered her a close friend – before she moved too far away for visits to be practical.

"Give her a kiss from me." Zembe responds with a heartfelt smile.

"Uh huh."

"I remember when we used to spend hours walking door to door fundraising for church. And on the street corners . . ." Zembe tries to remind Nomsulwa. "We would hold court in those days."

"Mama, I have a meeting to go to, I –"

Zembe launches in, stopping her escape. "I need a favour."

"I already called Mira and told him you wanted to speak with him. He'll get in touch. He just has his own schedule." Nomsulwa smiles at her small joke.

"Another favour." Zembe doesn't smile. "The foreigner who died, he was a water man –"

"So?" Nomsulwa jumps in. "Why do I care?"

Zembe continues as if she hadn't just been interrupted. "He worked for Amanzi's parent company and the company is, as you know, very close to the police services branch."

Nomsulwa isn't leaving, but she's certainly won't stay put for long either. Zembe speeds up her explanation. "The company is flying the daughter over here and has put my office in charge of taking care of her while she is in Johannesburg. That means I need to find a guide I can trust, fast." Now Nomsulwa really is turning around, as if to escape. "Where are you going?" She confronts Nomsulwa directly.

Nomsulwa stands still, legs taut and eyes big. "What can I do to help with that?" As if Zembe had levelled an accusation rather than a request. Then, before Zembe can answer her question, Nomsulwa starts to leave. "I really have to go to that meeting –"

"Wait. Don't walk away from me. You're the guide."

"You're crazy. I'm not going to be able to help you with this."

"You're going to have to. This is not a favour. It's an official request." Zembe walks forward, puts a hand on Nomsulwa's shoulder, and feels how tense the muscles are. She tries to be calmer, more friendly. "I haven't got enough information yet, I need more time." *Be grateful, Nomsulwa, that I didn't drag you down to the station that night.* "I need you to distract her, take her out, see the countryside, tour around. I need you to keep her busy." *Pause again, give her time to remember, to feel lucky and indebted.*

"Hayi-bo wena, you drunk? Not me, I can't." Nomsulwa walks up the stairs, stumbling a bit. Zembe follows her erratic path indoors.

"I could have turned you all in, I could have put you behind –"

"But you didn't." Nomsulwa spins and stands her ground. "You wouldn't because you resent the water men just as much as I do, as we all do. You hate every bit of what they've done here. You wanted those pipes gone. You were glad I was out there, doing what you didn't have the courage to do."

Zembe says very quietly, "I don't hate them enough to lose my job."

"Find someone else. I can't be in charge of some water man's kid."

"You're it. She arrives in four days. White girl, twenty-one years old. Be at the airport by eleven, it's the midday flight from Toronto. She'll be in the South African Airways terminal."

Zembe walks away.

"What's her name?" Nomsulwa calls after her.

"Claire Matthews."

Zembe does not look back. Nomsulwa will do it. She has to. The threat is real. Zembe doesn't like the idea of turning in this brave girl, but she will if she has to.

NOMSULWA ALMOST MAKES IT TO THE CAR. THEN SHE
feels sick to her stomach and turns around, dashing back
into her house. By the time she is on the road to the airport,
she is twenty minutes late.

79
–

She spent the past four days thinking of every possible
excuse to remove herself from the position of tour guide.
Each phone call was forcefully brushed aside by Zembe.
There is no choice. Either Nomsulwa shows up today or
she and her entire organization will be arrested for the pipe
theft. This reality sitting heavy on her chest, Nomsulwa
wonders what part of herself will shut down, what part of
her will turn off so that she can get through the task of
escorting this girl to and from her fancy downtown hotel.
For the first time in her life, she is thankful for her father, a
man who held life in pieces, always choosing which one
would rise to the surface. The kind of man who could break
your fingers one moment and then hold them in his cool,
broad hands with complete love the next.

The airport is on the opposite side of the city from
Phiri. She has been there once before, to send off a cousin
on his way to London for school. The entire family attended

his departure, shoving blankets and treats for the plane in his hands as he tried to escape. Nomsulwa hung back, fiercely jealous and nervous in the strange hall full of white men in business suits. One day, she swore, she would be the one with a scholarship, leaving on an airplane to study.

But then there had been a sick mother, and a cousin to keep out of trouble, and Nomsulwa had gotten her degree from the local university. A degree, sure, and with honours. But it is not worth much now.

The airport smells like cleaning fluid and men's cologne. She sidesteps ladies swathed in animal-print gossamer with large bags trundling behind them. Families are here this time, too, gathered in huge numbers to send off or receive their own prodigal sons. She doesn't look at faces, hoping to avoid recognition. She would have a hard time explaining her presence without giving away who she is picking up.

There is a scuffle on the left side of the hall. Crowds are being shifted this way and that as people gravitate towards the commotion. She follows a group of kids who were hovering around the vending machines to see what is going on. As she gets closer, she can hear the voice of a young woman yelling, "Give it back!" Another tourist fallen victim to the boys who hang around poaching unattended bags.

The woman in the centre of the gathering crowd still has one hand on her bag, while a tall boy backs away, looking very nervous about all the attention he is receiving.

The first thing Nomsulwa notices about Claire Matthews is that she looks incredibly familiar. Her colouring is all wrong.

Nothing like the pale ghost of the water man. But the eyes are the same. She is tiny; her face is scrunched and she is on the verge of exploding into tears, grabbing at her knapsack now securely in the arms of the tall boy searching for a place to run.

Before the boy has a chance to escape, Nomsulwa manages to scoot behind him.

"Shiya Buti," she says in a low voice. "Yeka isikhwama."

She holds out her left hand while tightening a vicious grip on the boy's shoulder. He winces. Bows his head, tries once to wriggle out of the hold, and then relents and passes the green-and-black bag to Nomsulwa.

"Dankie." Nomsulwa thanks him snidely before shoving him in the direction of the door. Those who were watching the interaction begin to pick up their own conversations and movement resumes all around Nomsulwa and the girl.

The second thing Nomsulwa realizes about Claire is that her dark hair and pale skin are unlike anything she has seen on a white woman before. There are no hard features, no tight mouth, and when she asks Nomsulwa to please give her her bag back, there is no whiney British accent, no hard clip of Afrikaans.

"I'm sorry, here you go." Nomsulwa reaches out with the knapsack.

"Thank you."

"No worries."

The girl sits down on the bench next to the baggage carousel.

"Are you Claire Matthews?" Nomsulwa asks, although she is already sure of the answer.

"Yes. Who are you?" A guarded expression covers Claire's face. She holds her bag tighter.

"I'm Nomsulwa. I've been sent to pick you up."

"I am meeting a police escort here."

Nomsulwa's not sure what to say to this. Claire is not budging, as if her escort couldn't possibly be the woman standing before her wearing an ill-fitting suit taken from the back of her closet.

"I'm it."

"You're a police officer?"

"Yes. I mean, no. I'm the escort."

"What is my father's name?"

"Peter Matthews." *The water man*, Nomsulwa thinks as she answers.

Claire gets her suitcase from under the bench. "I'm ready to go now," she says.

Nomsulwa reaches over for Claire's larger bag, but the white girl maintains a fast hold on the handle. Nomsulwa shrugs. They walk in tandem.

She had not, until this moment, contemplated that the girl would be a separate entity from the man, that the two could be individual people with different stories and histories. This girl, small, slight, tipping with the weight of the clothes she has brought for her African safari, is certainly not the man, angled, too tall, hair that blended into his skin that blended into his suit. The difference is a huge relief to Nomsulwa.

When they arrive in the parking lot, Nomsulwa directs Claire to her battered blue car. She is immediately self-conscious about the state of the paint and interior, and then just as quickly resents feeling that way. She throws the girl's bag in the trunk, gets into the driver's seat, and starts the engine without a word. They drive in silence, as though each is waiting for the other to capitulate and lose face.

Nomsulwa can smell Claire's nervousness and sadness like body odour. It seeps out of every crevice in the girl. She sees the will that is also there to keep her lips tightly clenched, to touch as little as possible of the small, dirty car, to take in almost nothing of the scenery around her – Nomsulwa realizes it's all part of the girl's futile effort to keep the smell in.

"You've been to Africa before?" Nomsulwa asks, conceding defeat.

"No," Claire answers, her voice less clipped.

"You'll like it here. It's the best place on earth." Nomsulwa smiles, and then doesn't know what to do because of course this is the farthest thing from the best place on earth, and Claire most certainly will not like South Africa. She stares at the road. Drive the girl to the hotel and get rid of her. This is not going to work.

"I've read a lot about South Africa and the work my father was doing," Claire answers quietly, eventually. "He was going to take me on the next trip."

She speaks almost like a child. Nomsulwa fakes another smile. She doesn't answer. She doubts that the water man would have taken his daughter further than the pool behind the air-conditioned hotel. Nomsulwa feels a little smug, for a second, before the reality of the dead man enters the conversation.

"I'm really sorry about your father," she chokes out.

Claire doesn't answer. Nomsulwa needs to get this girl out of the car.

"Do you know when I am supposed to meet with my dad's company?" Claire asks when they have gotten closer to the city and the large buildings can be seen through the front window.

"I know I'm supposed to take you to the police station in charge of the investigation tomorrow morning," Nomsulwa answers evenly.

"Oh." Claire slumps a little. Nomsulwa glances sideways, notices the parts of Claire that seem beyond her control: her hair curls at awkward angles from the base of her neck; her fingernails are bitten down to the skin with little scabs on the edges. She bites one now, catches Nomsulwa looking over, and quickly brings her hands down to her lap.

"I'm sure the company has left an itinerary for you at the hotel." Nomsulwa tries to reassure Claire, but she is really reassuring herself. Please let there be a full schedule, a plan for her so Nomsulwa can remain a glorified chauffeur. There is no way she'll get through this week – is it a week? – without it.

"How long are you visiting for?"

"My ticket home is for eleven days from now."

"Wow, that's a long time." What is she going to do for all that time?

"That's what my mother said." Claire pauses. "I want to see the places he worked, talk to the officers in charge of his case, talk to the men in charge of his schedule while he was here. There's a lot people don't know about my father, and maybe if they knew it, it would help them find –" Claire stops there. She folds her hands in her lap. Nomsulwa watches the road. She hears Claire shift in her seat. "I'd stay longer, but I'm starting law school soon. This is my only chance to come."

"Law school?"

"Yeah, that was the plan at least. Before . . ." Claire looks directly at Nomsulwa for the first time. Nomsulwa can sense her studying her face, the big hair and small jaw and big eyes. She imagines Claire taking in the way that Nomsulwa's hands are too large for the rest of her body and her clothes are tight over her arms. "He died trying to change things here. And I need to see what he was doing, what he didn't get to finish."

Nomsulwa nods, as if this is a satisfactory explanation for picking up and flying across the world to a strange and dangerous place and throwing yourself at the mercy of an anonymous company, an overworked police department, and a woman who would rather see you on the next plane home. Nomsulwa wonders if there is anything she could say right now that would convince this girl to turn around and go straight back to Canada. Only a small part of her admires the courage it took to make this trip.

The Regal Hotel is close to City Hall. Its exterior is the same slate-grey brick all the hotels on this strip chose. No windows, no doors other than the well-guarded revolving front door. High up, the windows begin, but they don't save the building from the severe impression it makes. A black man in a green uniform runs down to meet Nomsulwa's car. He opens the door and Claire steps out. Nomsulwa wants to drive away immediately. She wants to slap the small boys begging for change next to the steps who crack jokes about her beat-up car. She wants to run over the toe of the uniformed man snickering at the creak and whine the car makes as he closes the door behind Claire.

Instead, Nomsulwa cuts the engine and jumps out.

"I'll pick you up at nine-thirty tomorrow? To go to the station. Captain Afrika will be expecting you."

"Yes." Claire hesitates. Then she smiles at Nomsulwa, revealing white teeth too small for her mouth. "Thank you."

That is enough. Nomsulwa escapes, already dreading the morning and a repeat performance.

Nomsulwa calls Claire's hotel room at nine the next morning to make sure she is awake and ready to go. The phone rings three times and then a thick voice answers.

"Hello?"

"This is Nomsulwa. I am leaving now to come pick you up."

"Yes." Nomsulwa can hear Claire cough and then put the phone back up to her ear. The sheets rustle into the receiver muffling everything. Nomsulwa waits until there is silence again.

"I should be there in half an hour."

"Sure." Claire gives Nomsulwa her cellphone number and hangs up before Nomsulwa can say goodbye.

She turns to the outfit that she laid on the bed just minutes before the call. The grey slacks and dark-blue shirt look too conservative now, so she replaces them with white pants and a green sweater. When she has finished twisting her hair and smoothing the crinkled pants with a quickly heated iron, she takes a cold doughnut from the counter and runs out the door. She hasn't had her tea yet this morning and hopes that Zembe will have some brewing when they arrive. She can wait outside the door and enjoy a peaceful moment while the police and Claire have their meeting.

The drive to the hotel goes smoothly. As the hissing water towers fade into the distance behind her car, Nomsulwa watches the morning taxis bringing the day's workforce into the city. She would likely see many men she knows crammed inside the bursting vans, if only their jostled bodies weren't so obscured. Her car easily passes the slow taxi vans, but as she steps on the gas, the engine begins to knock in protest. She needs to get her car fixed. At this rate, she'll be lucky if she gets Claire to the Phiri police station at all.

The car is practically smoking when Nomsulwa arrives at the hotel. She leaves it, engine off, in the driveway to cool and passes the doorman ten rand to turn a blind eye to her intrusion. She enters the revolving front door and is stunned by the gold trim, the marble floor reflecting gold light, and the lavish chandelier with gold pendants hanging from its many branches.

It is breathtaking, but Nomsulwa has very little chance to take it in before a concierge sweeps down upon her.

"May I help you?" he asks with a British accent affected to cover the harder Afrikaans. The man blocks Nomsulwa's path, keeping her close to the door.

"I am here to pick up one of your guests. Claire Matthews."

"Perhaps you would prefer to wait outside. I will have her sent for." The man never loses his perfect smile, but Nomsulwa's jaw tightens. These same men are trained to let in black girls – done up and looking for clients – after dark. But in the daytime, they are quick to escort you back out onto the street.

"I would rather call her myself."

"It is hotel policy to have the front desk contact all guests when visitors arrive. Are you sure you would not rather wait by the door?"

"Just give me a second." Nomsulwa stands still, despite the man's efforts to push her into a corner of the room, finds Claire's number in her phone and punches CALL. It rings too many times and then moves through to voice-mail. The man cocks his head and purses his lips. Nomsulwa hits redial. Finally, there is a fumble on the other end of the line.

"Hello."

"Hi Claire, it's Nomsulwa. I'm downstairs in the lobby. Are you ready?"

"Umm . . ." There is a pause. "I'm not sure I'm ready."

"Okay, how much time do you need?"

"I'm not sure I'm going to make it today. I'm sorry. I just can't."

"I'm here already. Captain Afrika is waiting for you. It will only be a short meeting."

"I can't do it. I'm sorry." The phone goes dead and the concierge whips back around from the conversation he was having with one of his cronies farther into the golden hall.

"Not today, then?" he asks in a clipped tone.

Nomsulwa ignores him, turns around, and walks slowly, purposefully, out of the hotel. Her car starts on the second try and she almost intentionally mows down the hotel greeter stationed at the end of the driveway.

Spoiled fucking brat.

The highways are packed with morning traffic. It's a little after the work rush, but all those who were up late are still inching their way into the city centre.

It takes half an hour to get from Claire Matthews's hotel to the police station in Phiri.

Nomsulwa is in a rage by the time she throws open the screen door and confronts the two women pushing paper behind the reception desk.

"Where is Zembe?"

"Sawubona, sisi. What is it you would like?"

"I want to see Zembe."

Nomsulwa can hear Zembe's voice coming from a room close to the front. She looks beyond the cheerful reception she's negotiating and catches sight of a thick arm resting on the edge of a dark desk.

"Why do you wish to speak with Captain Afrika?" Nomsulwa doesn't answer the girl's inquiry; she simply sidesteps the long table and walks through to the main area of the station.

"Ima wena!" *Just wait!*

"Zembe!"

Zembe is on the phone. She holds up one finger and continues her conversation. Nomsulwa taps her fingers on the desk in a hard pattern, volume increasing with each repetition.

"Hold on, I'll have to call you back." She hangs up the phone and turns to Nomsulwa. "What happened? Is the Matthews girl okay? Why are you alone?"

"The Matthews girl decided not to leave the hotel today."

"Ahhh, poor thing was probably tired." Zembe's eyes fill with sympathy.

Nomsulwa is incredulous. "Poor thing? She made me drive all the way into the business district for nothing. Then, once the concierge had finished grilling me, she politely informed me that her highness didn't wish to be disturbed at this time. Bullshit. Sengidelile." *Enough.* "I came here to tell you in person that I am done with this job. I picked her up, that's enough."

"Nomsulwa, the girl lost her father. She's shaken up. Give her time."

"Voetsek."

"Hey now. We don't have a choice. The company insists we take care of this child. The police, right now, have to do what the company asks, orders from the national office. I need someone to watch her, make sure she doesn't get into trouble while she's here. If she wants to hide out in a hotel the whole time, all the better for us. Leave her. Call tonight and see if she wants to try again tomorrow."

Nomsulwa can see that Zembe is managing her, playing a part to quiet her down. *Don't coddle me*, she thinks, and gives her a warning stare. *Don't pretend that you understand this any better than I do.*

"Don't make me do this."

"This is not negotiable. I'll see you tomorrow morning at the same time, but bring her to police headquarters. The Commissioner wants to speak to her himself."

Zembe is firm in the face of Nomsulwa's angry frown. She waves her away as she lifts the receiver back up to her ear. Nomsulwa leaves, stomping her feet on the dusty station floor as she walks.

She can't return home. The competition between the smug face of the hotel concierge and the dismissive wave Zembe threw at her without a moment's concern over her troubles – she'll be too furious and take it out on Mira. He will be at her house for sure, slouched on the couch, beer in hand, watching the football game.

There was a time when Mira was invincible; now he is a man half-disappeared. More often than not his eyes are bloodshot when he comes to visit. He eats all her food and takes money from her purse. She would give up on him completely, but he still attends meetings, fires up the crowd like the old Mira, back again. And he is family, still there for Nomsulwa when she needs him most. He would give his life for her. He already has in so many ways.

She needs a drink, something familiar and bitter to help her forget the day.

HALF AN HOUR LATER, NOMSULWA ARRIVES AT Legends, in the club district. She walks past the doorman and through an imposing gate. Beyond the harsh exterior is a pebbled patio with picnic tables and umbrellas. The outdoor café is populated with people in casual summer sweats and peaked caps. The waitress, short and busty, gets to Nomsulwa's table almost before she does.

"What'choo'avin?" One word, with an expectant expression on her face.

"Black Label, in the bottle," Nomsulwa answers as she clambers over the bench and sits down. The couples around her turn to check her out, seated alone in her now wrinkled white pants. She recognizes a few faces and nods in their direction – Zandi and Susan, Christine and Mabusi. They are like cooing pigeons fawning over each other here in one of the few places where two women can intertwine legs while enjoying a cold drink. From the street, you would not know that Legends houses the largest lesbian bar in Johannesburg. It is well disguised with a big male bouncer and pictures of straight couples dancing on the exterior wall. The club itself is located near the end of the strip, where the space between buildings is a little too far to walk. Women know to drive directly here, but a group of men strolling in search of the next big night would rarely bother to make their way this far.

The security is necessary. This time last year, the most popular DJ at Legends got into a scuffle with some boys outside the club. Nomsulwa had been away that night, visiting her mother. It wasn't until the next morning that she heard about it. How everyone had assumed the fight was no big deal. How her friend was found the next day raped, beaten, and stabbed twenty-five times. They even put holes in the bottoms of her feet.

"Someone needed to make her a girl," the men arrested told the police, in the same breath denying participation in the murder.

The men were released six months later.

That was the last time Nomsulwa trusted the police to get anything right.

The waitress returns with the drink. She winks as she places it on the table. Nomsulwa hands her seven rand and takes a swig. The cool liquid and bitter taste calm her immediately. She relaxes into her seat, takes a moment to survey the crowd. Most of the women are clustered in larger groups, laughing and enjoying the shade provided by large white umbrellas. The picnic tables underneath are scattered with bottles. In this place, Nomsulwa feels like she is among family even when most of the faces belong to strangers.

A tall women peels off from one of the larger groups and walks over to Nomsulwa.

"Hey, girl." She is skinny with short hair relaxed so that it sticks to her head. Her smile is huge. She is wearing a pair of jeans and a baggy tank top displaying the logo for Loxion Kulca – advertising her ability to afford the nicest clothes in the South Gate Mall.

"Hi, Lindi." Nomsulwa positions herself to invite Lindi to sit next to her without seeming too eager.

"What you up to?"

"Nothing, ngizipholele. You know. I needed a break."

"All that toyi toying tiring you out?" Lindi jokes. She gives Nomsulwa a friendly nudge. Nomsulwa reaches for her hand before she can pull it away.

"Just needed a little distraction."

Lindi smiles.

It's too easy to be entertained. Lindi's thin body and deep black skin are beautiful. She moves like a girl who knows what it means to be wanted. And Nomsulwa has wanted her, watched her dance on many nights. But today her head needs more than a little flirtation to keep it off harder topics.

"I think I can help with that." Lindi waves over the waitress. "Can we get two vodkas? And throw in some oranges."

Lindi takes her hand back, but doesn't convince Nomsulwa that she wanted to.

"How's life?" Nomsulwa asks.

"The usual. I'm working in Durban, telemarketing. Making good money. Plus the surfing is nothing to scoff at."

"You surf?" Nomsulwa fiddles with her beer label.

"For sure, sisi. Better than you, I reckon."

"We will have to test that theory."

"Any time. You name it, I'll be there."

"Well," Nomsulwa fakes it, takes her chance to erase the day, "I don't want you going anywhere right now." She takes Lindi's hand back. Her skin is hot and dry. The vodkas arrive and Nomsulwa takes a big gulp of hers.

"Ach, slow down, sisi," Lindi chides her. "I need a chance to catch up."

"It's not going to be easy." Nomsulwa drains her glass and places the orange wedge in her mouth. The juice soothes the burn of the alcohol. Lindi laughs at her as she tries to extricate the peel from her lips. They kiss, both mouths wet with juice and vodka.

"Want to get out of here?" Lindi whispers.

On another day, Nomsulwa would have mocked the line. Today, she takes Lindi's hand and drops fifty rand on the table before walking off the patio into the parking lot.

THAT NIGHT, NOMSULWA DOESN'T SLEEP ENOUGH to dream and wakes up fuzzy and disoriented. Despite herself, her thoughts are full of Claire Matthews; Lindi's face has faded already from memory. The particular curve of dark hair on white skin that betrayed the girl in the car is all she can focus on. She waits for 7:30 to come. Finally, she dials. This time, the Matthews girl picks up after only two rings. Her voice sounds stronger.

"Hello?"

"Hi, it's Nomsulwa."

"Right. Hi."

"I was wondering if you feel up to going to the station today." Nomsulwa tries not to sound too sarcastic in her polite inquiry.

"Yeah. I mean, yes. Definitely. Yesterday was just a . . ." Claire's voice trails off and the thick sound of sleepiness seeps through. "Yesterday was a hard day. But I'm ready."

"I will be waiting outside at eight-thirty. Will you meet me out front?"

"Sure. I'll see you soon, then."

Her drive to the hotel is slower this time. She will arrive, pick up the girl, and drop her at the station, just as Zembe requested. Then she will leave. Next time, when Zembe calls for another favour, another tour for the water man's daughter, Nomsulwa will do what she should have done in the first place and refuse to help. She has discharged her obligation. Zembe has to see that.

NOMSULWA ARRIVES AND DOESN'T SEE CLAIRE. SHE idles outside for ten minutes before parking the car and entering the hotel. She steels herself for another inquisition from the hotel staff and it takes a moment for her to find a good spot, far enough away from the front desk to avoid attention as she scans the lobby.

Claire finally exits from the farthest set of elevators. She is wearing a pair of light-blue pants and a white shirt that hangs off of her small shoulders. She sees Nomsulwa and smiles, lets a little half-wave out before a man dashes out from behind the front desk and strides towards her.

"Claire Matthews?" Claire stops, confused, and nods.

"We have a number of messages for you. You didn't check in with the front desk yesterday."

"Yes, I know. I wasn't feeling well." Claire looks past the man at Nomsulwa when she says this.

The man hands Claire a small stack of pink slips. She stands still, reading each one, her face closing as she sorts through the pile. Claire crumples them all into a tight ball when she is finished and shoves them into her pocket. She looks around, unsure what to do next. Nomsulwa walks forward.

"Everything okay?" Nomsulwa sees the stress in Claire's small body. She suddenly feels responsible for her, which is, she realizes, exactly what Zembe was counting on.

"Yeah. Fine."

Nomsulwa isn't convinced, but reminds herself that her job is simply to deliver Claire to the police station. "Ready to go?" She turns towards the exit.

Claire hasn't moved. "My mother keeps calling." She looks up at the ceiling and takes a big, exasperated breath. "She's terrified. I called her when I arrived, but now she's asking if I'll turn around and come home. But I can't. I have to be here. Maybe I shouldn't have left her alone." She bites her lower lip and her angled face softens.

"Do you want to call her now, before we go?" Nomsulwa asks patiently, waiting for Claire to make a decision. But

Claire is immobile, paralyzed by the wad of pink messages in her pocket.

"She told me to come. Said I couldn't sit around the house all day, waiting by the phone for the police to call. She said that I needed to do *something*. And she was right. I needed to leave, to come find out for myself."

Nomsulwa thinks about her own mother. "But now you're gone and she's desperate to have you back. You know, she's worried, that's all."

"I know." Claire's voice gets quieter, like she is talking to a co-conspirator. "But I can't call and listen to her cry on the phone."

Nomsulwa understands what it means to escape that responsibility. "What if there's nothing to find out here? What if you left her for no reason."

"There is. There has to be something. He just got on a plane. He got on a plane and disappeared into thin air and that's not . . ." Claire searches for the end of her sentence.

"You should call your mother."

"She's my mother. Don't worry about it. I will." Claire begins to walk away, but this time Nomsulwa is the one to stay put.

"She's your responsibility now." Nomsulwa presses. "He's gone so you have to take care of her from now on."

"I will. Don't you think I know that?" Nomsulwa detects a tiny bit of anger and impatience in her voice.

"I know what it's like to have a dead father and a broken mother. That part I understand."

This Claire doesn't respond to, so Nomsulwa continues, walking past Claire to the exit as she talks. "It can feel like a huge weight and unfair and you can waste your whole life trying to make things better just so you can finally escape and that doesn't really ever happen."

"Look." Claire stops just before the door, blocking Nomsulwa's way. "That's not my life, okay? I'm going to start school when I get back home. I'm going to move out and get my own apartment and live my life. My father would have wanted that."

"Is that what *you* want?" They stand face to face, now.

Claire shifts her gaze to the ground, giving up on their staring contest. "All I want is to have him back."

Nomsulwa can't look at Claire any more. The feeling of wishing she knew nothing about water men is so overpowering it makes her feel like she might split in two. When she is with the fragile girl in front of her, all confusion and sadness, she regrets every moment of her life that brought her anywhere near the company and the police.

"We should get going." Nomsulwa barely manages to say.

"Yeah." Claire walks down the steps to the waiting car.

Nomsulwa gets into the driver's seat. She turns on the car and presses on the gas, hoping speed and the highway and the noise will erase the thoughts Claire has brought up in her.

Claire finally settles in and watches the road. Nomsulwa takes a deep breath and turns down the radio, now playing soft R&B.

Claire takes out the many crumpled pink messages once they are clearly out of the city. She smoothes out one message in particular. Nomsulwa glances over, but can't read the writing.

"It's the water company. They left me an itinerary and a phone number for Alvin something. So I guess I'll call him and see if they can't help me find my father's papers."

Nomsulwa imagines Claire alone in a cold office with pieces of her father everywhere. She pictures her surrounded by him and his life and how hard that must be. Maybe the girl in the car with her has more pride and strength than she gave her credit for. They drive in silence, only light radio in the background. The traffic smoothes by. They have just missed the rush hour minibus taxis and commuters in fast cars, and the road seems almost peaceful. Highway turns back into urban avenues between large buildings as they enter the government district.

"You ready?" Nomsulwa asks.

"I'm nervous," Claire says.

"You'll get through it."

"Yeah. . . . You'll come in with me?"

Nomsulwa is about to refuse. She can't imagine hearing one more word about the water man than she has to. Then she realizes that she is being offered a look into the investigation, a chance to learn what the police know. All the usual police leaks have dried up for this one. She is the only one with access. At least, this is what Nomsulwa tells herself when she nods.

"Thank you."

"Not a problem." Nomsulwa gives a grimace that was meant to be a supportive smile.

POLICE HEADQUARTERS IS LOCATED IN A TALL WHITE building. The avenues here are wide and the buildings are mostly grey and brown, separated by carefully tended lawns. There is a fountain in the median, also brown, with birds of paradise at the corners. Orange is the brightest colour around. But Claire might have missed all this because when they drive into the covered car lot, she looks, eyes wide and glassy, as if she has been asleep.

"We're here," Nomsulwa says.

"Yes."

The elevator takes a long time to reach the thirty-fourth floor and Nomsulwa says nothing the entire ride. The secretary waves them in with a weak smile. Claire pauses, lets Nomsulwa lead.

In the office the air is too cold from the AC wall unit behind the desk. Zembe perches on the edge of a side table, and a tall man Nomsulwa doesn't know rests in a chair behind Zembe.

Nomsulwa takes a stool from the corner and sits far away from Claire. Zembe gives her a hard look, but she ignores it despite the officer's wishes.

The Commissioner begins, explaining things very slowly, bit by bit painting the picture as gently as possible for Claire. His voice is deep and monotonous. They found Claire's father in the township, they don't want to upset her by going over again the details of her father's death that she and her mother were provided by phone, but they know who is responsible and all units are looking for the culprit. They believe her father was killed by a member of a local gang, likely for his money. They'll know more once the suspect is apprehended.

"Where was he found?" Claire stops the Commissioner in mid-sentence.

"In Phiri."

"But where? Show me a map so I can see *where*." She won't let this detail go.

The Commissioner reaches into a closed file on the desk and takes out a crude map.

"Here, on Lenkoe Street, between the two houses that meet up with Nsizwa. In this yard hidden from the street."

When the Commissioner removes the map, several photos fall out of the yellow folder. Claire reaches for these, and the Commissioner slides the photos back, out of reach.

"Show me those photos."

"Are you sure?" The man is incredulous, but seeing Claire's face he opens the file. Both Zembe and Nomsulwa lurch forward.

"No, let him," Claire says in a strange, high voice. "I need to see."

The man lays the pictures on the desk, facing Claire. Nomsulwa tries to avert her eyes but catches sight of an eyebrow, a hair, brown and curled. She sees a hand, white and yellow-rimmed from what looks like sand. It lies palm down, the back visible and bathed in light.

Claire reaches out and touches the last image where a gold ring wraps around the middle finger. The band displays three letters like swaying tree trunks intertwined: PEM.

"Where's his ring?"

"What?" Zembe asks.

"Where is his ring? I want his ring." Claire is still focused on the photo.

"It's in evidence," the Commissioner answers, voice firm.

"It's my property." Claire looks up, defiant.

"We'll send it to you with the rest of his effects once the case is closed," Zembe assures them both.

"That could be years. I need it now. Please?" Claire directs this last plea to Nomsulwa, who shrinks back. She can't get involved in police business.

"The ring." Claire motions with her hand. She stands up, raises her voice, "The ring is mine, ours. We need it at home." She seems wobbly on her feet, she sways. Nomsulwa gets to Claire in time to support her as she doubles over, retches twice, and throws up clear liquid on the office floor.

"Take her back to the hotel," Zembe orders, panic on her face.

Nomsulwa does as she's told, propping Claire up as they slowly make their way to the exit. Claire rests her head on Nomsulwa's shoulder, but straightens when they hit the outside air.

By the time they are on the main road to the hotel strip, Claire is sitting upright, staring ahead. She says nothing.

Nomsulwa parks the car and walks with Claire through the lobby and up to her room. Claire turns to her once they reach the door.

"I'm fine."

"No you're not."

"I just need to be alone." Claire's voice cracks. The embarrassment shines on her face like sweat.

Nomsulwa tries to say something reassuring, but before it can come out, Claire hardens her expression. She unlocks the door with the key card, enters the room, and closes the door without looking back. Nomsulwa stands there for a long minute listening to make sure Claire doesn't collapse, doesn't call for help, doesn't retch loudly again. After it becomes entirely quiet, she turns and retreats.

As soon as she is in her car she opens her cellphone and dials Mira.

"I think it's about time you started cooperating with Zembe. They have a suspect. . . . Member of a gang. . . . No, they didn't say a name. . . . They don't know that. You're safe."

SEVEN

When Zembe arrives back at the Phiri police station, Mira is in front of it. He seems to be surveying the building and the wide sandy parking lot that is empty too often. The green paint is faded, from rain mostly, but there is the occasional swatch of brighter colour where Zembe has made an officer paint over graffiti. A large tag, wonkily placed on a corner, reappears periodically – kids showing off the immunity of youth.

The structure has a central screen door, useless for keeping out the cold or many of the bugs. Mira starts towards it, slowly, unaware that he is being watched.

He has been here only once before. Zembe made sure it was the last time. She's not sure why. Certainly it was not because her heart went out to the tall, snide kid she arrested fifteen years ago, after a fruit cart was overturned, the owner kicked in the side before the boys ran away. Perhaps it was because he came with a sidekick: a fragile girl with huge hair and eyes that were light for her skin. She was too skinny to be beautiful, but she had a striking, head-turning smile, and a surprisingly loud voice.

—

THE ROOM SHE HELD MIRA IN THEN WAS BROWN with narrow windows near the ceiling that blocked out the light rather than filtering it in. Even the orange sunrise outside crept in as only a whisper of pale dust floating in front of Zembe's face. She looked hard at the boy in front of her. He was wiry, too tall, sneering. The insults came from him faster than Zembe could pick them up: "bitch, whore, slut, skinny, sick." Zembe waited them out. She waved away the other officer in the room, who had inched closer to the boy and rested his hand around his gun. When the boy finally ran out of curses, Zembe placed her hand on his arm and jerked him hard. "Shutup wena."

She patrolled the streets every day. She saw these tsotsis, gangsters, slouched against corner store walls, smoking awkwardly rolled cigarettes and ganja. They spoke in tsotsitaal, a bastard Afrikaans that is incomprehensible even when it is heard at a normal volume. Usually Zembe heard their slurs only in screams that followed her as she drove. She didn't know these boys by name, but she knew their mothers. They talked to one another at the windows of the nearest spaza. They complained about their sons who stole food in the middle of the night but wouldn't come in to sit for a family meal. Kids who took money from their mothers' purses, even though they could see that their families were struggling.

In the same breath, the women told stories about their sons as babies, how curious they were, how active and strong. They carried pictures of young, smiling boys, the images creased from folding and refolding.

Outside the office, Zembe heard a racket. A girl's voice called the boy's name out over and over again. "Mira. Mira!" She screamed as only teenage girls can scream. "Leave him alone!" There was a scuffle. The door rattled, officers tried to hold the girl back, but she made it anyway and flung herself through the door into the small room.

Mira looked shocked. The sneer, the slouch, gone. He ran to the girl, surprising Zembe into releasing her grip on him.

"Sisi," he whispered fiercely. "Get out of here."

Nomsulwa ignored him. She marched up to Zembe, thrusting aside the other officers' attempts to gently restrain her. She was so small, so slight, the adults in the room were scared they would break her if they grabbed too hard.

"It was me. Leave him alone."

Zembe was surprised and smiled despite herself at the gall of this small thing. She really thought that the police would believe a skinny girl overturned the entire fruit cart, launched it off the platform in the market, and took off with a bag of fruit? All by herself? The boy she was standing in front of was a well-known runner, moving up in the township world, friends with boys who were older and stole things much more valuable than some mangoes from a cart.

Mira held Nomsulwa by the shoulders and turned her to face him. He shook her, whispering the entire time as if the secret could stay between them. "Thula wena. Voetsek. Hamba manje! Hamba!"

"I won't go. I won't go. I won't let you go to jail." Nomsulwa slammed small fists into the boy's chest. She cried, big open tears. She was obviously terrified. Mira closed her into his long arms. He held her while she shuddered. They seemed completely unaware of the audience of officers gathered around them. The men were hanging back, letting Zembe lead the way. Even though they were all the same rank, it was her collar and, besides, crying children are women's business.

108
–
That night, after cajoling the fruit stand owner into dropping the charges and accepting instead a month's work from the boy, Zembe knocked on Nomsulwa's door. An older woman answered, eyes tired and hands thin.

"Mama Sithu. We need to talk about Nomsulwa and Mira."

Zembe explained, frankly, to the woman in front of her about the crowd her daughter was running with. She also told her about Mira's actions in the station, the way he comforted her daughter.

"They are family," Nomsulwa's mother offered. "uMira is a good boy. Good boy with a hard father."

They agreed that Mira would move in with the Sithus, go to school, eat meals at home. If Nomsulwa was insistent on spending time with her cousin, then the two women would turn the cousin into someone worth spending time with.

When Zembe left, Mama Sithu hugged her bigger and longer than it looked like she could. Small women with huge fire, Zembe thought. Then she said, "Nomsulwa is special, Mama. Something about her. She is a force."

"It's her name. 'Purity' is too large a burden for a girl. I told her father that, but he would not listen."

"Perhaps it is her mother." Zembe smiled.

"I wish I had that much influence over her."

"I think she is more like you than you realize," Zembe offered before turning to leave.

Their plan, surprisingly, worked. Zembe checked in weekly, then every month or so, and soon she and Mama Sithu spent their visits sipping tea and parsing township gossip rather than worrying about the children.

Then the electricity and water men came, and Nomsulwa and Mira found a new way to run afoul of Zembe.

109

—

"You here to see me, bhuti?" Zembe stops Mira before he gets through the door.

"Yebo, Mama. uNomsulwa told me to come."

"I know your friend is back in town."

"I have lots of friends, Mama." Mira turns, leans against the wall, and lights a hand-rolled cigarette.

"I am interested in one friend in particular. Kholizwe."

"What makes you think he is in town?" Mira exhales, looking around at the street, squinting for a look at the goings-on, even though the police station is a good two blocks from the tightly packed Phiri centre.

"Don't waste my time. Just give me the name of the shebeen he's using this time."

Mira doesn't let his eyes meet Zembe's. He shuffles his feet and makes a big show of pondering the request. Then he shrugs his shoulders, stomps out the cigarette even though it is only half smoked, and starts to walk away.

Before Zembe can protest, Mira tosses over his shoulder, "I saw him last at Tiger's. But you didn't hear it from me."

Zembe watches him walk for almost a minute before heading inside. She turns at the front desk to enter the wide room that holds the desks and lockers of her officers.

"I need three men."

One of the two people in the room turns to her. He is an older officer, hired on to the force before Zembe, but stuck on the same assignment for too long because of intermittent alcoholism.

"I'm not supposed to start rounds of Zone 2 until they get back with the buggy."

Zembe turns to Tosh, who is standing behind her. "You free?"

"Sure." He walks to the desk and picks up a second holster.

"Hold here for a moment, both of you, we need to find one more."

"One more?" Sipho's low voice sounds from behind the partition. He walks in and stands next to Zembe.

"What are you doing here?"

"Helping, it turns out, although I thought I was just checking up on you. Was ordered to, in fact, see if the Phiri station was handling things."

"Fucking national," Zembe says under her breath.

"Now, now." Sipho puts a hand on her shoulder. "If it wasn't for national you'd be one man short. Where are we going, anyhow?"

"I have a lead on Kholizwe's location."

Sipho pauses. "Are you sure we shouldn't call in backup for this? We have no way to know how he'll react when we take him."

"We aren't taking him."

"We aren't?" Sipho sits in the chair on the other side of Tosh's desk. He looks at Zembe with resigned eyes, as though he knows this is going to be a fight.

"We have no evidence, no way of knowing if he's responsible. I'm not sending him into hiding until we know for sure."

"And how will we know for sure?" The two officers watch the back-and-forth between Sipho and Zembe. Zembe wishes he would take the condescension out of his voice.

"I have a way."

"And I'm supposed to trust you?"

Zembe doesn't respond. She motions for her two offic-ers to follow her. "I'll go without you if I have to," she says.

Sipho follows her without further protest, deciding, she guesses, to wait it out and see what unfolds. Zembe under-stands that approaching Kholizwe without arresting him may cause him to run anyway. But she won't risk arresting him only to have him turned loose a few days later. A man with a record would usually be ushered quickly into the criminal court system and given a government lawyer, who, when offered a stiff sentence, would agree and have their client shipped off to jail. Kholizwe, unfortunately, can afford to pay for a real lawyer. A white lawyer. That can equal freedom, or at least a light sentence. When she gets him for this murder, Zembe wants it to stick.

The men pile into Zembe's own car and begin the trip to Tiger's. No one speaks. Sipho grunts while texting on his cellphone; Tosh drums out an imaginary beat on his thigh. Zembe can tell they are nervous. She is nervous too, but she drives smoothly, forcing her hands to hold the wheel lightly, to move the gearshift slowly.

TIGER'S SHEBEEN IS A TUMBLEDOWN BOX OF METAL and wood on the outskirts of Phiri's lok'shini. At night it brims with teenagers clutching large bottles of beer, but during the day a few men sit, drinking and playing dominoes. A woman is behind the counter, head down on her hands. No sign of Kholizwe. Zembe walks in alone once the group of them have established that the gang leader is nowhere in sight.

"Wake up!" Zembe taps the woman on the side of the head. She doesn't move, just groans, so Zembe tries to physically pry her head up from the bar. The woman looks at Zembe for a second before closing her eyes again. Zembe gives up and turns to the old men playing dominoes.

"I'm looking for Kholizwe."

The men laugh. The table, uneven on its legs, shakes and one of the domino pieces falls, revealing its dotted side to the man's opponent.

"Voetsek," the man mutters.

"Is he here?"

"Does it look like he's here?" the opponent grunts.

"He was here yesterday. I need to know where he went."

"Out." The men aren't afraid to give Kholizwe up. They seem nonplussed about the possibility of his return.

"Is he coming back?"

"Don't know." The man sitting closest to Zembe places a tile on the growing pattern of dominoes, then he smacks his fist on the table triumphantly.

"Ha!"

"Nah, can't place it there, you didn't announce." The men descend into an argument. Spit flies and fists slam. The table wobbles dangerously and the men seem unaware of the impending collapse of their game.

When the table settles, the man with the overactive fist mumbles to Zembe, "uKholizwe is meeting with the happy men from lok'shini two."

His opponent laughs. "Yeah, happy is a needle and an ice cream cone."

"Yebo, bhuti. Yebo," the fist answers, chuckling as he gently lays down a double six.

Zembe doesn't say thank you or wait to see the end of the game. She walks quickly away from them and back out the door.

"Sipho, let's get back in the car. He's not here."

"Are we going back to the station?"

"No, he's in Zone 4, at the heroin house. Let's drive there and see if we can't track him down."

The older officer groans audibly. Zembe ignores him and gets back into the car. They drive a roundabout route to the east side of downtown Soweto. Trawling the streets runs them past at least four groups of tsotsis who point at Zembe, kick dust behind her tires. But none of them hide the gang leader.

"Let's head to the far side of the house. I'll drive around from the back while you set up a perimeter," Zembe instructs. They approach the white shack stuck between two red brick structures. She sees the flash of a familiar face on the south corner as soon as her vehicle noses around to the front. She mutters into her radio and drives the car around to where Kholizwe can see it. Before opening the door, she prays: *Keep my soul, and deliver me; let me not be ashamed for I put my trust in You. In Jesus Christ, Amen.*

Zembe signals Sipho and the other two officers to stand back by the doors of her car. Sipho starts to protest and Zembe shoots him a hard look. She is running point on this one, irrespective of rank. After a second of hesitation, he and the others find their spots and place their feet shoulder-width apart, hands hovering over their hips, ready to draw when necessary. Zembe walks towards the man at the front of the house alone.

Kholizwe's eyes are set deep in their sockets. Triplet scars adorn his left temple. His face is wide and flat with pointed cheekbones, and his lips are too thin. So thin that when he sneers his teeth take over his face, so thin that the spit he aims at Zembe's feet can escape easily. Zembe turns to him, facing her broad shoulders towards his slumped frame. She doesn't allow herself to show any reaction.

"Watch yourself, bhuti."

Kholizwe leans back and puts his hands in his pockets, revealing the bright silver of two handguns tucked into matching holsters.

Kholizwe is the mascot spirit of Phiri gang culture. He is nowhere and at the same time on the lips of all the nine-year-olds acting out shootouts on their mothers' front walks. He has survived two gang wars and a five-year stint in Sun City. He is only twenty-four. Zembe met him when he first joined Thug Life: children, twelve to sixteen years old, training for life in the real gangs. They mostly deal in tik, a bastard version of crystal meth that promises a longer high than crack if you're willing to pay the twenty rand extra. Zembe was on the team that put him away for armed robbery after the gang rape and murder of four high school students on their school's playground. They had been lucky to pin him with anything. In Sun City, Kholizwe joined the 28s and rose quickly. By the end of his five years he owned his own cell in the prison and had at least ten men under him.

Zembe doesn't ask him about the guns, but she lets her own jacket fall open, revealing her pair of police-issued RAP 401s in a subtle grey-black. Now they are even. It is daytime, but the street corner where Kholizwe has stationed himself for the day is as deserted as Zembe's own block after dark.

"I killed the last pig who showed me his gun."

The tsotsitaal is harsh from his lips. It cuts, showing the ragged piecemeal of the language. Tsotsitaal is a weapon for Kholizwe, partly because everything he says is weighted with truth. He doesn't boast because he doesn't have to.

"What do you want, pig? Or sow, shouldn't I call you a sow?"

Zembe steps forward and comes within a foot of Kholizwe's face. He merely glances at the line of policemen, now with their guns drawn. *Keep my soul, and deliver me – I put my trust in You*, Zembe repeats to herself.

"You know what I'm looking for." She tugs on the collar of her own shirt, illustrating.

Kholizwe adjusts his T-shirt. The rim of the cloth is dark brown from sweat and days of wear. The material is soft and almost thin enough to see through.

"Fuck you."

Zembe doesn't move. The officers step closer. She sees Kholizwe consider his options, look to the door, now blocked by a man with a gun. Finally, he takes his fingers and pulls the neck of his shirt down, revealing muscled skin and a black tattoo.

He is adorned with a line of ink with numerous slashes across it, like the image of a cartoon scar. Each slash represents a body: a man or woman Zembe's team dredged out of the stream that runs behind the shantytown, a prisoner who ended up hanged in his cell when his friends were all conspicuously absent, a fellow gang member who got out of line and then was "transferred" to another location. Kholizwe documents his kills religiously. The station has pictures of that tattoo's development from before he even entered Sun City. It cannot be used as evidence in court, it's not helpful when pinning crimes on him, but it tips them off, tells them they are looking at the right guy, the right organization. Zembe remembers the four raw lines, red from the recent injections of ink, that he showed her the day after the four girls were murdered. The smile and the raised tattoo skin. Those images haunted Zembe for the full two years of investigation and trial.

Zembe looks at the tattoo now. Her surprise at the lack of red, raw marks causes her to step back, forgetting for a second the showdown she is in.

"Looking for something, officer?" Kholizwe's voice is a whisper.

"There's nothing here," Zembe yells to her backup.

"I would leave now, pig. If you know what's good for you." Spoken like an observation.

Zembe stares at him, using every ounce of prayer and restraint to avoid hitting him. But eventually, grudgingly, she does as she's told.

The rest of the gang will be harder to pin down. If Kholizwe has no new tattoo he didn't order the kill. Zembe backs away from Kholizwe's eyes and worn shirt and lazy grin.

"You came here to pin another on me?" he yells to her. "You can't frame me again."

The door shifts behind him and a small boy peeks out. There is a large welt over the left side of his face so that he looks almost like a younger version of his boss. He doesn't try to hide the fear all those guns cause and quickly disappears back inside the building.

When Zembe is back in the car and driving towards the station, Sipho launches into her.

"What was that?"

"He didn't do it."

"How can you know?"

Zembe pulls the car over now that they are a few blocks away from Kholizwe's corner. She faces Sipho. "Every time he orders a kill, or someone dies on his watch, he marks it on his shoulder. There's nothing there. No new tattoo."

"So maybe he didn't get one this time. Or he hasn't done it yet."

"Listen." Zembe hesitates for a moment, unsure about talking to her superior in this way in front of the other officers. Sipho's belligerent face eggs her on. "I know this guy. I followed him for years. There are no exceptions to this rule. And he doesn't wait."

Zembe turns back to the road, ignites the engine, and drives the full way back to the station in silence. She assumes that Sipho is thinking of ways to circumvent her on this and bring Kholizwe in for questioning. She doesn't care. If Kholizwe wasn't involved in the murder it must have been a rogue member, or another gang copycatting the 28s' M.O.

Or it wasn't a gang murder at all.

THE NEXT MORNING, ZEMBE FINDS A NOTE ON HER desk written in the curly cursive of the girl who watches the front in the morning.

Need a list of all people Matthews met with while he was here.
Sipho

Zembe is not sure why Sipho hasn't been given this information already. But knowing her own difficulty in getting Dadoo to talk about anything but the gang investigation, she's sure the national office has been reluctant to press the water company for any information that indicates a shift in focus.

Before she heads back downtown she puts four officers on a search for other men connected with the Soweto gang system. What crimes the gangs don't commit themselves, the members generally hear about after the fact. It's been over two weeks since the water man landed in Phiri, and still, gang members, who congregated like skin spots on every corner before the murder, are nowhere to be found. Zembe's sources tell her they went underground when the news of the murder got out. She could have figured that one out on her own.

Zembe doesn't like the idea of returning to Dadoo's office. She drives into the business district, passes by the Regal Hotel, and realizes that Dadoo's office is not far from where the Matthews kid is staying. She makes a mental note to remember to check in with Nomsulwa.

Inside the building, the same four guards are squished up against the marble walls. One grins at Zembe as she waves her hand to get the attention of the receptionist. This time the woman urges her into the elevator on her own after getting permission from upstairs. Zembe presses the button for the fourteenth floor and hopes she has recalled the number correctly.

On her first visit, she hadn't noticed that the reception area of Dadoo's floor is covered in the Amanzi logo. A friendly personified water tap adorns the front desk. Water posters, like the ones Zembe sees every day near her house, line the walls. She takes time to absorb the office itself. "Water Is Precious" is written on the wall over the front desk in all eleven languages of South Africa. The phrases follow each other in a line down to the floor. A small mound of water brochures sits on the coffee table in between chairs. She flips through them while she waits for Dadoo.

Over thirty minutes later, a tall woman in a black skirt and matching jacket approaches her.

"Captain Afrika?"

"Yes."

"Mr. Dadoo is in a meeting. Is there something I can do for you?"

"I need some more information concerning Mr. Matthews's stay here. I was hoping Mr. Dadoo could help me."

"He asked me to fulfill any request you might have."

"Fine. I want a list of everyone Mr. Matthews saw while he was here."

"I will see what I can do. Please wait here."

The woman waddles back into the office, leaving Zembe with the brochures. She flips through the same one she's already read twice. It details the new, improved tamper-detection system on the "Atlantic" water meter.

The meter itself looks much like the ones already installed in the township. It is white and small. But the computer screen is larger and the plastic casing, according to the ad, is lined with wires. Any movement of the casing and all water is cut off.

It is nearly an hour before the woman returns.

"Mr. Dadoo can see you now."

"Oh, great." Zembe follows the woman back to the offices. She pretends a heartfelt thank you and sits in the same room she met Dadoo in before. He slides into the office almost immediately after the woman leaves.

"So sorry to keep you. I had a meeting I couldn't avoid. Perhaps if you had called beforehand –"

Zembe cuts him off. "I needed the information right away. Our deadline is very tight."

"I understand." Dadoo is just as grim as always. "Have there been any developments?"

"Yes, we have decided to expand the investigation slightly. We need more information about other people who might have come into contact with Matthews while he was here."

"I heard that the new theory was that this was a copycat murder, someone pretending to be part of a strong gang."

Zembe silently curses Sipho. She knew he wouldn't trust her to follow up with the gangs on her own. "It could be that, but I'm looking to cover all of our bases. I need to see whether there are any other avenues to explore. While the gang investigation continues."

Dadoo picks up the only piece of paper on the desk. "Here is the list you requested. I've excluded hotel staff, I assume you can look into them on your own."

"Thank you."

The list is short, about fifteen names. Many of them are familiar to Zembe. She is confused and looks to Dadoo.

"There are at least five city councillors on this list."

"Yes. We meet with the local politicians to ensure a safe delivery of our services."

"But the services were not being delivered safely. Pipes were being stolen, some right in Phiri."

"That was one of the things we discussed."

"How did the councillors respond?"

"Well."

"Meaning?"

"They listened to our concerns and suggested some alternative solutions."

"Alternative solutions?"

"Means by which the opposition could be controlled."

"What means?" Zembe presses, an idea already forming.

"We like to incorporate public appeal strategies into all our projects."

"They asked for money, didn't they?"

"We give a large amount of money to local infrastructure, including some to the councillors for ad campaigns aimed at increasing support for the new water system."

"How much did they ask for this time?"

"It wasn't a fixed amount. More like a discussion of the funds we would need to get the job done."

"So it wasn't the usual cash grab. The bribes the councillors expect . . ." Zembe lets her voice trail off.

"Our company does not engage in criminal activity. And I resent the suggestion, Ms. Afrika. Unless you have other questions, I must get back to work."

Zembe can see Dadoo tapping his pencil impatiently. She stands up and holds out her hand. "Thank you very much, Mr. Dadoo."

123

"My pleasure." Dadoo's handshake is weak and he barely takes time to drop Zembe's hand before showing her out the door.

In the lobby, the guards have changed their shift and the grinning man has been replaced by a lanky kid, no older than eighteen, with acne plotting a course around his chin. He keeps his hand on his gun while scanning the room.

Zembe nods to the security quartet and ducks into the sun.

EIGHT

MIRA IS YELLING AT NOMSULWA LOUDLY ENOUGH that the small children playing outside of the house have moved a little farther down the street. When he gets angry, the vein in the centre of his forehead sticks out, splitting his head in two. Nomsulwa focuses on the vein because the mouth is contorted and frothing.

"Mira, this is not up for discussion. I can't do it. I can't be around her."

"You can't afford not to follow her. Next to the white girl you'll be able to find out things Zembe wouldn't dream of telling you herself – where the gang investigation is going, who the suspects are, who they've arrested. Can't you see how important that is?"

"I get it. But we know what's important. Zembe told you herself. They're after the 28s. Warn who you want to."

"One stupid meeting doesn't give us the information we need," Mira says.

"It will have to."

Mira swings around violently and punches the wall. The plaster splinters and caves. A hole larger than his fist opens. He retracts his hand, the knuckles now split and bloody.

Nomsulwa is momentarily stunned. The boy she loves and the man punching walls don't reconcile.

"Look what you've done."

"Forget the fucking wall."

"You'd better be on your way out the door to get plaster to repair it."

Nomsulwa turns her back on Mira and walks towards her couch in the far corner of the room. Mira clamps down on her shoulder, he whips her around. "Don't walk away, sis. I need this. We need this. You have to go back. Things could change. We need to know if they find anything else."

Face to face, Nomsulwa can see the panic in her cousin. He really believes that Nomsulwa's time with the white girl, overhearing bits and pieces of the investigation, will help. He's not necessarily wrong. But it's not an option.

"I can't be around her any more. I can't look at her eyes, be near her." Nomsulwa sinks into the living room chair. "It's too much."

"It's hard. I know."

Nomsulwa lets out her breath. She waits a second before looking at Mira, now sitting next to her. He is quiet. The sunlight falls in through the living room window and lands at their feet. Dust plays games in the air, darting in and out of swirling patterns.

"She is different from him. I thought it would be easier to hate her but –"

"Do you remember who her father is? The monster she is here to mourn?"

"Yes. Which is why I need to get out." Nomsulwa collects herself. "I need to wash my hands of this altogether. It's too much. She's . . . she's too much. Too easy to take care of, to be around."

"You mean she is too nice?" Mira snorts. "All the better. Use it. Use her."

"I can't," Nomsulwa finally admits, letting the weight of it fill with the words. It feels like a confession. Mira puts his arm around her, but he doesn't let the argument go.

"This is not a vacation, not the beginning of a grand love affair. Everything is at stake – our lives, the township. I'm not going to let one charming white girl stand in our way."

The room is silent. The kids on the street yell as one hits the ball past a fielder. Nomsulwa leans on Mira's bony shoulder. He holds her. The phone rings.

"Shit." Nomsulwa gets up and answers. "Hello?"

Mira wanders towards the television. He moves to turn it on, but Nomsulwa violently waves him off.

"Yeah. I'm glad you called, Zembe. I have to talk to you about the Matthews girl. . . . Yeah, I know. . . . What?"

Mira perks up at Nomsulwa's rising tone.

"She what? . . . Are you sure? . . . Can't you drive her? . . . No. I don't want that either. I'll see you in a few." Nomsulwa hangs up.

"What happened?"

"Claire is at the Phiri police station. Zembe needs me there. She says I have no choice."

"Why is she there?"

"I have no bloody idea."

Nomsulwa stands frozen for a moment. She looks down at her shirt and jeans and walks quickly to the bathroom. She washes herself, ties her hair back from her face. She gets a new shirt and frowns at her pants, emerges a little less fraught, but not nearly ready to see Claire again.

"You look great, sis," Mira says, and as Nomsulwa rushes out the door, she swears she sees him smile.

CLAIRE IS SITTING ON A BENCH IN THE SMALL FRONT room of the Phiri police department building. The heat from the day, bearable in the open air, is constricting on the other side of the wood doors. She is frowning at an old woman sitting next to her. The woman looks over at Claire intermittently and sucks her teeth in disapproval. The interaction is amusing and Nomsulwa watches for a minute, motioning for the woman at the front desk to keep silent. Finally, Nomsulwa sits down next to the mama. "Sawubona mama, unjani?"

"Ngikhona, kodwa, this silly girl wandered through my front yard. All alone. I had to leave my stove to bring her here."

"A white girl? Wandering the township alone? Hmm." Nomsulwa feigns surprise. "Not too smart."

Claire looks like she might burst into tears, which stops Nomsulwa short. She can see Claire bunched and tense with frustration and decides not to press the joke. What Nomsulwa would have said, had the woman been gone and the girl in front of her half as difficult to deal with, was that it was both ridiculous and impressive to take a taxi into the township on your own. It was brave to exit the car in the middle of Phiri, let alone wander through the deserted neighbourhoods, away from the foot traffic of the main square. Nomsulwa would probably also have cursed out the hotel employee who let a white girl into a township taxi on her own.

Instead, she leans in and says, "I think she'll be okay now. You can go back to your cooking."

The old woman squeezes Nomsulwa's hand and stands up. She sucks her teeth one more time at Claire and leaves the station.

Claire begins defending herself before Nomsulwa has a chance to say hello. "It was the middle of the day. I don't get why people are making such a big deal about this."

"Where were you trying to go?"

"The place where he was found." Claire answers directly, as if it were a normal destination.

"Then how did you end up all the way on the other side of town in this lady's yard?"

"I'm not sure." Claire crosses her arms. Nomsulwa battles the instinct to put her arms around Claire's scrunched shoulders until they relax.

"Listen, Claire. It's dangerous in the township. For everyone, it's dangerous, but especially for you. White people are targets. They have money. They have connections."

"You think I don't know this place is dangerous? Did you forget what happened here? But I wanted to see where he was found." Claire's voice is less sure, quieter. "I needed to see the place he died. And there was no other way."

"You should have called me."

"Yeah, well, I didn't want to put you out."

Nomsulwa answers without thinking. "Taking you around is my job right now. You need to call me or you'll get us both in trouble."

Zembe emerges from the back room and interrupts Nomsulwa's attempt to explain herself.

"Why weren't you with her?" she demands of Nomsulwa.

Claire answers for both of them. "I didn't call her. I'm perfectly capable of finding my way around on my own."

The policewoman sighs. "Ms. Matthews, the township is no place for a white girl to venture on her own. You must ensure that you have an escort at all times. It is for your own safety."

"I was interested in seeing the site," Claire offers, as if it is a defence.

"It is nothing but a sandy yard. We have fully investigated the area and the houses and streets that surround it. What exactly did you think you would find that we missed?"

Claire doesn't answer.

"You must leave the investigating to the police. You must trust us."

"Why should I do that when you've found out nothing?" Claire snaps back.

"Police investigations take time, they are complicated."

"But you know who did it."

"We have ideas. But no confirmed suspects."

The woman at the front desk motions for Zembe to come over, and Nomsulwa and Claire sit side by side on the hard bench like chastened children while they wait. When Zembe returns she won't look Nomsulwa in the eye.

"Nomsulwa will take you back to the hotel since the remainder of your money was stolen."

Nomsulwa turns a surprised face to Claire. She had missed that part of the story.

"I need to speak to you about something before you go." Claire abandons her seat and stands, slight compared to the policewoman's girth. "Is there anyway you can clear his personal effects early? Or some of them. My family – my mother and I – would really appreciate getting his ring back."

"Miss Matthews." Zembe takes a breath, but Nomsulwa can tell she's not really considering the request. "The rules are in place for a reason. We need all evidence in our possession until the case is concluded. If even one piece is missing, we might not be able to put the criminal behind bars. And you wouldn't want that, would you?" She speaks to Claire like she is a child; Nomsulwa can see how angry Claire is behind her polite expression.

"I understand, but surely the ring has no evidence in particular on it."

"We have yet to determine that for certain."

"You could, though, determine that for certain today and then let me come pick up the ring before I leave. Please," Nomsulwa can see Claire trying a new strategy, hoping for sympathy, "he was going to give me that ring on my first day of law school. He wanted me to have it before I started."

"I'm sorry. I really am. But it's not possible. I wouldn't be able to, even if I thought it was a good idea. This is a high-profile case and the evidence protocols must be followed." Zembe raises her voice, exasperated. Nomsulwa moves to protect Claire from the lashing she is sure she is about to receive. "Nomsulwa is your guide for a reason. If you attempt to venture out alone again you will only slow me down and make the work I need to do for the investigation take longer. As you can imagine, the longer it takes to find the culprit the less likely it is that he will be found. And I am sure you don't want to be responsible for any delay."

Zembe dismisses them both with nothing but a wave and a glare at Nomsulwa. They walk out the double doors and over the noisy wooden front porch. White paint peels from the signposts that demarcate the parking area, where Nomsulwa's car sits alone in the far corner.

"What happened to your taxi money?" Nomsulwa asks.

"It's stupid. I gave the driver a big bill when I paid and he kept the change."

"What do you mean?"

"He just sat there, refused to give it back, and when I got out, he took off."

Now Nomsulwa is chortling like a boy in a schoolyard. "You must have been shocked!"

"Well, it wasn't ideal." Claire smiles for the first time.

They both get into the car.

"I'll take you to the township tomorrow, if you want. On a proper tour."

"And you'll take me to the site, the place they found him?"

"Yeah, that too."

"Thanks, Nomsulwa." Claire's relieved expression relaxes her face, softens her eyes so she doesn't look quite as heart-broken as usual.

NINE

THAT NIGHT, NOMSULWA GOES TO BED WITH THE SUN.
After dropping Claire off at the hotel, she returned home and
spent the afternoon in her garden. Mira came by for dinner
and quizzed her on what she had found out from her station
visit. She ignored his inquiries. He left soon after eating to visit
his girlfriend and Nomsulwa was alone in the house at last.

The next morning, she wakes up to the phone buzzing
against the uneven surface of her bedside table. She ignores
it. When the phone rings again she thinks it must be her
mother or Mira. No one else would call twice in a row.

"Yes?" Nomsulwa forgoes any formal greeting.

"Miss Sithu?"

"Er . . . hello."

"This is Mr. Dadoo, from the water company. Captain
Afrika tells me that you are Ms. Matthews's driver."

Nomsulwa sits up in bed. Her T-shirt falls off her left
shoulder and hangs on her elbow. She tugs her hair with
her hand, trying to wake up by pulling on it. "I'm taking care
of her now and then, yes."

"I am going to show her the township where her father
was working. I want to show her the work we've done.

What he was establishing there. I'm sure it will make her feel better, proud, of her father and the company."

"Okay." *She works fast*, Nomsulwa thinks. Claire must have arranged an entire day of township tours between Nomsulwa and this man. It will be easier this way, with the distraction of the water official. She just prays he doesn't bring up the pipe theft or the recent unrest. It will not be easy explaining any of that to the water man's daughter.

Nomsulwa follows Dadoo's instructions, pulls into the driveway of the hotel, and waits for Claire to come out. When she does, her face looks as delicate as ever, but puffy, a little creased. When she finally settles into the car, Nomsulwa has the urge to smooth the skin with her thumb. Instead, she flips the valet boy the finger as the two girls drive out to the street.

"You okay?" Nomsulwa asks.

"Yeah, just overslept. Do I look awful?"

"No." She swallows. *Turn around and face the road.* "You look good, cool."

"Thanks. I'm nervous."

They enter Phiri proper directly from the highway, drive past nothing but desert and a large rundown boarding house, and then, suddenly, they are in the middle of a busy town. There are women with large baskets filled with clothes ambling down the edge of the road. Men weave between them, ankles exposed under short overalls. Children are milling around in the front yards and alleys between the houses and shacks wearing their crinkled school uniforms.

Farther inside Phiri, women huddle on corners chatting, shifting baskets from one hip to the other. Nomsulwa and Claire pass a small, two-storey apartment building painted a fading pink. Underneath the outdoor stairway is a small store with a large Coca-Cola ad pasted above the door. Across the street is a church with a concrete yard surrounding the circular building. A quote from the Bible is written in big black letters on its wall:

INGOBA UNKULUNKULU WALITHANDA IZWE KANGAKA, WAZE WANIKELA NGENDODANA YAKHE AYIZALAYO EYODWA, UKUZE BONKE ABAKHOLWA YIYO BANGAFI, BABE NOKU-PHILA OKUNAPHAKADE.

JOHN 3:16

"What does that mean?" Claire asks Nomsulwa.

"Umm, well it roughly means, uh, God loves the world and he gave the gift of his only son so that people who believe in him, those people would have life forever."

"Oh." Claire tries to make sense of the broken translation in her head as they drive past the church building. Nomsulwa feels embarrassed about her inability to sound off the smooth words of the Bible that everyone else knows by heart.

Claire waits a moment, then blurts out, "We had my dad's funeral in a church. My mother organized it. . . . He would have hated that. Dad took me to church once. Said I had to see for myself what I was missing. When I told him it was a bunch of boring junk he just smiled and we walked out."

"Boring junk, eh? Hah." Nomsulwa hasn't heard anyone go that far before. Not that she hasn't thought it herself. She tries to imagine the funeral. In her head it is an open casket, a priest bent over the wood box, greeting family members as they lean in to examine the dead man. The dead father, Nomsulwa corrects herself.

"When did you have it, the funeral, I mean?"

"A week ago." Claire becomes very quiet.

"That is fast."

Claire answers, but her voice sounds shaky. Nomsulwa knows she should just shut up and drive, but she lets Claire explain anyway. "It *was* quick. I didn't have time to get ready for it. My mother could do nothing else. The moment we found out, she started planning. . . . It was horrible."

"Were there a lot of people there?"

"A lot? I don't know, maybe a hundred." Claire trails off. She is really about to cry now and Nomsulwa realizes that she has gone too far. Instead of staying soft and fragile, Claire's voice gets an edge to it. "Look, could we talk about something else?"

"Sorry, I was just making conversation." Nomsulwa sounds defensive despite herself. She grips the steering wheel tighter.

"Are we close?"

"Close?"

"To where we're meeting Alvin?"

"Um, it shouldn't be too long now."

Claire says nothing more, just looks out the window, brooding and stiff.

The town centre falls behind and the car enters the grid of a new neighbourhood. Here there are brick houses between the shacks. The streets become a little wider and fewer people can be seen outside. At a main intersection there is one small store with "Bongani's Spaza" written over the entrance. Sitting high above the building on a metal post is a billboard:

GCIN'AMANZI. WATER IS PRECIOUS, DON'T WASTE IT!

On the billboard, a little girl with pigtails braided tight to her head is sipping out of a glass. In the upper right-hand corner is a cartoon water tap.

Nomsulwa notices Claire staring at the billboard, grits her teeth, and gives a forced smile.

"Mmm-hmm. That's Amanzi."

"What does 'gcin'amanzi' mean?" The car picks up speed slightly, kicking more dust up around the windows. There are no stores now; the landscape becomes more desolate.

"Save water." Nomsulwa doesn't look at Claire as she says this. She turns left, pulls over, and gets out of the car.

Alvin is waiting. His van, swathed in Amanzi logos, idles, the air conditioning going strong. He is in a suit, khaki-coloured, with a white shirt and a black tie. His shoes are impeccably clean, they repel dirt as he steps on the ground, sending the road dust up in clouds.

"Ms. Matthews, my name is Alvin. We spoke on the phone. It is nice to meet you."

Alvin shakes Claire's hand even though Nomsulwa got to his car first. Nomsulwa shrinks back, almost huddling in the shadow. She waits for them to begin their walk and then meanders behind. He begins by opening the door to the small shop kitty-corner to his parking space.

"This is the main office for Phiri. It's not much to look at, but it does the trick for us. We hire local people to run the counter and complete the maintenance. Water creates many jobs for the people of the community."

Alvin pauses and nods at the huge man behind the counter. The man steps aside to let Alvin and Claire pass. Nomsulwa stays near the door.

"There is a computer here that measures out water for the people of the township. They come in and we fill up the keys for their meters."

"Do you find the computers are working well? My father worried about bringing such sophisticated computer systems to the townships."

Alvin is taken aback by Claire's question; Nomsulwa can see him catch himself as he tries to answer. Turns out neither of them had expected her to know anything at all about the water system. "Oh yes, it has not been a problem. The computers we use now are relatively simple. Though we hope that will change." Alvin shifts gears back to the tour. "This little office is the centre of the water system. Having the township residents go through this step helps us regulate their water intake. Also, having them pay teaches them a new level of respect for water conservation. Phiri used to be one of the worst offenders in water mismanagement. Now, they have one of the best conservation records in Soweto."

"They use less water here than anywhere else?" Claire is impressed.

Nomsulwa stays silent. The teller is staring hard at her. She ignores him and continues listening to Alvin.

"Your father's goal was to make sure that every household was hooked up to this water system."

"Even though the company didn't want to expand here." Claire smiles at Nomsulwa, as if she's adding this in for her benefit.

"Yes. Though it has proven to be quite advantageous, for the company and the township. It was a real stroke of genius to expand our water distribution system to the poorest areas of the city. We have, in part, your father to thank for that."

Alvin pauses for a long time. Claire stands closer to him and waits for him to continue. She looks at him with a palpable hope for more.

"Let's walk through the township, then, shall we? You can get a sense of what our water means to these people."

ACROSS FROM THE COMMUNITY CENTRE AND THE park with hand-painted designs on squat concrete pillars, a crew of workmen is laying pipe on the main thoroughfare

139

of the township, despite how hard the ground must be to dig this time of year. Nomsulwa is surprised that the company has attempted to continue with their infrastructure development in spite of the rainy winter's approach. She is also surprised that she didn't hear about it beforehand. She has been too distracted to focus properly on her work.

"This pipe will feed clean water to all of the houses in this neighbourhood. Once it is laid, it will last for generations before repairs must be done. This way the township builds solid infrastructure to assist development."

Nomsulwa falls back, hoping to lose Alvin's speech to Claire in the wind between them. She wishes she were giving Claire her own tour, one that would fill her with the same anger Nomsulwa feels for the pipe-laying men from the city and this businessman who probably goes home to a Sandton mansion with gates and wired fences. Then she remembers that the girl with her is one of them, the product of the highest level of company management. How could she understand?

Alvin is enthusiastic when he speaks. His head jerks with each explanation, arms and hands moving in pointed, aggressive movements. Claire leans close to him. Nomsulwa trails them. On the far side of town, where the houses are a little larger and the shantytown can't be seen from the road, Alvin stops abruptly at one and knocks on a wooden door. Claire lingers behind him. She doesn't ask any questions but she turns to check in with Nomsulwa. Her face is open, her eyes friendly and clear. Nomsulwa suddenly feels flushed. She straightens and smiles, but the glance quickly passes and

Claire refocuses on Alvin. It feels like that was the first time she's looked at Nomsulwa all day.

This house is separate from all the others. The yard is impeccably maintained, with bare patches that are as evenly swept as the grass is cut. A satellite dish hangs off the front, proudly displayed to passersby, and it cuts a small shadow on the roof of a shiny Volkswagen parked in the makeshift driveway. The door opens and Mama Ndaba stands there, grease still shining on her hands, apron clutched behind her back.

"Hello, Mr. Dadoo. Nice to see you. Won't you come in?" And then to Nomsulwa, "Sawubona, sisi." Mama Ndaba's body hunches as she shuffles out of the way. She won't meet Nomsulwa's eyes. Nomsulwa stares straight at her pinched face, counting the wrinkles, waiting for some acknowledgement. Mama Ndaba gives her nothing, only escapes to the kitchen to brew tea. Nomsulwa had not known that this house was on the Amanzi payroll. But here they are, welcomed and served by this real township lady, no doubt for a handsome payment that she'll receive when the guests of the water company have left.

Claire looks at Nomsulwa for a second time. "Do you know her?" she asks quietly.

"Yes, a little."

Alvin merely shifts in his seat at this confession. Claire smiles. Nomsulwa looks away to the kitchen, waiting to see what will come next.

Mama Ndaba enters the main room with a tray of tea. The cloth lining the tray matches the curtains and the two

141

couches that the three guests sink into. There is a lot of white in the house, more than Nomsulwa remembers from other visits. *Must take a lot of water to keep this clean*, she thinks to herself. The tea is hot and tastes very thick; cream instead of milk. Alvin sips loudly and Claire sniffs at the lip of her cup, testing the temperature before trying. Mama Ndaba lowers herself very slowly into a chair.

142
–

Alvin puts his cup down, and lays his hand on Mama Ndaba's lined palm.

"How are things, Mama?" Alvin emphasizes the word "Mama," giving it a nasal quality.

"Well, thank you."

"This is a very important guest of ours, the daughter of one of our most important friends. I told her you could tell her a little about how the water runs in your house."

Badly, Nomsulwa thinks to herself, *not at all, half the month*. Mama Ndaba only nods and then walks back to the kitchen. She returns with her metal key.

"The Amanzi gives me credit on my key. I use it to make the taps run for the month. If I want extra water I can buy it. But I don't need to every month. Just when I have guests and there is more washing."

Claire smiles at the woman. Mama Ndaba doesn't look at anyone. Instead, she fiddles with the little key, letting it fall into her hand, flipping it over, feeling the smooth tab on the top and pushing it out to her fingers again.

"How were things before Amanzi?" Alvin prompts her.

This time Mama Ndaba pauses for a long time. She finally

sneaks a look at Nomsulwa. Nomsulwa steels herself for the answer. The two women eye each other warily, testing how far the other will go. Mama Ndaba gives in first.

"Before there was so little water. The pipes would break, spill their water onto the ground. It was a big waste."

Nomsulwa stands up and walks out of the house, muttering something about needing some air.

Outside the air is dusty and comforting. The bleach smell from inside Mama Ndaba's white house is out of Nomsulwa's nose within minutes. She is furious, seething under the afternoon sun, but there is nowhere for her anger to go. For a fleeting moment she considers returning to the living room, confronting the Amanzi man and his township mouthpiece But there is no use. Alvin would have a smooth answer – a lie – for every point, and Claire, no matter how much time they spend together, is still the daughter of the water man. Nomsulwa reminds herself to be vigilant with the white girl. They have nothing in common. Remember that.

143
–

THE TOUR ENDS IN A GRAND CIRCLE, RIGHT BACK IN front of the water office. The store is packed, as usual, and the big man eyes Nomsulwa a second time as she passes in front of the open door. Old women suck their teeth at Alvin and his guests. They throw their coins on the counter and hand over their metal keys.

"That is all I have to show you here, but you should feel free to visit our office in the city. We have much more information there."

Sure we will, Nomsulwa thinks.

"Your father spent a lot of time there, planning all of this for the people of South Africa."

Damn, that did it. Claire's almost on her tippy-toes.

"Really, Alvin, I would love that."

Alvin nods to Claire and then Nomsulwa. He gets into his car and rolls down the window.

"You have my number."

"Of course. I will call soon."

Nomsulwa smiles so briefly at Alvin that the left side of her face falls before the right side has a chance to perk up.

Claire lets the bliss around her settle for a moment before she places a hand on Alvin's window.

"Alvin. My dad's case. I thought there'd be developments by now."

Alvin is caught off guard at the sudden change in Claire's attitude. He stumbles over the words. His hand shoots out, almost, Nomsulwa thinks, to attempt to roll up his window. Then he resigns himself to the question and looks directly at Claire. "I can't help you, Claire. The police are your best option."

"I met with them," Claire presses. "They wouldn't tell me anything."

"I'll make sure someone gets in touch with you." Alvin says this on the fly. As he turns the key, his front wheel kicks dust into Claire's face and she steps back into the centre of the road. Her shirt is smudged with dirt now and her face is changed, twisted, unrecognizable. She looks ugly angry.

Nomsulwa studies the ugliness and sees in it so much familiarity. Claire angry is easier to deal with than Claire sad or happy or confused.

Out of the corner of her eye Nomsulwa sees the man at the water counter excuse himself past the crowd and start towards her. He is larger without the counter to obscure his body, and though Nomsulwa would confront him on her own, with Claire there she is nervous. She takes Claire's arm and leads her down the street. Claire stops, trying to head for the car, but the man cuts off their route. Nomsulwa guides Claire left, avoiding the man's eyes, and they walk around the corner.

"Let's walk for a little while longer."

They keep moving. The man is still watching them, but his body is stuck just where he can still keep an eye on his storefront. When he is completely out of sight, Nomsulwa relaxes.

"Why was he following you?" Claire asks.

"We don't get along."

"Because . . . ?" she presses.

"I work with the women." Nomsulwa pauses, trying to figure out how to explain what she does. "I work with people here in Phiri, help them get enough electricity and water for the month. Sometimes that means convincing that man to give up water credits for a little less than he'd like to charge." *Or bypassing him completely*, she thinks.

"You mean like a subsidy program? You do that as well as work for the police?"

145

"I don't work for the police." Claire looks very confused. "I should have explained. I am helping Zembe, looking after you, but in general I run a civil society organization. Here in Phiri."

Claire seems wary but stays close, lets Nomsulwa keep holding her arm. They walk like that, both knowing that to pull away would be more awkward than staying where they are. "A civil society organization that does what?"

"Here, let me show you."

She leads Claire out of the lok'shini and into the residential area. People are out on the streets here. They stop and stare at the white girl. Grandfathers with spittle on their lips tip their hats. Grandmothers huddled on their front steps wave wildly like schoolchildren. The order of things is turned upside down by Claire's presence.

There is a standing tap in the corner of a cement yard up ahead, where the road peters out into gravel. A black iron fence cuts the space between the road and the old woman's land. The tap is slender, arching over at the end. It is turned on. A white bucket sits underneath receiving a steady drip drip of water. Claire peers over the gate at the bucket.

"This is the way most people in the township get their water. They have a company-issued tap, it dribbles out water slowly, and when there is no more free water allotted, the tap shuts off."

"But we just saw a house with a tap inside. When she runs out of water, she can buy credits for extra."

"Not everyone has that kind of money. If you can't pay, you get a standing tap and no chance to buy extra water."

"So it's a financial management thing? Like cutting people off so they can't build up debt?"

"No." Nomsulwa can't stop herself. "It's a making money thing, like why spend the money bringing taps into this woman's house if she's never going to pay."

Claire frowns, looks at Nomsulwa as though she were a stranger.

"Hey, we should keep walking." Nomsulwa tries to lighten her tone. Claire stands with her back to Nomsulwa, staring at the tap.

"It's overflowing. Shouldn't you let the people who live here know?"

Before Nomsulwa has a chance to move Claire back onto the road, a very old woman shuffles out from behind the house. She doesn't look up at the white girl hanging off her fence.

"Your bucket is full."

The woman doesn't acknowledge Claire.

"Translate for me, Nomsulwa. Tell her her bucket is full."

"Ngiyaxolisa, Mama," Nomsulwa almost whispers. *Sorry, Mama.*

The old woman stops at the tap, turns it off, and looks up at the two strangers in front of her.

"Thank you, ma'am." The old woman drops the phrase at Claire's feet. Lifts the bucket and shuffles back towards the house.

"My cousin and I work with women to lobby the company for more water. We march and hold protests, but we also work within the township to distribute water from areas with free access to those parts of Phiri and the surrounding neighbourhoods that are already on the pay system."

"Look, how much free water does each house get?"

"Six thousand litres."

"See, that's a lot. The water company charges the heaviest users to subsidize the infrastructure improvements. How else are you supposed to improve things when you have a bankrupt government?"

Nomsulwa almost loses her patience. "You alone use over a thousand litres a month just flushing the toilet. For us, the allotment only ever lasts two weeks. The rest of the time we borrow, steal, wait, and hope the end of the month comes quickly. Sometimes people here walk to the edge of town where the rainwater collects in the gullies next to the highway. They get some water from there."

"That's impossible," Claire answers matter-of-factly. "My father's company provides clean water, it doesn't cut it off. That doesn't make sense, even for a business. It loses them customers."

"Who cares about customers who can't pay?" Nomsulwa says under her breath, and Claire either doesn't hear her or chooses to walk quietly rather than argue in the middle of the street.

At the next house without a tap in front Nomsulwa stops and whistles from the gate. A very young boy runs out and skids to a stop.

"Ja, Simphiwe, can I see your water meter?"

The boy runs back into his house.

A woman only a little older than Claire follows Simphiwe back out.

"Sawubona, Nomsulwa! Unjani?" she calls.

"Ngialright." Nomsulwa falls back a little as she answers, playing up the casual nature of her response. "Ngisacela ukubona iwater meter?"

"Sure, fine." The woman smiles at Claire. "Hello," she says. Her accent is almost British, different from the English of the older women Claire has met in the township. "Are you visiting?"

"Yes, from Canada."

"I love Canada. We had a student here once from a place called . . . um . . . Calgan?"

"Calgary?" Claire hazards a guess. She is being polite, but her expression is tight and Nomsulwa can tell that she is not happy about their unfinished argument.

"Yebo! That's it, you've got it. Are you from there too?"

"No, I'm from a city on the other side of the country. Toronto."

"Toronto." The woman rolls the *r* and the last *t* explodes into the *o*.

"Come on in. Simphiwe will show you that damn meter. It's full today. Well, you know, the beginning of the month. I have to keep washing out back."

"Ngiyabonga, sisi." *Thank you.*

Simphiwe skips as he leads the two women to the metal grate beside the house. Nomsulwa makes sure Claire is following before she leaves the road and enters the yard. When they reach the spot, Simphiwe stoops and opens the lid. Inside is an innocuous-looking white box. It has a rudimentary computer panel, the same as a calculator, and a small Amanzi logo on the side of the casing. The numbers are hard to read in the sun and, even when Nomsulwa cups her hand over the top of the box, the numbers seem to dance in the shadows, changing from 8s to 3s to 7s with each slight tilt of Nomsulwa's fingers.

"Simphiwe, you got the key?"

Simphiwe jumps up and runs inside. He comes out moments later with a metal stick.

"This is how you fill the meter. The computer adds money to this key and the box reads your credit when you place the round head in this hole. Here, try it."

Claire clumsily fits the key into the meter and then quickly takes it out. She hands it back to Nomsulwa.

"For most families around here, this meter runs their life. They check the box every day. They scramble for pennies to pay the water man. Still, the meters run out so quickly –"

"It's not my father's company that shuts off the water. It's the government, their system is so inefficient. They had to hire my father to come here and help them reorganize water delivery methods."

"Before Amanzi took over the water was provided free all year round. The cutoffs came with the private company. I help people distribute the water so that they can survive even when their taps have been turned off. We're working now on a campaign to raise the free water limit. There's a lawyer from the city, a white woman, who is going to help us bring our case to court."

"You're going to sue my father's company?" Claire gets up and backs away.

Nomsulwa stops talking then and stands up too. She pushes her hand on Simphiwe's shoulders, smiling before gently sending him towards his house. Then she heads for the road.

Claire hangs back, not following right away. When she does speak, she yells from behind, "My dad was *fixing* the infrastructure. His job was getting more water to the township in a more efficient way. He doesn't – didn't . . . cut off water." Claire waits for Nomsulwa to acknowledge her.

Nomsulwa smiles weakly back and puts out her hand. "We are suing the government, trying to up the free water allotment. Come on, let's keep walking."

Claire stops for a second. Nomsulwa will apologize if that is what is required to keep Claire walking beside her. But she hopes she can get away with this, a smile, a gesture, a chance to avoid the topic of water altogether. She knows she is not entitled to take this part of Claire's father away from her, but she wants so badly to share the truth with Claire. There is a part of her that wants the triumph of making the water man's daughter see what they have done to her township.

Claire walks forward. They let the confrontation fall behind them. When she is in step with Nomsulwa she says quietly, "I'm sorry I yelled. I know that my father hadn't done everything he wanted to do here, that the water wasn't running properly and the system was inefficient. He needed help from people like you who are willing to fight the government for more money, more investment in township infrastructure. That was his passion."

Nomsulwa doesn't respond. She sees Claire's hopefulness, the same look of reverence that she had for Alvin.

"What you do is incredible. It's exactly the kind of thing he would have loved." Claire stops speaking.

Nomsulwa knows that her job is to deliver Claire safely to the hotel, to smile and nod and give in to the white girl beside her. She hopes for the strength to do it. She thinks about Claire brave and defiant in the police station waiting room, about her small and fragile in her arms after the meeting with the Commissioner. Those two thoughts keep her from saying anything more.

Less than a block away there is a group of young kids playing cricket with a board and a tennis ball. Three sticks are stuck at crazy angles into the hard road to make a wicket. The tallest boy winds up for a pitch and the batter cracks it. Claire breaks from Nomsulwa and runs after the ball. She catches it on the second bounce, teetering on the edge of road and scraggly grass.

The kids crack up, doubled over and pointing.

"Bheka umlungu!" the batter screams. Claire just stands there triumphantly, allowing the joke to go on while she decides where to throw the ball.

"Do you know how to play?" Nomsulwa yells over the racket.

"Play what?"

"Cricket!" Nomsulwa is laughing now too.

"Oh . . . no. I thought it was baseball." Claire looks a little crestfallen, but smiles nonetheless.

A little girl, stuck way back where few balls go, comes up to Nomsulwa.

"What is she saying, Mama?" she asks.

"She wants to play, Sana."

The girl thinks for a moment. Then she runs to the pitcher and whispers something in his ear. The tall boy is gentle and bends down while the girl speaks. He looks back at Claire and nods to the girl.

"They say you can play if you want," Nomsulwa explains. She catches Claire staring at the small girl.

"Only if you do."

"Fine." Nomsulwa claps her hands in a great show and sends the fielders into fits of mirth. Claire gives Nomsulwa a real smile. Nomsulwa watches her ready herself for the next play.

They field for a good half hour before Nomsulwa hears the mamas begin to call their children inside.

"Let's go, Claire. We should head back to the car."

"Okay, you." Claire runs up and playfully punches Nomsulwa's shoulder. Then she slides her arm into Nomsulwa's. "That was so much fun! Kids at home never get to play in the streets like that. There are cars and old women worried about their flower gardens."

153

"Yeah, there's definitely space around here."

"Is that what you used to do as a kid? Were you a cricket star then, too?"

Nomsulwa wants to answer yes. She wants to build up Claire's image of her, innocent child with a cricket bat. Instead of lying, she stays silent.

The street clears out quickly. Dusk in the township paints the sky a million shades of red and purple. Claire stands with her back to Nomsulwa and stares. Nomsulwa moves to be beside her and exhales audibly.

"Amazing, isn't it?"

Claire doesn't answer, just stands lightly touching the side of Nomsulwa's body. Nomsulwa can't move, aware of every place their arms touch.

"I need to see where they found him." Claire puts distance between them.

"There's nothing there but a sand yard."

"So you've seen it?"

"The whole township has."

"Take me there. Captain Afrika told me I shouldn't try to go there without you."

"She told you not to bother going there at all."

"You promised you would take me."

"Quickly. We'll go quickly. In the car. It's safer that way." Nomsulwa regrets giving in the moment it is out of her mouth. It is getting dark. They should have left the township already. Zembe is going to kill her if she finds out.

"Great." Claire walks ahead quickly and arrives at the car before Nomsulwa.

On the short drive neither of them speaks. They pull up to two houses side by side. Hidden between them, and set back from the street, is a yard. Laundry lines hang over the dust. Corners of white sheets trail in the wind, picking up an orange coating from the ground. The waning sunlight streams through the fabric, patterns the surface of the sheets, and then splits into glinting pieces around the yard. Nomsulwa gets out; she walks to where the mosaic hits her feet. She dips her toe into the sunlight, then motions for Claire to step through the hanging laundry. An older woman shuffles up behind Claire before she has a chance to move.

"Hey, you. What do you want?" Her accent is thick and she scowls fiercely.

Nomsulwa steps between them. "Ungakhathazeki, Mama, angeke sithathe isikhathi eside."

The woman continues to speak English. "Who is this?"

"The daughter of the man they found here."

"Oh, wena? For real? Very bad thing that, very bad."

Nomsulwa nods.

"Okay." The last word is said in a singsong. *Ooo kayyy.* The woman tuts and presses Claire's hand into her enormous chest. Claire stands awkwardly, letting herself be tugged forward.

"My child. So sorry for your loss." She turns around and moves away from the sun into her house. She tuts to herself

155
–

as she leaves, half whistling condolences even once she is well inside.

"This is it?" Claire is speaking very softly now.

"Under these lines. Right about here." Nomsulwa goes to stand in between the two largest sheets.

Claire doesn't move. The ground has been swept in many different directions. Large tracks, like brush strokes, cross each other in the orange. There is no crime scene outline, no tape to mark the spot.

Claire walks to where Nomsulwa motioned. Her shoes leave clear prints. She sits down – more of a collapse, really – then lies on the ground. The orange dust sprinkles lightly over her as she presses her whole body onto the warmth of the sand. She lies there for a full five minutes, eyes closed.

Nomsulwa stands back with her arms crossed, trying to not look at the still body at her feet. She waits for an eternity. She studies the dusty yard under the yellowed washing, dirty sheets blowing out their musty odour, houses falling on either side. She can't look at the ground so she looks everywhere else until small sounds from the sand catch her attention.

Claire is crying. Her tears run down her cheeks, collect in the maze of her ears, and then drop down. Orange clumps form. Darker than the dry ground, they make a pattern that mixes with the sun's mosaic and creates a golden spotted halo constantly moving around her head. Nomsulwa helps Claire off the ground and into the car. She tries to dust her

156
–

off before sitting her down, but the dust is stubborn. It will not leave Claire's delicate skin and hair.

Claire wipes her eyes. She sits with her feet hanging out of the open door and fiddles with her thumbs in her lap. Nomsulwa doesn't dare disturb her. She sits in the driver's seat, waiting for some indication that they can begin the drive home. The argument from the day has disappeared. So has the water company, the township, there is only the girl in front of her and the pain she is so obviously feeling. Nomsulwa wants to take it away.

Claire moves her feet inside and closes the door. She speaks before Nomsulwa has a chance to readjust into a driving position. "I thought I'd, you know, feel something."

Nomsulwa searches for a response.

"He wasn't there."

Claire turns to face her, orange sand streaked with clear rivulets where the tears have fallen. It looks like face paint, and the small smile Claire attempts crinkles her skin and causes a short shower of dust to fall on her hands. They are sitting close now, Claire's brave smile and Nomsulwa's grave expression. Nomsulwa tries to relax her mouth, provide a serene mask of sympathy in response to Claire's attempt at endurance. They hang there, the two faces, inches from each other, feeling the heat leave the air, the welcome cold settle in, hearing the night's insects begin their chorus.

TEN

158 – ZEMBE PERUSES THE INTERVIEW SCHEDULE ONE more time before leaving the office. There are a number of familiar names – Trevor Phadi, Sinethemba Langa – but the senior councillor on the list is Mandla Matshikwe. He has been elected in Phiri District Three for four terms running, unheard of in the heated struggles of local politics. Matshikwe is notorious for throwing large parties for his supporters throughout the year, and she has visited his house many times before on noise complaints. The kids often get rowdy and end up crossing through quiet neighbourhood yards still calling reverie to the sky. She has had to cart many of them home to disapproving mothers.

When Zembe arrives, the compound is quiet. The red-brick house hides behind a large iron gate. The front yard is covered in concrete tile, and one tree extends almost to the pinnacle of the slender second storey. Matshikwe's house is the tallest in the neighbourhood.

A young boy sweeps the front yard as she heads up the front walk.

"How are you, Mama?"

"Fine, and you?"

"Fine." He continues with his slow work around the garden.

Zembe rings the bell and an older woman opens the door. Her mouth is pursed and she says nothing after a cursory nod in Zembe's direction. She waits on the threshold until Matshikwe emerges at the far end of the front hall.

"Come in," he bellows.

Zembe enters and shakes his hand before following him into the living room. The house is as impressive on the inside as the outside. A brand new forty-two-inch TV sits in the middle of the living room, a doily adorning the top. Big windows sporting patterned safety bars let light in. The curtains are trimmed with lace that matches the TV's doily. Crystal glasses line the standing cabinet. A large portrait of Matshikwe and his wife with their four children is hung above the largest couch. Another, smaller portrait features Matshikwe on his own.

The councillor's wife waits to greet her, and Zembe takes Mrs. Matshikwe's hand in hers and comments on the beautiful decorating in the room.

"Ngiyabonga, Mama Afrika," Mrs. Matshikwe answers proudly, then leaves the living room to Zembe and the councillor.

"Mandla, I came to speak to you briefly about the white man who was found in Phiri recently."

"Oh, yes." Matshikwe's broad forehead wrinkles with concern. "I heard about that. A very awful event."

159
–

"Mr. Dadoo from the Amanzi office told me that you had a meeting with him the day he died. I was wondering if you could tell me what the meeting was about."

"We met, a number of us from the community, to talk about how to keep the water meters working well. You see, there have been . . . problems."

"What sort of problems?" Zembe is fishing; she knows what Matshikwe is referring to.

"Some . . . people have been tampering with the meters. Others have been expressing concern with the way the water is being delivered. It makes the company's job very difficult, you see."

"Did Mr. Matthews know about this before you met with him?"

"Oh yes, the company called the meeting to discuss just that. We are so interested in helping the Amanzi people with this, you see. It is good to see thirsty people finally get water."

"How is it that *you* have been helping Amanzi?"

"We do so many things, talk to the people, help provide security for the workers transporting pipe steel in and out of the township. We even helped lay a series of pipes last week in a ceremony in the new District Three neighbourhood." Matshikwe gestures vaguely in the direction of the township. He rubs his hands over his thick thighs.

"Very nice place there."

"Oh yes, new houses, all owned. None are rented."

Matshikwe beams. Zembe pauses and gives the room another sweep of her eyes.

"What did you decide to do about the water distribution . . . in the meeting with Matthews?"

"We discussed some . . . fees that would allow myself and the other councillors to garner more community support for the meters."

"You mean advertising?"

"Not exactly. Advertising has been ineffective so far in halting the conflict. But it is similar. We have been having so many troubles with this program and needed a little extra . . . support, like I said before."

Bribes. Matshikwe is getting nervous. She wants to talk him down, tell him that her division is not in the dark about the money flowing from all corners of the city to Matshikwe's office for a myriad of "causes" and "special interests." He is not alone.

Bribes are as good a motive as any. Maybe Matthews refused to give the money. Maybe he was in the township delivering the money that night. Either way, Matshikwe wasn't going to own up to anything alone. Zembe would need to use the other councillors against him, encourage them to talk to avoid a harsh sentence.

"Just one more question, Mandla."

"Yes?"

"Where were you the night Mr. Matthews was killed?"

"At home, my wife had our neighbours over for dinner. I was watching TV. The women will all confirm this."

Zembe had no doubt they would.

———

IF SHE HOPES TO CATCH MATSHIKWE IN A LIE, Zembe will have to work outside of his circle of influence. Those under the protection or care of the councillor will not be interested in talking to her once word of the investigation's new direction gets out. She needs a political rival.

The councillor in District Five, Trevor Phadi, has attempted more than once to instigate another clearing of informal settlements. He has successfully appealed to the federal government to send in a fleet of bulldozers to destroy the thousands of homes on the back plain of his geographical area. It keeps his richer voters happy, appeasing fears of rising crime rates from the large numbers of displaced people in their backyard. It also creates chaos for those displaced. While some decide to abandon the site after the destruction of their shacks, most simply scrounge enough money to rebuild out of scrap material left behind or purchased from junkyards near Johannesburg. Matshikwe got a lot of quick votes by opposing the bulldozing. Those in his less-affluent district with family or friends in the informal settlement are interested in seeing the shacks protected.

Phadi's name is on the list of attendees at the Amanzi meeting. Zembe wonders how the two councillors behaved in the same room with a bribe on the table. She is hoping that the animosity between them hasn't settled down.

Phadi is not at his house. Unlike Matshikwe, he spends most of the workday actually in the office. He is a more industrious politician, one who assumes that hard work can translate into votes from the community. Although Zembe disagrees with his policies, she must admit that his quiet demeanour and naïve faith make him an attractive candidate.

Zembe sees Phadi's shocking white hair first, bobbing in the middle of a small crowd of men in overalls near a cell-phone store. His skinny frame is weighed down by a friendly belly, and his hair tufts out from his head, hiding his wide ears and framing his broad forehead. He smiles when he sees Zembe approach. She gives a cursory nod.

"We don't see you much in these parts, Mama."

Zembe thinks this might be a jab, his way of emphasizing the complaints he calls in about the need for increased street patrols. She chooses not to engage.

"Do you have a minute?"

"Well, I am on the campaign trail, as they say. Spreading the word. Not His word, but a good message nonetheless."

"I'm sure." She grimaces at the flippant reference to Him.

"Care to take a pamphlet?" He holds out a single sheet of paper in front of her. There is a black-and-white picture of the informal settlement across the top and a dense block of type below. At the bottom are big black letters: "QEDA UBUGEBENGU. VOTELA UPHADI." *Reduce crime. Vote Phadi.*

"No thanks." Zembe sits on a ledge beside the store. "Have a seat."

Phadi complies, resting his bag of paper on his knee and massaging his shoulder. "Old bones," he offers in apology for his distraction.

"Tell me about the meeting with the water company."

"What is there to tell? We met with a man from Canada and Alvin Dadoo. We talked about how to deliver the water services, how to create more support for the company. It lasted all day, but honestly not much was accomplished."

"How did Mr. Matshikwe and the man from Canada get along during the meeting?"

"You know Mandla. He's a bully and never respectful. There was a conflict. An argument about some fees we were promised by the company. But it seemed to have all been smoothed over by the end of the night."

"The night? How long was the meeting?"

"We went to a bar, after the meeting. Matshikwe had organized for women to be there to greet us, show the visiting businessman a good time. He really is a pig." Phadi stomps his foot when he says this, and even that act seems refined coming from him. Zembe is amazed at the serenity he maintains when talking about his rival.

"Did Matshikwe go home with the white man?"

"Honestly, the white man disappeared with a girl a quarter his age. When he finally got back inside the bar, Mr. Dadoo took him home. I left soon after, but came straight back here. I'm sure Mandla was at the bar all night. He had a girl too."

"Did you see who Matthews, I mean the white man, did you see who he left with?"

"Yeah, pretty thing, didn't look up to that kind of work. Mandla probably recruited her from the elementary school." Phadi shakes his head.

"So the girl could have gone home with him?"

"Could have. I didn't see her, though."

When Zembe leaves Phadi, he seems glad to return to his pamphlets. She needs to talk to Matshikwe and get the name of the girl Matthews was with after the meeting, confront him about his lie. Could she be lucky enough to have found the owner of the beer receipt? The young girl sits next to him at the hotel bar, maybe she was invited there, she orders a beer, lures him outside with the promise of sex. National found nothing at the hotel, but Zembe's not sure they checked the grounds. At the time they had all assumed Matthews was killed in the township. There may be something they missed.

ELEVEN

THE NEXT MORNING, NOMSULWA SETS OFF FOR THE country. When she left Claire at the hotel the night before, neither of them had suggested meeting today. Nomsulwa has a chance to catch up on her work.

After an hour in the car, kwaito music blaring to close out any wayward thoughts, she arrives at her mother's house, parks around the corner from the main structure, and sneaks back towards the shed. The slate-grey bricks shine out onto the street, glinting and reflecting almost like the shantytown metal. The walk is carefully gardened, her own handiwork, and the front door emerges out of a bed of green. She checks the window and confirms that the television is on. She can picture her mother, huddled on the couch watching her soaps. Likely, she is wearing her pyjamas from the night before, coughing during commercials, a cup of tea, now lukewarm, resting against her lips. Nomsulwa crouches down the side wall, careful that her footsteps not make any noise on the gravel driveway, and makes it to the shed out back without being heard. She needs to reassure herself about the pipes before she can face her mother's illness, the unfilled prescriptions, the scattered mess of the living room. Then she'll draw her mother a bath and bring her hot tea, try to tidy up that depressing house.

The door opens easily and the chickens begin their protests before she even crosses the threshold. The room is dark and filled with the chalky, putrid smell of chicken shit. Feathers float in the stuffy air. Nomsulwa can feel them brush against her bare arms as she walks forward, closing the door behind her. Her shoe hits solid metal and she turns to the task at hand.

Nomsulwa uncovers the steel and begins to shift each pipe, counting as she goes: one, two, three, she reaches to the left side to feel underneath, four, five, six, then the right, seven, eight, nine, ten. She walks to the very back wall where the last three pipes were laid under thick canvas cloth, lifts a corner, and feels underneath. She stops. Feels again. Closes the cloth, looks around, opens it again, feels the two pipes nestled in the soft floor of the shed. Just two. Nomsulwa's joints freeze up. She looks around frantically, as if someone could have misplaced three metres of solid steel. Immediately she imagines police investigators confiscating the missing pipe, comparing the steel with that of the Phiri water line, and showing up ready to arrest Nomsulwa's mother. She imagines tsotsis stumbling across the stash and stealing away some for themselves. She almost wishes these scenarios were true. What really happened, what she knows must have happened, is worse. Four men lifting the steel pipe in the dead of night and a pickup truck delivering it to the black corners of the Saturday market. Mira.

—

NOMSULWA SPEEDS ALONG THE HIGHWAY BACK TO PHIRI. She drives into the community centre parking lot and runs to the side entrance, which leads to winding hallways lined with pictures of women of all ages dressed in red, carrying placards with protest slogans painted in black. She and Mira carefully pasted these colour printouts to the cracking walls. They blasted music in the halls as they reorganized the filing cabinet, filling it with water bills and overdue statements organized by neighbourhood, then by street, and now by family. The township names run in alphabetical order, overflowing with Amanzi bills.

The main office is on the left-hand side, just before the hall leads back into the waiting room. Mira is sitting at the computer, which creaks every time he clicks the mouse. He hammers the number one key hard three times before it gives and lets him move on. The screen makes his skin look green. He is so much darker than Nomsulwa. They don't really look related at all. But by now everyone is so used to seeing them together that their odd pairing has become a single, cohesive unit. They make sense together, Mira and Nomsulwa. They are a team.

"Ukwenzeleni kodwa lokho, Mira?" *Why did you do it?*

"What? Oh, hey, sisi, I'm just recopying the statements for the Ndebele family."

"I told you it was too dangerous. How could you?" Nomsulwa keeps her voice even. Her words sink in, and Mira turns completely to face her.

"I didn't have a choice."

"What did you do with it? Tell me you still have it. You didn't sell it yet, you didn't."

"I met that thick man from the metal corner at a field near your mother's house. We exchanged there. It's done, Nomsulwa. You didn't want to be involved."

"No."

Mira rises but stays back from where Nomsulwa stands.
"It's not your place to tell me no."

"Who do you think runs this organization? Who's in charge of those pipes you are selling off? It's me, Mira. You snuck into my chicken coop and stole something that belonged to me, to the movement."

"We agreed. We would hire protection. But I can't get that kind of manpower without payment and I made a decision. Kholizwe is on the warpath. I needed to pay."

"We already gave Kholizwe his payment. We gave a pipe to him before we took the rest to my mother's."

"Yes, but his men were restless. They said we cheated them."

"How much did you get for it?"

"Two thousand rand."

"And how much did you pay out?"

Mira pauses, caught in his lie. "The four of us split it."

"That's what I thought. That was our money, the movement's money, and you blew it on Black Label and cigarettes."

"What do you care? What are you giving back? I haven't seen you in here with those American bills the white bitch carries with her."

"You want me to steal from her now, too? After everything."

"After everything she did to us!" Mira is furious. "Without them, the water men, none of this would have happened."

"She's not a water man."

"She may as well be. And don't you forget it."

"You should have come to me. I would have found you the money. Don't you see what trouble those pipes are? I'm trying to protect you, protect us." Nomsulwa moves into the room, away from the door, closer to Mira.

"Do you even understand how much you owe me, what I did for you? You got me into this mess to begin with. I think I'll take care of myself from here on in."

"We were a team." Nomsulwa retorts.

"No. I cleaned up your mess. It's what I always do." Mira walks out the door, past Nomsulwa. He shoves her as he passes, the fury so uncontrollable he is shaking.

When he is gone, the office seems smaller. The pipes and the men from the 28s and Mira's voice, angry, fill the silent room. He's right, Nomsulwa thinks. Without me he would be happily causing trouble with his tsotsi friends, not running from the police, making backroom deals for stolen steel, spending all day organizing fruitless protests and boycotts.

Walking back to her car, Nomsulwa surveys the neighbourhood. A group of boys wrestle in the lot next to the centre's front door. A girl hangs on the outside of the scuffle, yelling encouragement to her comrades. She has scraped knees. Dust lightens the ends of her hair, clings to the oil her mother combed through it that morning in an attempt to relax the strands. The familiarity, so like her and her child-hood comrades-in-arms, makes Nomsulwa feel dizzy – the hard part inside her, the part she can't open up, knocks against her chest, tightening everything, reminding her how everything has changed.

NOMSULWA'S HOUSE FEELS EMPTY WITHOUT MIRA there. She sleeps badly, then sits in the bed in the morning and listens for the sounds of the neighbourhood, hoping they will fill the space he used to occupy. Nomsulwa notices her-self fingering her cellphone, flipping through the missed calls. Rechecking, as if the list of names could change from one second to the next. She is waiting for Mira, and thinking of their conversation yesterday makes Nomsulwa think of Claire.

Nomsulwa fights the feeling, distracts herself with the preparation of a big breakfast of fresh fat cakes until half her block, she's sure, is filled with the acrid smell of oil frying. It gets into her hair and her clothes, and when she can't take it any longer, she ducks into the bathroom, runs her head under cold water, smoothes her twists with a little wax, changes her clothes, and smells her arms carefully to make sure the fat is off them. Then she picks up the phone again.

The rings begin and Nomsulwa gears herself up to leave a chipper message. *Just checking in. Wouldn't want a repeat of that township visit.* No, wait, that will put Claire on the defensive. *Just checking in. Thought you might want some company.* No, that sounds more needy than Nomsulwa had hoped.

But Nomsulwa doesn't get the chance to leave a message.

"Hello?" Claire answers. Why did she call Claire? Was it duty or loneliness?

"Hi. It's Nomsulwa. I was just calling to check in, see how you are doing."

"Oh. I'm fine, thanks."

Nothing more. Nomsulwa does not give in and interrogate the girl about her activities, her life away from her driver.

"Okay, well, I just needed to make sure you were all right. No more running off on your own, okay?"

"If you're not busy, I would like to get out of the hotel today."

Nomsulwa agrees to be there in an hour. She tries to think of somewhere they can go that won't have anything to do with the company or the township. She rushes to the mirror again and sees how her hair has fallen too far to one side and the twists are too thin at the head and too loose at the bottom. She's sure she still smells like oil. She gets her bag and leaves the house, sits on her front porch, hoping the dusty air around her will make her smell more normal. Or more like Claire.

She sits very still, arms slightly apart from her body, willing the air to rush through her. But it is a hot, quiet day. No wind. Just children running down her block in small groups, their school uniforms on and no school anywhere nearby. Truants. And then a few teenage boys who whistle or suck their teeth at Nomsulwa. She flips them off with a smile. They laugh with one another and return the favour in a friendly way. She sees no one she knows.

OUTSIDE THE HOTEL, NOMSULWA WAITS, IGNORING the glares of the doormen. She watches the front door, calm now because Claire is coming down and they will spend the day together enjoying the sights. She thinks she might take her to the Apartheid Museum, a place every student in the country visits before high school graduation. When Nomsulwa first saw it, it was a brand new building, and she was so moved, witnessing all the clever ways their history had been squeezed into "interactive" displays. How easily hope can pervert the world around you.

When Claire arrives, she walks smiling, but with her arms crossed across her narrow chest. She stops at the car, deftly navigates the stuck passenger-side door, and sits down.

"I was thinking today we could go see his hotel," she says, as if it is a suggestion to see the local zoo or museum.

"We could do that." Nomsulwa pauses. "Or we could go see the Apartheid Museum. It's the most famous museum in Africa."

Claire nods. "We can do that, after the hotel."

"I'm not even sure what we can see there, Claire." Nomsulwa holds out her hands, giving up.

"I've been to his office, and to the township. Now I need to see where he stayed."

"Maybe you should wait and get Alvin to take you. I don't even know which hotel it is."

"The Central Sun."

"Right. Well, I didn't know it. I've never been there. I think he'd get you better access."

"We can try. If it doesn't work, I'll call the Dadoo guy."

"I don't know . . ." Nomsulwa stalls. She thinks of Mira's reaction if he knew she was going to that hotel.

"I've been here for over a week and found nothing. This is the last place I can think of to look."

"What are you looking for?"

"Can you just take me? I'll know it when I see it." Claire is very sure of herself. She sits upright, posture full of confidence. Nomsulwa gives in and steers out onto the main road.

As they drive, Claire shifts back and forth, full of nervous energy. Nomsulwa wants to put out a hand and stop her moving. She wants to warn her against getting her hopes up. Whatever Claire expects to find at the Central Sun, Nomsulwa is pretty sure it won't be there.

The differences between the Central Sun and Claire's hotel are minor. Really, they all boil down to scale. The Central Sun is the largest hotel in the district and it is sufficiently out of the way so that it looms even larger; there are no big buildings to offset it. Nomsulwa flips her collar up around her neck and flicks her twisted hair to one side. She keeps her head down in case there is any problem.

Claire walks quickly and Nomsulwa hangs back, keeping close enough to Claire that it is clear they are together, but letting Claire be the one to greet each new face. As they get inside, Claire walks directly to the front desk and smiles a big smile. Nomsulwa pretends to be very interested in the art on the far wall. She does not stare up at the decorated ceiling and does not study the lobby that is more like a wide avenue, lined with restaurants and shops. She hears Claire ask sweetly for the manager and then drum her fingers on the desk, impatient now, so close to something but not sure what it is. Nomsulwa feels a sense of dread. When the manager emerges, Claire introduces herself. There is a pause.

"My father," Claire explains further, "he was staying in this hotel right before he died."

There is silence.

"He worked for the water company," Claire offers.

The manager clues in. He stumbles on his words. "Of course, of course. Yes, yes, very sad. He was a . . . a . . . valued guest here."

"Do you have a record of which room he stayed in?" Her voice has become higher.

"Perhaps." The man starts to click at the keys. Nomsulwa peeks around and surveys the busy room. People are moving through it in makeshift queues, suits following suits. No one notices the others around them.

Claire turns while Nomsulwa is watching. She catches her eye and smiles. "Don't worry," she says to Nomsulwa. "This is something I need to do."

"Here it is. The fifteenth floor, room 1521. It is one of our executive suites."

175
–

"Can I go see it?"

"See it?" The man pauses. Nomsulwa wonders what he thought Claire was looking for when she asked for the room number if she didn't want to actually go there. Numerology?

"Please. I've come all the way from Canada." Claire's voice climbs higher again. "I just want to see it."

"We have a guest checking in to that room this afternoon."

"I will be quick."

"The police have already cleared it for occupation."

"I won't touch anything. I just want to peek in."

The man sighs. Then he motions for one of the bellmen. "Take them to 1521."

"Thank you," Claire says before pushing off from the desk, waving Nomsulwa over, and following the bellman to the elevators.

The elevator plays choral music, unlike anything Nomsulwa has ever heard before: soft, round, high like a child, but full like a chorus of men. The music moves as slowly as the elevator, and Claire reaches out to squeeze Nomsulwa's hand twice before they reach the fifteenth floor. Nomsulwa keeps her head down. She doesn't let her fingers wrap themselves around Claire's.

In the hall, Claire leads the way and finds the right number on the door. Then she steps back and makes room for the bellman to open the door. "Thank you," she says, as he steps back to let them enter. He hesitates, but Claire closes the door firmly on him before he can say anything.

The interior of the room is cream and beige. The two colours, so close, they blend into each other. In the middle of the wallpaper a swatch of deep red runs around the room. It matches the stripes on the curtains and the pattern on the bedspread. The neutral room. The crack of red. It seems violent.

Claire walks through the bedroom towards the bathroom. She peers in. Nomsulwa follows, her curiosity moving her feet before she chooses to. It is an enormous room, bigger than Nomsulwa's living room and kitchen combined, made of cream-and-beige marble. No red, save for the toiletries wrapped in red paper peppering the wide two-sink counter across from the sloping cream bathtub. A separate shower stall has a round head that hangs like a cloud over the floor. Turn on the tap and you could have your own personal rainstorm. There is no sign that anyone living ever touched the room.

Nomsulwa is still staring at the bathroom when Claire leaves. She hears scratching from the other room. Then a thud.

Claire has thrown herself on the bed. She is tugging at the pillows, the endless pile of pillows, and throwing them one by one on the floor. She lifts up the covers and works her way under them. She scratches at the sheets until they pull up, revealing more padding, and under that the satin sheen of the mattress. Claire slams her open palm into the wall above the bed and it causes the canopy, strung with gauzy curtains, to sway.

"He's fucking nowhere," Claire says to no one.

"The room has been cleaned," Nomsulwa offers. As if that logic would make sense to Claire.

"I know the room's been cleaned. But you can't clean a ghost. It lingers, it hovers and waits for its people to find it." Claire is speaking with a great deal of authority. The ridiculous words seem almost plausible.

178
–

"Claire. This isn't a good idea. Let's go back." Nomsulwa tries to be gentle as she takes Claire's arm. Claire is still clutching at the sheets. Her knuckles are white.

"He's not here. Where is he?"

Nomsulwa doesn't know how to answer the question, and Claire's distress is disturbing. Nomsulwa wants to go, but she can't leave without the girl.

"Camon, sis." Nomsulwa moves her hands under Claire's armpits, lifting now. She's so light. Claire leaves the bed without further coaxing, but as soon as she's standing she breaks from Nomsulwa's grip and goes back to the bathroom. Nomsulwa follows and watches her take each red-wrapped package from the counter and stuff it into a pocket. She clutches the bigger items, the soap and tissues, in her hands. Little swatches of red peek out from her hips and through her fingers. She matches the room now, all pale with red accents. And her cheeks are red, too. And her neck.

"I'm ready to go now," she says.

"Okay." Nomsulwa goes first, trusting Claire to follow. Willing her to leave the place quickly, without a scene. Nothing to draw attention to them.

In the elevator, Nomsulwa leans over to Claire. "How are you going to get past the front desk with all those toiletries?"

Claire looks down, as though she's forgotten she's clutching the collection of soaps. "I don't know."

"Here, give me some." Nomsulwa takes the shower cap and the small bottle of conditioner and puts them in her pocket. They bulge out.

"You're going to get us caught," Claire observes.

"I'm not the one who just tore up a hotel room for no reason," Nomsulwa retorts.

The elevator announces the lobby. Claire nervously pushes the contraband deeper into her pockets. "We need to find a side exit."

"There's one in the restaurant, but we don't need it. Just walk quickly, look confident, trust me." Nomsulwa leads the way, sauntering as if her pockets aren't filled with red cardboard boxes. She hopes Claire is doing the same. The man at the front desk nods curtly as they pass, but he says nothing and returns to the paperwork on the high table in front of him.

The lobby recedes, the outside air is thick with car exhaust. People are everywhere. Nomsulwa's car is waiting for them.

Claire lets out a breath. "You marched out of there like you owned the place. It was incredible!"

"Best trick in the book, act like you belong and no one ever notices you."

"Thank you." Claire's face is serious and stoic, like the pieces of the hotel room in her pocket are calming her down some.

"Let's get out of here before anyone notices."

Claire puts her hand on Nomsulwa's arm. "I couldn't have done that without you. It's like when you're around I'm a little invincible."

"You're safer when you're with me." Nomsulwa says more to herself than to Claire and then she puts her hand on the small of Claire's back and leads her to the car door.

TWELVE

Z<small>EMBE RINGS THE DOORBELL AGAIN AT</small> M<small>ANDLA</small>
Matshikwe's house. Mandla's wife shows up looking perfect
and frazzled at the same time. She has her best dress on, but
her hands are dripping wet, as though she was taken away
from her sink.

Inside, Zembe can hear loud laughter and the deep
voices of men in argument.

"Mama Afrika. What a pleasant surprise," Mama
Matshikwe says, clearly not believing her own niceties.

"Sorry to barge in, but I must speak with Mandla immediately. It is urgent."

"We are in the middle of dinner."

"And I am in the middle of a murder investigation. Tell
him to meet me out here."

Defeated, Mama Matshikwe trudges back inside. The
laughter stops. Chairs scrape across the floor. Zembe looks
up at the sky, the colour changes from a light pink to a
deeper red. Night has begun. Dust grounds itself around her.
The sounds of cars and people fade. It is peaceful.

That peace is broken when Mandla exits his front
door. He has his napkin in one hand and a scowl on his

face. He wipes his mouth before holding both palms up in front of him.

"What could be so urgent that you would interrupt a man's dinner? When I am entertaining important guests, no less."

"What could be so important that you would lie to the police to protect it?"

"I have no idea what you are talking about."

"I know, Mandla. I know that you went out after the meeting with the water men. I know that you were out late, that the men took home girls. No confirmation from your wife about a nice dinner at home is going to save you."

"It's bullshit."

"I can prove it."

"How?"

"I've found the girls," Zembe bluffs. Phadi had, in his most disdainful voice, alluded to Mandla's choice cut from the local elementary school. Zembe is hoping, praying, that Phadi's suspicions are not far from the truth: local girls to whom she would have access. The high schools in the area have not reported any activity involving their students. But the chances that some administrator would notice such goings-on, let alone report them, are slim.

Mandla pauses, but not so long that Zembe feels the surge of success.

"There are no girls for you to find."

Zembe snaps at him. "With the girls I've got, I can start an audit, find out everything, legal or not, your office has been spending money on. We'll begin with campaign contributions, and then move down the line to your personal accounts. This is a dead white man we're talking about. A foreigner from one of the most powerful companies in the country. There are unlimited funds. National has an entire team working the case. If I tell them you are the missing link, they'll go after you with so much fervour you won't understand what the word 'investigation' means any more."

"You've got nothing."

Zembe sighs. She takes in the night's arrival. And then, because she is the chief of police and she wants Mandla to remember that, she closes her jacket, turns around, and walks off without a word. It takes just seconds for Mandla to follow her.

"Sisi. Look. Ima!"

Zembe stops at the gate. A group of curious men stops across the street and Mandla lowers his voice when he gets close.

"We went to a club, a bar, after the meeting. It was not my idea. That Indian man wanted it to happen. Said it would be a good idea to loosen things up after the meeting. There *were* girls. Not mine. But girls. The white man went off with one of them. He came back into the club after that. We saw him leave with the Indian man. They were drunk, but fine. I swear."

Zembe listens with her arms crossed in front of her chest. She pauses for a moment when Mandla, now panting a little, paunchy, suffering from serious consternation, finishes. Then she leaves. He yells after her, "That's all I know. Sisi." She doesn't turn back. The word will spread now, the councillors will be on alert. They will all know that one of their own is a suspect. But Zembe has other worries.

Dadoo is withholding information, and, she suspects, it's not just because he is trying to be difficult.

184
–
Zembe finds a note on her desk when she gets back to her office. She picks it up and walks out again, into the main room.

"Who took this message? When did it come in?"

"About an hour ago."

"And they are sure these are the same pipes, the ones dug up in Phiri?"

"The man on the phone sounded sure, but I didn't think it was my place to ask more questions." The officer lowers her eyes.

"Okay. Thank you."

"Zembe?"

"Hmmh?"

"Sipho Thizwe has been telephoning for you. He's called four times in the past hour."

"Thanks."

Zembe walks back into her office and shuts the door. She crumples the message and opens the Matthews file. She begins to log her interviews, following the trail from Dadoo to Matshikwe and then to the young girl. Within the hour, there is a tentative rap on the glass window of her office door. She puts down her pen and closes the file. She takes a long time standing up. A female voice, muffled, starts talking before Zembe crosses the room.

"Regional Director Thizwe is here to see you."

"Tell him I'm not back yet."

". . . Ummm, Captain?" The young officer hasn't left.

"What?"

"He knows you're here. I told him already."

Zembe collects herself. "Show him in." What was she thinking? That she could avoid him forever? Seconds later, there is her boss, bald head, tall body, leaning over her desk.

"I know as much as you do. I got a phone call. A pipe was sold in the market. That's it, Sipho."

"That's not it. You got a phone call, then what, what did you do? Who did you send to investigate? Let me speak to them."

"My office is full up with work from the water man. You think I have officers to spare for some stupid investigation into lost steel? I've only known for an hour." That should fend him off. How is she expected to head two investigations in addition to the station's regular duties? *Go away now, Sipho. Please.*

"They say it was sold to them by a boy, tall and thin, with almost no hair –"

"That could be anyone!"

Sipho sidles up beside Zembe's chair. He perches on the desk, which only adds to his height. He bends down, almost menacing. "But you have an inkling, a little suspicion, no? You know who it *could* be."

"I'm busy, Sipho. You have to leave me to do my work."

"Ha! So you do know. I knew it. I want to see her by morning. I want to have a little chat with our friend the pipe thief."

"Her?"

"Are you playing dumb with me, Zembe? It's a girl, the one who runs the electricity mamas. Am I right?"

"Yes, but –"

"– but nothing. Come on, I'm not isilima, not an idiot. Who else would have orchestrated this." Sipho does not pose this as a question.

"But it was a boy who sold the pipe."

"It was. I want to find him, too."

"Listen to me." Zembe speaks very slowly, she looks at Sipho, keeping her eyes directly on him no matter how much she wants to look away. She acts like the innocent she should be. "I don't have a clue who went to the market. I have no evidence that Nomsulwa had anything to do with the theft. If I find something, ngizoshesha ngikushayele ucingo." *I'll call you immediately.*

"I expect a call by the end of next week." Sipho stands up and leaves.

Zembe's heart contracts in her chest with a mix of anxiety and fallen hopes. She spins the creaky chair in a circle and takes in her office, the cracked walls, the peeling paint, the musty smell that circulates endlessly around her as she works. She wonders why she is still here. Still playing the game with the township, letting them have just enough of their own law to keep them happy. It used to be a survival mechanism, but Zembe worries that after so many years she has more faith in the ramshackle order imposed by taxi drivers and community workers than the judges in the city.

Zembe thinks about packing it in early for the day, taking the afternoon for herself. She could spend some time in the church's big main room while the preacher prepares for Sunday, then do some shopping. She might actually get a full head of cabbage if she gets to the vegetable stand now instead of batting off the other latecomers in a rush to scrounge food for dinner from the day's leftovers. She makes the move to leave: picks up her bag and places her phone and datebook inside, piles the papers on her desk in two separate groupings, small and big. She takes the open file on her desk and locks it in the bottom left-hand drawer.

Zembe does leave, but she heads to the community centre. She greets a young woman poring over a solitaire game at the front desk.

"Is Mira in? Do you know?"

"Angazi, sis. If he is, though, he'll be back in the corner office. They always hole up in there. Especially on weekends."

"They?"

"Him and those no-good boys. Eish, tsotsis, the lot of them."

"Thanks, Masindi." Zembe brushes by her before finishing her thank you. She winds through the maze-like hallway to get to the back of the building. The centre is built like a riot-proof boarding house, small rooms off a hallway that cannot possibly fit more than one person at a time. Zembe would believe that this design was purposeful if it weren't for the fact that the entire complex was built less than ten years ago – a time when the whole country pretended it could live in peaceful harmony.

Mira pops suddenly from a doorway in the last stretch of hallway. Her body bumps into him and the wall all at once. She collects herself, but not before Mira backs up and scoffs at her attempt to adjust her vest and bag.

"We, ngulube." *Hey, pig.*

"What did you say, boy?" Zembe can see Mira caught off guard by her aggression. She is caught off guard by how angry she feels. It is not the first time the local tsotsis have mouthed off to her. Maybe it is the claustrophobic hallway and the sheer height of this boy that gets to her. But he has always been confrontational and ungrateful for all Zembe has done for him.

"Voetsek."

"You shut your mouth, bhuti, before the help you're about to get disappears. I am here to fix your mistake. But if I decide to get annoyed, it will be worse for you than for me, uyangizwa?" *Understand?*

Mira starts to kick the floor like a surly child. His sullen face only makes her more angry. "Is Nomsulwa here?"

"No, she's probably with that white girl you stuck her with."

"The Matthews girl . . ." Zembe's voice trails off.

"What do you want?" Mira puffs himself up again. Zembe notes a meanness in his face that makes her feel the tiniest bit scared. He cracks his knuckles, probably a nervous habit, but she winces a little at the sound.

"One of the pipes turned up at the market. Do you know anything about it?"

"No. Why would I know about the pipes? The ones that went missing?" Mira feigns ignorance.

"Siphukuphuku! *Idiot!* I saw you run behind a house like a coward. Now, one of the men reported to be involved looks a lot like you."

Mira doesn't pause long before capitulating. "We needed money, for water for Phiri extension. We had no choice."

"Damn. You're all in trouble this time." Zembe is thinking of Nomsulwa, how she has to get her away from those pipes before they are found by the police.

"We had no choice."

"Ubuduphunga, just stupid. . . . The chief knows. Now I have no choice but to focus fully on recovering them."

"Are you warning me?"

"I'm letting you know that the PCF's mistake has forced my hand."

"You shouldn't do this, Mama, there are people who need that money."

"I have no choice." Zembe walks out, hoping against hope that Mira gets the message to Nomsulwa and the two of them at least find some way to remove themselves from the stolen pipe. She wants to recover the pipes, but doesn't want to arrest the leadership of the PCF in the process. "Just make sure you are nowhere near those pipes. I can't put this off much longer."

189

Zembe walks through the now empty community centre. When she finally makes it out of the maze, Masindi is packing up for the day.

"Did you find him?"

"Yebo, thanks, sisi."

"I don't like that boy. There's too much thug in him."

"I know what you mean." Zembe squeezes Masindi's arm and heads out to her car. It's late enough that dinner and an hour of TV will keep Zembe occupied until it is time for bed. She drives slowly, comforted by the company of her township closing up for the day. Hidden behind the tinted glass of the police car, Zembe feels like she is flipping through old family photos, familiar but surprising. Memories you forgot you had.

THIRTEEN

AFTER DROPPING CLAIRE AT HER HOTEL, NOMSULWA
drives fast down the highway away from the city. When
she arrives home, despite her exhaustion, she cannot relax.
She surveys the main room, the kitchen with bread, milk,
and fruit in disarray on the counter, the floor with missing
tiles and tracks of dirt that reappear despite her constant
sweeping. Then ants, ants that make their way along the
wall, a long line from the garden. Nomsulwa grabs her
spray bottle and cloth and attacks the bugs from the front.
She sprays and wipes and repeats: ridiculous, useless, but
she can't stop herself.

Nomsulwa recleans the spot next to the door, she rubs
the off-white wall with all the force she has, allows the movement of her hand to distract her a little from her morning.

The phone rings, excusing her from the task at hand.
She places the bottle and cloth in the corner and picks up.
A voice on the other end says the usual greeting, but
Nomsulwa is distracted by the line of ants, already growing
again, winding their way along the wall.

"Sorry, what?" Nomsulwa catches herself.

"Nomsulwa, it's Pim." Why is Mira's girlfriend calling her?

"Hi, Pim. How's Aluta? How's the baby?"

"Fine, fine, they're both fine. As well as can be expected."

Nomsulwa doesn't ask how her husband is.

"Mira asked me to call you. His phone is out of minutes. He's at the community centre, but he needs to see you."

Sure, Nomsulwa thinks. *Because if he called me himself he'd have to deal with our fight. And I'd have another chance to yell.*

"I'm exhausted, Pim. Really. Was up most of the night. Can you get him to call me tomorrow?"

"Can't you just head down there for a minute? He seems really upset."

Nomsulwa clenches her teeth. Mira knew that if Pim asked, she'd say yes.

"Fine, how long will he be there?"

"Another hour at least, I think."

"Then I'll go."

"Thanks, sis."

"Oh, and Pim? Aluta, are you sure she's okay?"

"She's making it out of her room most days now. And she ate breakfast with us yesterday. It's a good thing he stopped before he . . ." Pim can't continue.

"I'll find a time to come by," Nomsulwa promises.

NOMSULWA WATCHES MIRA FROM THE DOORWAY OF the wide room. The sunset squeaks through the dirty windows. It throws shadows on the floor. In the dark centre, Mira stands in front of an older woman. He gestures emphatically and his head moves in her direction over and over again.

When Nomsulwa sees him she forgets to be mad. The sting of their confrontation didn't even last two days. She imagines sneaking up and tickling his sides until he can no longer continue explaining the next meeting's agenda or the pickup time for the emergency water supply. Instead, she waits for him to finish. The woman begins to leave and he turns towards the offices with his hands shoved deep into his pockets. His pants are too short and the cuffs wave like eager flags around his ankles. Nomsulwa watches the flapping as Mira approaches, not wanting to see his face.

"Glad you came, sisi."

She hesitates, not sure what to say.

"I got your message."

Mira looks at Nomsulwa. He seems to study every line from the corner of her eyes to her chin. Then he smiles. "I'm glad you came."

"You told Pim you needed to talk to me. So, out with it." She's not going to relax. He tried to take everything from her because she spent a few days downtown on a police assignment. She forces herself to be on guard with him, to forget that he is family.

"Ag, sisi. You can't stay angry with me forever."

"You acted like an idiot. We could be in trouble for this, me more than you, and you knew that."

Mira pauses, as if contemplating Nomsulwa's charge. But he takes a deep breath and continues, less friendly, less soft. "If you hadn't threatened to lock me up we could have moved the pipe before the police had time to jump on the market. You should have let us do what we thought was best. You always have to control everything, Nomsulwa, you take it in your hands and won't let anyone else in."

Nomsulwa backs away from her cousin.

"You called me." She offers this and turns to walk out.

"Lalela! I did call you . . . I need your help. I had a visit from Zembe."

She stops and wheels back towards the office. "I told you . . ." She is speechless. "We are done for now . . . the movement –"

"No. She came to warn us. We have a little time to make this all go away."

"What are you talking about? We're in trouble either way. If we don't sell them, she will find them and we'll be through. If we do sell them, we'll be caught in a second. Again, finished. God, Mira, how could you?"

"She doesn't want you arrested. She needs you to look after the white girl. Now all we have to do is execute our plan a little faster. The heat's just been turned up. We sell the pipes and use the money."

"You mean *blow* the money."

"No, I found a project, a good one. Well, it found us. And then we can get the money out of sight, out of town right away. There will be nothing connecting us to the pipes when it is done."

Nomsulwa wonders what Mira has in mind. It takes as much work for the organization to spend money properly as it does to raise it. And it can't just be used to buy more water. The water company would notice if their community of women suddenly had an influx of coins to spend filling up their meters.

Seeing her hesitate, Mira continues. "We got a call from Kwanele –"

"Kwanele called?"

"He asked to speak with you, but when I said you weren't around he told me about the crisis in Victoria. The cholera outbreak isn't being contained. They have found a sanitation engineer willing to help, but there is no money for a facility. They've asked for a government grant and received nothing. We can give them the start-up funds they need. He sounds desperate . . . well, as desperate as he ever sounds."

"I'm not sure what you need me to do. Go sell the pipes. Send him the money."

"Nomsulwa, you have to see him again. You have to be willing to work with him again. He needs help. They've lost over thirty-five people already. They may have to move everything."

"I'll call him."

"You should be the one to deliver the money. You set up the project so that I can hand the money off to you when the sale is complete."

"I have Claire to worry about, remember? The key to the police information? I can't go spend my days out in the desert."

"Take her with you."

Mira's face is plaintive. How can she think about the white girl when this is their chance to complete the pipe project more successfully than they ever imagined? Being needed again feels good. Feels familiar. This is her real life. She nods her head without thinking too hard about what she is agreeing to.

"How are you going to sell the pipes without tipping off the police? Zembe might not want me arrested, but she certainly wants those pipes back."

Mira lowers his voice conspiratorially. "We have a comrade from the eastern townships who owns farmland outside the city. We're going to transport it there, bury it, and then bring the buyers to the land."

"What buyers?"

"The man from the market. With that many pipes it makes sense for him to send his men far from the town, away from prying eyes. He has already agreed to hire a car and four boys who don't ever work in Phiri to load and drive the steel to his sister's shop out of town. You always wanted to wait to make the sale when things had died down, but it's just as easy to sell now. And we have reason to hurry."

Nomsulwa hates to admit it, but the plan makes sense. If the black market merchants send new runners to pick up the pipes, no one will be tipped off to their location. And if they go far enough out of town, finding the piece of land where the pipes are buried will be next to impossible without a tipoff. Kwanele's town is close. She could be up there by the end of the morning. Maybe with a little nudging,

Claire would be willing to come with her. That would keep her out of trouble with Zembe, too.

"I'll see what I can put in place. Either way, go ahead with the sale. This is good work, Mira." Nomsulwa squeezes his arm. It feels so skinny, no different than when they were kids. "Thank you."

"For what?"

"For figuring this out, for leaving me out of it and off the police radar."

"Of course."

Mira looks at the ground. He must be blushing. Nomsulwa wants to hug him, but gives him a final friendly shove and leaves.

CLAIRE IS SITTING ON THE BED. OUTSIDE THE WINDOW, the sky is darkening fast. The room smells like sleep and Claire. Nomsulwa can pick out the two smells distinctly. One heavy, sweet: sleep; the other high and sharp, like musk and lilies: Claire. Nomsulwa can feel sweat collecting behind her knees and across her forehead. She wishes it weren't so damn hot in the room. She notices a line of perspiration on Claire's lip and then forces herself back to the task at hand.

"The company has asked me to take you to another part of the city. A township, really, where your father worked." As soon as the lie is out Nomsulwa feels better. She doesn't bother to think about how she will align her story with the conversation with Dadoo that Claire will inevitably have. She just focuses on the hopeful expression on Claire's face.

"I have some work to do there too, so it would be great for both of us to go. If you're up for it."

"I was hoping to do more research here. I've been thinking about what you said and I think there's a way for the water company to change its billing structure and redistribute the cost so that the townships aren't hit so hard."

Nomsulwa licks her lips. She is getting nervous, one lie running into another. Her normal state of being these days, she thinks. "Well, this is a big water project. It's a newly settled community. A famous one. And the company put in the system of pipes and water delivery from scratch. It might be a good test case . . . for your research." Nomsulwa can barely get the last words out.

"They're trying to get me out of their way, aren't they, the company." Claire says this more to herself than Nomsulwa. "Rushing me off to one anonymous water project after another."

"Come, Claire. I'd like you to see the work that I do, too."

Claire purses her lips and frowns. Nomsulwa steels herself for the rejection.

"If it's only a short trip, I guess. We can go, sure, why not."

"Pack a bag with a few things. We'll probably have to stay a night or two." Nomsulwa feels a jolt of excitement when she admits this. Claire shows no change in demeanour. "We'll take off first thing in the morning."

"Okay."

"Great. Then I'll see you early tomorrow morning."

Nomsulwa exits awkwardly, but she is smiling. Claire

will come, even if it seems like a plot to keep her away from the investigation. Even if Nomsulwa had to make up stories to make it happen. For a second she imagines they are preparing for a vacation. When the door to the hotel room closes, she lets reality slip away just enough to feel excited.

FOURTEEN

DADOO'S SECRETARY WAS CURT ON THE PHONE. Zembe pressed her for details of the man's whereabouts and finally, after more cajoling than she would have liked, the secretary revealed that Dadoo was at the treatment plant northwest of the city.

"The towers near the highway?" Zembe asked.

"The very ones," the secretary answered dryly. "So, you see, he cannot be reached at the moment."

Zembe is not interested in exchanging phone calls with the man who lied about Matthews's whereabouts the night he died. This warrants a face-to-face confrontation. Surprising him at work would give Zembe an advantage.

The treatment plant was the proud industrial bellwether for Johannesburg's townships. When the plant, erected almost a decade earlier, began operation, the townships celebrated. Here, with the towers so close to their small homes, was the promise of equal rights, equal treatment. Zembe celebrated too, sure that the new plant indicated governmental commitment to improved service. No more broken pipes, no more service cut-offs because of pressure problems. The bulbous concrete sisters rise higher than anything for miles around. Their open lids emit steam constantly, and a sad, stale smell blankets the immediate area around them.

Inside the plant things are different. Visitors meet the alternating hot noise of machinery and quiet, cool, stagnant ponds. Everything is intricately wound around itself. Pipes move in incredible patterns around the walkway, which travels at complicated angles around the reservoirs. Zembe has been told by the man at the front desk that Dadoo is in the left antechamber. When Zembe looks at him blankly, he radios the workgroup.

"Can you tell Dadoo a –" The man raises his eyes at Zembe.

"Captain Zembe Afrika."

"– a Captain Afrika is here to see him. . . . Right. Ja." He tells Zembe, "You're to meet him there. Follow the blue grate. It will lead you." Then he turns back to his computer screen.

Zembe sees Dadoo before he sees her. He is bent over a large sheet of white paper, running one chubby finger down a list. The smell in this part of the plant is particularly strong. She fights the instinct to cover her nose. It is too sweet, too plastic, as if the air can't really have oxygen among all those chemicals.

"Mr. Dadoo." Zembe taps him on the shoulder.

"A moment, please," Dadoo says into the paper.

Zembe waits. Takes in the noise around her, lets it wash over her. She has to maintain her composure, but this plant is more unfamiliar than she expected. A person could be lost in here. A body, too. Zembe shakes her head. She wonders for a moment why Dadoo wouldn't bring Matthews here, rather than an abandoned yard in the township. The body would never have been found. But then she realizes that she has just slotted the regional director of Amanzi into the role of murderer. May as well accuse the President himself of treason and call it a day.

"Yes, Ms. Afrika. What is so urgent that it could not wait until I was back in the office?"

"I want to go over the night Matthews died again."

"I have told you everything I know." Dadoo takes off the hard hat perched on his oblong head and wipes the sweat from his temples.

"Perhaps we could go somewhere a little quieter." Zembe has to yell, even though Dadoo is not five feet from her. He sighs, says something Zembe can't hear to the man working next to him, and then leads the way out of the maze of pipes towards one of the pools of murky water. The noise recedes. The smell intensifies, but Zembe won't let herself react.

"Okay. Again. Start from the meeting."

"The meeting was in his hotel. It went late. When I left, Peter was at the bar." Dadoo makes an exasperated noise.

"And you did not go anywhere? After that?"

Dadoo pauses. For a second, Zembe thinks that she might have stumbled across the wall, that point at which the effort of lying outweighs the benefits and people give up on the charade.

"I left him at that hotel and went home. He was with the councillors. There were many people there when I left."

"You did not go to a bar in the entertainment district? You did not drink and dance until late that night? You did not escort Matthews home to his hotel – alone?"

Dadoo is a small man. He's all wiry limbs and bulky middle. So it is surprising when the man Zembe outsizes two to one turns on her ready to pounce.

"Don't bloody come to my plant, interrupt my day, and accuse me of lying! Your parameters are clear. Investigate the gang system in that township you live in. Figure out who dumped him in an abandoned yard and arrest them."

Zembe stands firm in her spot next to the pool of water. "I am trying to investigate a murder, Mr. Dadoo. A murder investigation is not like a carjacking. It's not a question of taking a few statements and then finding the car, blown out and abandoned in the suspect's front yard. I need to recreate the night, look at all the angles."

"You want to look at all the angles?" Dadoo's excited bobbing gets worse with Zembe's calm response. "Look at those thugs in the township who attack my men, run them off their yards with knives and sticks, dig up the pipes we bury to run water to their houses. Last time Peter and I were there, our tires were slashed. Did you look into that? The night before our meeting, an entire block of piping was stolen. If you want to find people with the inclination and the motive for this kind of monstrous . . ." Dadoo catches his breath, "monstrous . . ." he says more quietly, "thing, then perhaps you should look at your own people."

Zembe prides herself on her ability to maintain her composure. Throughout her career, as hotheaded young men lost promotions and assignments because of blow-ups on the job, a suspect who said the wrong thing during an arrest, Zembe kept calm. She has turned it into an art, this keeping calm. But the way Dadoo is now panting, satisfied after his tirade, the way he said, "your own people" . . . Zembe can feel something building inside her and she knows, just as she knows the time to wake up every morning for church, she knows she will not be able to control herself this time.

"Thank you for your time," Zembe mumbles. She walks past Dadoo, along the walkway, and follows the chugging mess of machinery to the front entrance. As she walks she lets the methodic whoosh of steam and pipe calm her. She resolves to investigate Dadoo like he's the only suspect they have. She resolves to force his fat head on that stick-like neck to explode with frustration when he sees the kind of manpower and scrutiny Zembe will bring down on him.

Once out in the open air, Zembe notices her hands are shaking.

THE FOLLOWING DAY, ZEMBE ARRIVES AT THE OFFICE ready to redirect her men to the water company's offices. Over the long drive home from the plant and the quiet night in front of the television half-listening to the parade of soap operas on Simunye, Zembe planned: If Mandla and Dadoo

204
–

had an arrangement that Matthews threatened, they would have had more than enough motive for a murder. Money, Zembe knew, was at the heart of almost all township murders, heartbreak and anger being too commonplace to warrant wasting bullets. Mandla understood township geography, and he knew about the 28s, their methods and their telltale post-mortem mangling of the corpse. Dadoo had the cars, the access. Matthews trusted him.

But, instead of the quiet hum of an office beginning the day, Zembe walks into a massive mobilization in the Phiri police station. Sipho is standing just inside the main doorway on his cellphone. He is barking orders, while Tosh, frightened and earnest, runs back and forth moving officers around the wide-open room that houses the detectives' desks.

Sipho's voice rises. "I need three extra men and one more car. . . . No, not national, no city guys, please. Send me someone from another district near here and make sure they're well-behaved. I'm going to canvas the township. . . . Yes, I know it's a long shot . . . just get me the men and the car."

Zembe walks up to Sipho and doesn't wait for him to finish his call. "What's going on here?"

"I don't know what you said to Dadoo, but he's furious. He wants us to scour the township, find any evidence linking known PCF members to the murder."

"A canvas makes no sense. People gossip, give us false information. They hate us too much out here, Sipho. There is nothing to gain from giving information and a lot to gain from making us run around on false errands. There's a reason we never do this."

"We know the area where the PCF is strongest. That will help us weed out the false stories from the real ones. Anyway, it doesn't matter what we think. National's orders. Thanks to you, we now know just how many strings Dadoo has to pull."

"You've told the officers to focus on PCF houses?"

"Yebo."

"This is a witch hunt."

"Might be. Then again, if you'd found the steel they stole, we might not have been faced with this problem in the first place." Sipho turns around and continues giving orders to the officers. It takes another twenty minutes for the room to clear out. Sipho walks towards the door.

"Leaving me to sort out all the crap this is liable to bring in?"

"Yebo, sisi. It's your fault this happened. What did you say to Dadoo, anyway?"

Zembe opens her mouth to tell Sipho her theory. She at least could warn him that Dadoo is lying. But Sipho's expectant look, his frown, cause her to rethink her strategy. Openly pursuing Dadoo will lead to nothing. She needs to find a back door to the truth.

"Nothing. I asked him his whereabouts the night of the murder."

"Humph. Bit of an overreaction. Ah, well. Maybe we'll find those pipes in this chase down the rabbit hole."

I doubt it, Zembe thinks to herself. She nods to Sipho

and retreats into her office. No time to warn Mira. She prays he has had a chance to move the steel. She settles in, sure now that she will have to look into the councillors and Dadoo on her own.

ZEMBE IS SURPRISED WHEN A FEMALE OFFICER returns to the station only an hour later with an older woman in tow. She is stooped. Her skin is worn, leathery against her pronounced cheekbones. Her lips purse in a constant expression of disapproval and she is still clutching her wooden spoon in her left hand.

"Sanibonani." Zembe removes herself from behind her desk where she has been searching through the paltry file the office has on Matshikwe. "Ninjani?"

Zembe's officer launches right into an explanation. "Mama Afrika, she heard something that night. She lives close and she heard –"

Zembe puts one finger on her lips and silences the young officer. She turns to the woman. She recognizes her from many community meetings. She is active in the PCF. Florence. Her name is Florence.

"Sawubona mama, tell me what you told this officer."

Florence begins to speak very quickly. "I live right by Pim's spaza. The street next to it."

The officer interrupts again. "It's right in the neighbourhood. Other PCF women live in her area."

"Thula wena," Zembe says to the officer, and then motions for the woman to continue. Inside, her heart is sinking.

"The night this sisi was speaking about there was a commotion outside. Very early. The dogs were barking and scrapping."

"Which night, Mama?"

"The night before they found the water man."

"Did you see anything?"

"No, I didn't do laundry that week. The water ran out before I had a chance. There's no other reason to go out back. The walk over the sand is too hard on my legs."

It's not much to go on. Zembe understands that this could easily have been someone cutting through the back-yard, early for work or drunk late. It could have been a smaller animal, like a rabbit, caught between a pair of dogs. She will not think about what else it could mean now. Instead, she picks up her bag and motions Florence to lead them out of the station into the buggy.

The drive is short, a few blocks to the main street, then into the winding, smaller paths of Phiri. Zembe stops in front of Florence's house, opens the door for the old woman, and follows her to the backyard. Two dogs are lying in the heat. Their tongues are hanging out of their mouths, pink and shimmering. Little piles of excrement sit like carvings on the outskirts of the area where the dogs lie. It stinks back here, even with the wind. Zembe picks her way around the shit. The dogs do not budge.

"These dogs, Mama?"

"Yebo. Those."

Zembe reaches to the ground and feels the sandy bed.

208
–

Her hand scrapes the grains and then touches hard surface, concrete. The sand is a uniform yellow. If there is any evidence it might have filtered through onto the concrete floor.

Zembe stands up and asks Florence for a broom or brush.

"Anything you have inside, Mama."

Florence returns with a small hand broom and a dustpan.

Zembe stoops and sweeps, centering on the area closest to the dogs. Her officer, abandoning Florence on the stoop, begins to clear the periphery, giving her room to work alone. As they move away the covering the stink intensifies. It is only the wind that saves Zembe from choking on the high acid smell of urine and shit. The concrete reveals itself, pockmarked and cracked from so many years of wear. The dogs stand, and the smaller one begins to follow her lead, scratching at the ground, sniffing for treasure buried in the hard earth.

It takes ten minutes for Zembe to clear the sand from the centre of the yard. In front of Florence and the officer is a stain, large enough to be from more than a small mishap, rusted enough to be unmistakable: blood. She walks around it, measuring roughly with her feet. This is not big enough for a murder scene. Perhaps it is a foot in diameter – a little smudge on one end might extend that measurement to a foot and a half. No one committed murder in this yard, but something bled onto the ground. It could have been an injury; it could have been a missing heart. Then again, it could have been an unlucky rabbit.

Stains that are older than three months are useless and Zembe has to take a sample assuming it will be too old to analyze. She takes out a kit she has brought with her, just in case, and scrapes three samples from the stained area and two from the outlying area to use as controls. Then she takes out her cellphone and dials the office.

"I've found something. Send down three officers and a large sieve."

"Where will I find that?" The man on the other end of the phone sounds panicked at the thought of not fulfilling this request. Perhaps the pressure of this case has been affecting the other officers more than Zembe has realized.

"Get them to take the buggy to their houses. They can find their own sieves, then meet me at the corner of Tshiawelo and Phisanterkraal."

Zembe motions for the young officer beside her to get into the buggy.

"Go find a sieve too. We have to be sure to catch any trace evidence in this yard."

The woman nods and crosses the street to the car door.

Florence, undisturbed by the deep red-brown mark in her backyard or the police officer standing with her arms crossed waiting for reinforcements to arrive, wanders back into her kitchen, wooden spoon back in her hand.

Zembe will send the samples to the paternity unit. The forensics lab, one of three in the country, will be too slow, even with the priority given to this case. It has been only a couple of years since they began DNA testing and Zembe would need a court order to get her sample in the door. She has used the paternity unit before, and a blood-type match will be enough – at least enough to derail her attack on the Amanzi official. She has no choice. She imagines the gross bobbing of Dadoo's head as he hears, satisfied that he was right. It infuriates her. She hopes that the sample comes back as animal, or old, or corrupted – anything to make it clear that this hunt for township troublemakers is a waste of time.

211

—

ZEMBE ACTS AS THOUGH SHE IS UNDER A TIGHT deadline. She has a grace period while the blood sample is processed, but she knows that the window of opportunity to pursue Dadoo is closing. She opens the file and takes out a photocopy of the Central Sun bar receipt found near Matthews's body: 11:53 p.m. and a single beer. The receipt places Matthews in the hotel bar just before closing. Matshikwe and Dadoo could have both been there, ready to pounce.

Zembe finds the name of the officer supervising the hotel investigation and dials the national office.

"Hello, this is Captain Afrika calling. Is," she checks the name again, "Siya Lulethi there?"

A scratchy voice announces the Joburg traffic news while Zembe waits. She sits for at least five minutes drumming her fingers in time to the background sounds. Her fingers fall left to right and then reverse their order, they purr on the desktop.

"Hello, Lulethi here."

"Sawubona sisi, unjani? It is Zembe Afrika speaking."

"Ngisaphila. Wena?"

"Nami ngiyaphila. I am calling about the Matthews case."

"The dead white guy? Must be causing you quite a headache. It's been a long time and you've got nothing, I hear."

"You've been talking to Sipho." Zembe grimaces on her end, but maintains a high-pitched, friendly tone.

"He did stop by. How can I help you?"

"I see that you did the interviews at the Central Sun. I was wondering if you found anything interesting there."

"It's a dead end, sisi. The staff all account for their whereabouts that night. Half of them couldn't tell Matthews from any of the other company men who run through there."

"What about the room?"

"We did a search, nothing. The bed wasn't slept in the night he died, which fits with the time of death. All usable fingerprints found in the room belonged to hotel staff. They were all on the database at the hotel. All irregulars belonged to the victim."

"What about the rest of the hotel?"

"What do you mean, sisi?"

"Did you search the rest of the hotel? Other rooms? The dining room? The bar?"

"There was no need."

"Did you get a list of guests and patrons in the bar and restaurant?"

"No. There were no signs of a struggle. Plus, the guy

was killed in the township, not in a busy hotel in the middle of downtown."

"Not necessarily."

"What do you mean?"

"We have no evidence he was killed in Phiri."

"But you found bloodstains in a nearby backyard."

"I know. Listen, thank you for your help."

"You don't think he was killed in town, do you?"

"I don't know what to think."

"You won't find anything at the hotel, sisi. Trust me."

Zembe doesn't want to continue this conversation. The more she tells this officer the more Sipho will know. She doesn't want him back in her office breathing down her neck over a little hunch.

"Do me a favour. Don't say anything to Sipho just yet, okay?"

"Whatever you say. I don't want to get involved in this mess."

"Thanks, I guess. Sala kahle."

"Okay, Afrika. Talk to you later."

Zembe goes to the hotel in her own car. She parks in the driveway and shows the eager doorman her credentials before bounding up the staircase to the revolving front door. She ignores the whoosh of cold air and glinting lights in the lobby, does not turn her head up and wonder at the adorned ceiling, the religious paintings on the wall that use oil paint not faded or marred by dust.

The man at the front desk greets her with a bland expression. She responds by sliding her badge over the counter. He turns to the back room, and it is only a minute before an older coloured man in a suit emerges, clearly the manager. He knows immediately what the police visit is about and seems quite frustrated by the return of meddlesome cops.

"We have opened that room already, ma'am. Your officers spent a week combing through the place. When they left we were assured that the investigation in our hotel was closed."

"I understand. But it's not the room I'm interested in."

"I see." The man's face falls. Zembe can see him predicting a whole new set of closures. Police presence in an international hotel can't do much for business.

"I need to speak with the staff from the bar the night Mr. Matthews went missing."

"I believe our staff were cleared of any involvement in the matter." He makes no move to assist Zembe.

"I just want to talk to them about what they remember. Nothing formal."

The man sighs and picks up the telephone. After muttering into the receiver for a minute, he pokes his head out towards Zembe.

"Misha, one of our bartenders, will be with you momentarily. The other staff from that night are not on shift today, you will have to check back later."

"Can I get their names?" Zembe asks.

He mutters into his phone some more.

"Josef Alben. Thabo cleaned up before closing. And then Misha . . ."

Zembe jots the names down on the cover of the file

and lowers herself onto one of the antique benches situated just to the side of the front desk. Now she has time to study the room. It is like a church, but one worshipping a different god. The colours, all red and gold, are wrong for the size of the room. There are no windows, but it is so bright from all the lights, Zembe wishes she had brought sunglasses.

A young woman enters, tentative and beautiful. She pushes her blonde hair behind her ears and sits at the other end of the bench.

"Misha?"

"Mmm-hmm," she answers, hands rubbing each other in her lap.

"Were you working the bar three weeks ago? It was a Tuesday night, the night before the water company executive was found murdered."

"Mmm-hmm."

"That night, do you remember a group of men? There would have been several of them. They came in late."

"A lot of them?"

"Yes, a white man, at least one black man, an Indian man, maybe more. They might have had girls with them."

"No, ma'am."

"You don't remember that night?" Zembe doesn't want to push too hard.

"I remember there was a table of drunk men but they were all coloured. They came in late, very drunk. I remember them because I had to take the loudest one up to his room."

"Is this something the bartenders do often here?" Zembe can't understand why the shy girl is moonlighting as an escort for the hotel.

"Oh no, nothing like that. I just, er . . . encouraged him to follow me out of the bar. He was getting out of hand. By the time we got into his room he was on the verge of passing out. I left him on the floor, actually, sound asleep."

216

"Oh." Zembe pauses. "And you're quite sure there was no Indian man with a white man, a Canadian?"

"Wait. There was a pair of men at the bar. I didn't talk to them, but I heard them arguing. I'm pretty sure one was American or, I guess, Canadian. Maybe the other guy was Indian."

"Arguing?"

"The one guy, he, ummm." Misha is thinking of a way to put it. Zembe can see her editing. She gives her an encouraging nod, hoping to end the censorship. "He kind of yelled at the other guy, the white guy. I mean, he was frustrated that he was drunk and there was some mention of punishment, and I didn't really want to know, you know? I'm not sure what he did then, but he was gone by the time I got downstairs."

"And the white man?"

"Gone too."

"Anyone else in the bar?"

"I'm sure there were others at that time. There may have been some girls. But there always are one or two picking up a client around that time. I really only remember kicking Fika out at the end of the night. He's a regular. Stays here all the time when he is in town from Durbs. Sat with us till the bitter end. I did a sweep of the place and closed up shop with Thabo."

"That took how long?"

"About twenty minutes altogether."

"Did either of the men order a beer?"

"A beer? No. We wouldn't have served them if they did. They were sloshed. Honest."

Misha has gained steam, is feeling more comfortable. But she has entirely confused Zembe. This story doesn't match Dadoo's version, confirming that he's hiding something. But it doesn't put Mandla at the scene at all. She finds it hard to believe that the little Indian man from the water company lured Matthews outside, into a taxi, took him to the township, and killed him. Mandla must have been involved somehow.

FIFTEEN

218
–
NOMSULWA CAN'T BELIEVE THE LANDSCAPE FLYING by the car window as they approach Victoria. This township was once a flagship, the most celebrated community project since Mandela's victory. The roads were maintained, and sculpted flower beds greeted heads of state, even Bill Clinton himself, as they entered the compound.

But now, it looks like they could be back in Phiri.

The brick-lined beds are still there, but the flowering plants are all dried up. The houses, set back from the road, have peeling exteriors, and many of the impressive structures have disappeared altogether. It feels like a ghost town.

Nomsulwa told Claire about the compound during the hour drive. It was established by a group of women who refused to accept the government-issued houses. Instead of allowing a village of small boxes to be erected by government contractors, they demanded the money allotted for each structure, sourced the material from their own area, and gathered their neighbours to help with construction.

Their success was unprecedented. They replaced the tiny, one-room boxes other government-assisted townships survived in with full-sized houses, including living rooms and dining rooms and enough bedrooms for a small family. They had front yards and fences, and everything was done for not a cent more than the government granted.

Kwanele was at the centre of that movement. He took the idea of the elders and made it into a reality. His lobbying in eGoli was the beginning of a project that put the municipal government to shame.

The last time Nomsulwa was here it was a vacation of sorts. They were meeting an organizing group from a township nearby, and Kwanele invited her back to the compound. It wasn't a love affair. More like politics spilling into the bedroom. But when Nomsulwa finally extricated herself from the boy, he was fuming and she was on the first bus home.

It had taken a lot for him to call her. She recognized that. But then she had no idea things had become so bad.

The community centre is still the most beautiful building Nomsulwa has ever seen. Long, sloping lines frame stained-glass windows that, despite their lack of religious imagery, seem holy. Every wall is lined with dark wood panels, and the front door is framed by two tall, manicured trees forming a lush awning.

Claire is equally amazed by the scene – the building must seem even more impressive given the contrast with the now debilitated village.

"Is this a church?" Claire asks.

"No. The community centre. It's where we'll be staying."

"Is this where my dad stayed?"

Nomsulwa thinks about lying, if only to get a broad smile, a sigh, from the girl next to her. But all she can manage is a half-truth. "Maybe. I'm not sure."

It worries her, this inability to manipulate the water man's daughter, but she is saved from dwelling on her weakness by a rap on the driver's side window. Kwanele stands there, handsome, in white pants and a brown button-down shirt. His wide face, given by his San mother, and dark skin, from his father, work to create a truly unique-looking man. Nomsulwa had forgotten how attractive he is.

Kwanele wraps an arm around Nomsulwa and carries Claire's bag in his other hand. He escorts them through the doorway and the front hall.

"You'll be staying up there, in the dorm rooms." He motions towards a lofted space on the left-hand side of the large inner room. "Yours is the room with the two twin beds, on the right when you get up the stairs." Nomsulwa nods. "Would you like a second to settle in and put down your bags?"

Before either of them has a chance to respond, a voice chimes in from behind the trio. "Since when does she settle in anywhere?" Then, a big laugh.

"Neil!" Nomsulwa exclaims and folds the older man in a large hug. His guitar, strapped to his back at all times, bumps against them and lets out a note in protest. "I didn't know you would be here."

"Wouldn't miss your return, my girl."

Claire introduces herself to Neil without needing encouragement. "Hi, I'm Claire. Nomsulwa's . . . friend."

"I know. You're the reason we get to see her again, I hear." Neil winks at Nomsulwa, referencing her urgent call the night before to ensure that the boys at the centre would play along with the charade.

"Neil is one of my oldest comrades. And, if you're lucky, he'll sing you a song or two later." Nomsulwa moves closer to Claire, talking to her as if it's a secret, though she knows that Neil can hear.

"Yes, yes, all in good time. Now get upstairs and get out of those city clothes." Neil is more forceful than Kwanele: he physically pushes Claire's small frame towards the bedroom stairs. Nomsulwa hurries to catch up. She gives Kwanele a small eye roll as she leaves, as if to say, *Duty calls.*

The bedroom is tiny, one window, two beds only a few inches apart, and a few shelves to lay out clothes on. Claire sits on the bed nearest to the window and Nomsulwa stands watching her for a moment. Her hands are placed oddly in her lap and she is looking at the ceiling with a slack face. Nomsulwa sits next to her and flops backwards, resting against the wall.

"This place isn't how I imagined it."

"It isn't how I described it," Nomsulwa answers quickly. "When I was here last, the place was amazing, beautiful houses, front yards with vegetable gardens, they were even thinking of redoing the school. Now it's like an empty shell."

"You said the water system was failing. Is all this because the access was cut off?"

"I guess we'll find out. But I've seen it happen before. These communities are isolated, they have no neighbours to borrow water from; if the central source is contaminated, the whole town suffers."

"And the company has a plant here."

"Yes, but the price of water is too high."

"Higher than in the city?"

Nomsulwa wants to explain that the company doesn't care if people in the country rot away the way they do when it happens in their own backyard, but Claire has such a look of concentration, as if water is a problem she can figure out. It is the calmest Nomsulwa has seen her since she arrived. "Yes. The rate is higher, and the people poorer."

"But this is an example of what could happen in the townships?"

"Yes. Exactly." For a second, Nomsulwa lets herself hope that Claire is getting it.

"This is the problem my father always talked about – what happens to places with no access to anything." Nomsulwa can't say anything. "He was out here to develop the infrastructure. It was going to make things better." Claire finishes with a firm tone.

Nomsulwa takes a deep breath. "I know."

"The pipes cost money and so the company had to charge. He was always battling it out with the government, frustrated because they wouldn't follow through on their funding promises. This was their only option."

"If we don't get downstairs soon, the food will be cold."

Nomsulwa moves to leave; she needs to get out of the bedroom and back downstairs with Kwanele before she says something she regrets.

"I feel closer to him out here, like I might finally find what he left behind. Thank you for bringing me." Claire takes the lead out the door. Nomsulwa doesn't ask what she's talking about. She's too scared of the answer and certainly hopes that the ghost of the water man, if there is a ghost, is very far away from her.

223
–

The room is full of people. Steaming curry fills two bowls on the far end of a large table. There is creamed spinach and sausages from the braai and cornbread, and someone put some lettuce in a bowl, no doubt a nod to their white guest.

Before they can sit down, Kwanele is up and next to them.

"Hey, Claire, you want a little tour of the area after we eat?"

"Sure."

"You're lucky," Nomsulwa says. "Since Kwanele retired from the resistance, he's become the best tour guide in the country."

"I haven't retired, Nomsulwa. I've joined a different team."

"One that won't sell us out?" Nomsulwa looks over to Claire as if she's in on the dig, but she has a blank expression.

"We're confusing her." Kwanele smiles. He's about to make another remark when Nomsulwa interrupts him.

"Kwanele was part of MK."

"MK?" Claire asks.

"Umkhonto we Sizwe, the armed wing of the ANC during the struggle against Apartheid. A bunch of boys, kids from the townships, escaped South Africa to train in foreign army camps and then returned to fight a guerrilla war against the white government. We disbanded years ago. Now I lead tours, talk to groups about my life in MK and the state of things today." Kwanele pauses. "Most tourists have explanations of this stuff in their guides. Which one are you using?"

"She doesn't need some book. She has us," Nomsulwa interrupts.

"Yeah, sure." Kwanele laughs while shaking his head. "Well, go get some food quickly. Then we'll take off."

"Stick to the salad and the sausage," Nomsulwa warns Claire quietly. Claire walks over, scoops huge piles of steamed curry and creamed spinach on her plate, ignoring the salad. Nomsulwa could tell her that the lettuce will just go to waste if she doesn't eat it, but she follows suit and digs into the curry.

WHEN THEY FINISH EATING, KWANELE MOTIONS for them to head outside. Once on the road, evidence of the surrounding village creeps in. Soon they are passing groups of people. Nomsulwa greets the men and women as they walk by. They stare openly at Claire and ignore the white girl's guide and companion. Small children run up to them.

"Sicela imali, sicela?" they ask Kwanele. He bends down to each one, ruffles their hair or throws a ball for them. He answers, "Anginayo bantwana."

"Do you understand them?" Kwanele asks Claire.

"No. Are they asking for food?"

"Money."

"Oh."

"If you are asked, just say *an–gi–na–yo*. It means, 'I don't have it.'"

Claire tries the word under her breath. Nomsulwa wonders why these children don't flock directly to Claire, the white woman in the crowd. But it seems they know Kwanele, expect him to answer yes now and again. They trust him, and their eyes, when he bends down, are hopeful.

Within a few blocks, Nomsulwa's pant legs are rimmed in the deep red sand that covers the area north of Johannesburg. Its presence changes the palette of the township. It seems to make everything more desperate, more desolate. The children, begging, are new here, like they peeled off the walls of the houses with the paint. Where are the school uniforms? Nomsulwa thinks. Why are they not at the playground or the church?

There is an order to small-town life. Without the transience of a big city, children, men, and women have places. They belong to someone, have a schedule others understand and expect. People are not better by nature in this township, but the ways they are destructive are known by their neighbours, are tracked and mitigated. So the drunk is still a drunk. But someone might stop by and take away his gun before things get out of hand.

That order, those checks and balances, mean that daytime is calm and nighttime is quiet.

But not today. The children are part of the problem, their constant clamouring for attention as the group wanders through the streets of Victoria. But the adults around them do nothing to shoo them inside or to their proper destination. They don't call to the younger children and have them feed the chickens rather than run around causing trouble. The adults sit on their stoops and watch the scene and half-wave to Kwanele as he passes.

The township is dying. Nomsulwa can see its people disappearing in front of her.

"This is the main church. It's the first building we built here." Kwanele stops them in front of a broad building with white walls and a black roof. Claire moves towards the door, but Kwanele waits outside and keeps talking. "Across the street you can see the field of government-subsidized houses." He points to where a crop of brightly painted boxes pepper a sparse field.

"That's what Victoria used to look like. Each house is the same inside. The size of a bathroom with no running water and two windows. We are the first community that rejected that planned assistance. Instead, we bought this land from the government." Kwanele stamps his feet at the edge of the churchyard. "It was part of a pilot project of sorts, an experiment. We were going to take the raw cash used to build a township and create better structures using volunteers rather than city contractors."

Claire turns around. "Like a barn-raising. Nomsulwa explained it to me. It sounds like a brilliant idea."

"It was," Nomsulwa says.

"We started with the houses first. Built twenty of them in the first year. The few families that opted for government houses were furious when they compared their bathroom-sized buildings with the palaces some women put together. More came, and we built them houses, too. We built a school and the community centre and, with grant money from America, we put a playground just off the main street."

"Will we visit those places, too?" Claire asks.

Kwanele ignores the question, too engrossed in his own storytelling. "But the water infrastructure. Well, we shouldn't have trusted the government with that one, either."

Kwanele walks towards a house just down from the church. It's one of the nicer ones on the street, though all the houses in this part of town have gardens and fences and front doors made of solid wood. Kwanele knocks on the door and a young woman, no older than Nomsulwa, answers. She looks tired, but when Kwanele introduces Nomsulwa, her face brightens.

"Ah, the woman who has come to save us!" she says in Zulu, and she walks out of the doorway to give Nomsulwa a huge embrace.

"Who is the white girl?" the woman asks when they finish their hug.

"A friend of mine, from Canada. This is Claire." This last part in English clues Claire in and she reaches to shake hands.

"Hello, I'm Claire Matthews."

"Thembi. Good to see you." Thembi answers in English, but her accent is thick. She quickly switches back to Zulu. "What's she doing here?"

"Nomsulwa has to take care of her – some favour for the police back in Phiri. But don't worry yourself. She's no trouble." Kwanele soothes the woman with the pinched look on her face.

228

–

Thembi seems to realize that they are still outside and ushers the three of them into her house. She explains in English, slowly, for Claire.

"We built this house four years ago. It cost 11,000 rand, the same amount for the bright pink and blue houses over the hill. I am a young woman, with a job part-time at the cellphone station, but even I get to live in this place."

She motions to the interior, all of it meticulously clean and decorated in matching blue cloth. There are separate rooms for the dining area and couch. The kitchen is bordered by a half-wall, and two doors in the back look as though they lead to a bedroom and bathroom. It is bigger than Nomsulwa's house, bigger than the place her mother lives now. Certainly, the house this young woman lives in, in the only town for miles, would impress the richer residents of Phiri. It is astounding what Kwanele accomplished here.

Claire notices it too. "This must have taken forever to build."

"Can I make you some tea?" Thembi interrupts.

"Yes, please," Kwanele answers for all of them.

"We did it all in one day. Impressive, neh?" Kwanele

leans in to join the conversation. "You should see when they build. The music . . . and the beer and food. Someone always puts up a goat or sheep and the women cook a meal, ychoo! What a meal. It's worth the work. You get fed!"

"You've helped build a house?" Claire almost laughs when she asks Nomsulwa the question.

"Of course. Just one of the skills I picked up along the way."

Claire gives Nomsulwa a sideways glance. Nomsulwa 229
smiles back.

Thembi returns with the tea and the four of them sit around the dining-room table. Nomsulwa opens the conversation in Zulu with Thembi. She hears about the loss of Thembi's youngest son. How he got sick early on, before they knew that the river was contaminated, and how she brought him to the clinic too late.

"I've been boiling my water ever since, but even that I can't do for much longer. The electricity is too expensive and my arrears are so great that they're going to cut me off soon."

Nomsulwa nods. The story is familiar. How can you treat water in a home where no one has enough money to run the stove?

Kwanele begins explaining to Nomsulwa about the sanitation engineer they found. Nomsulwa listens, but notices that Claire has turned away from them and is staring out the window at a pair of girls scuffling over a jump rope. Kwanele follows her eyes and then switches to English for Claire's benefit.

"The sanitation engineer says with some money he can treat the local water. We can bypass the company's pipes altogether. Forget about private fees and start a real source for the community."

Nomsulwa elaborates for Thembi. "It's not a permanent solution, but with the money we raised, we can treat enough water to get you through the year."

230
–

"Can you really? You have the money for us in the city?" Thembi grasps Nomsulwa's hand.

Kwanele focuses on Claire, who is now very interested in the conversation. Nomsulwa realizes that her attempts to hide the purpose of their visit are about to be undone. She holds her breath and hopes that Kwanele chooses his words carefully. "A few months ago the community suffered a cholera outbreak. We lost a lot of our people." He explains in English.

"But my father's company is in the process of putting in a treatment and distribution centre here, isn't it?"

Kwanele opens his mouth to speak and Nomsulwa stretches out her foot and nudges his leg beneath the table. "Their system is too expensive for many of our residents. They have no taps and use the river instead."

"What about standing taps? Surely you can set those up near the settlements with no actual kitchens," Claire adds hopefully.

"We have yet to, er . . ." Kwanele looks at Nomsulwa again, ". . . convince the water company that the taps would be a good investment. But Nomsulwa has found us a solution. She has money from the city that we can use to build our own filtration system."

"To bypass the company?"

"It's our only choice right now. We can't provide clean water from a contaminated river forever, but it will give us time to find a new site and decide how best to start over."

Thembi interjects in Zulu again, urging Kwanele to invest in distribution as well as filtration.

"Are you ready to head back?" Nomsulwa asks Claire quietly as Kwanele and Thembi return to their conversation.

Claire shakes her head. "We should stay longer. This is important. The company isn't providing the water, so someone has to. I'm glad you're here, doing this."

Claire's response is surprising. For the first time, she doesn't defend Amanzi or her father. Nomsulwa should feel relieved, but instead she feels guilt. She has no right to let Claire see this. Alvin's tour of the township was the story the water man's daughter was meant to hear.

THEY ARE QUIET ON THE WALK BACK TO THE COMMUNITY centre. Nomsulwa, especially, doesn't feel like talking about the abandoned structures they pass on their way home. Kwanele walks a little ahead of the women, his shoulders falling in and his head hanging. Living with this every day has broken him. Nomsulwa can see it. After the visit with Thembi, he can't even fake a tour any longer.

Claire doesn't seem to expect one. Instead she whispers to Nomsulwa, "Are you all right?"

"Yeah, just frustrated," Nomsulwa answers.

"Me too." Claire reaches out and puts her hand on Nomsulwa's arm.

It's strange, Nomsulwa realizes, that she should be comforted by Claire and not the other way around, out here in the middle of nowhere where she has been promised something of her dead father. If Nomsulwa could put herself in Claire's shoes it would overwhelm her. Worse than imagining Thembi holding her dying son or Kwanele watching the elders waste away.

Kwanele is still ahead, out of earshot.

"I just keep thinking I could have stopped this, the cholera outbreak. If he," she motions ahead to Kwanele, "hadn't been so damn stubborn, if he'd told me about it earlier."

"But how would you have done it? You can't ship water in from communities that have access to a free supply. There are no neighbours for miles."

"No. You're right. It's not as simple. But we could have organized, we could have protested. These women just stood here waiting for their families to die. They were so helpless."

"I'm not sure you're right," Claire says softly, seemingly unsure about her objection. "These women built houses from scratch; they built that community centre and church and everything else in their town. It was probably impossible to believe when their own land betrayed them. They were stunned, not helpless, and when that wore off, they called you, immediately."

Nomsulwa is thankful for Claire's quiet voice and comforting hand. "You know, that's the hardest part. The water you have drunk your whole life suddenly becomes poison. It's too hard to believe, so sometimes you don't."

"I think I have a new appreciation for 'hard to believe'," Claire replies with a smile as they walk the last stretch towards the compound.

THAT NIGHT, THE SOUNDS OF THE DESERT OVERWHELM their small bedroom. They lie, barely a foot from each other, neither sleeping. Nomsulwa can hear the irregular breathing of Claire awake.

"Are you asleep?" Claire asks when Nomsulwa turns over to face the wall.

"No."

"I'm not either." There is a pause. "I keep imagining him here, sleeping in these beds. It's strange. I still expect him to sweep in and turn it all around. Get a grant, give everyone a new, perfect kitchen with running water from a clean well . . . I guess you never grow out of that idea of fathers."

"Maybe not," Nomsulwa agrees, but the idea of the water man as an angel with wings annoys her.

"He was always like that. The person who made everything better."

"We should get some sleep."

"Yeah . . . Nomsulwa? . . . He would have liked you."

"Ha. I'm not that good with fathers." Nomsulwa attempts to keep her tone light.

"My father would have seen how incredible you are."

Nomsulwa doesn't answer. Claire's breathing evens out and turns into a light snore. Nomsulwa closes her eyes and wills herself to sleep, refusing to move until she has fallen. She dreams of water men. In her sleep, she punishes the man for each death. A long line of women who look a lot like Thembi pass by them as he cries out. In the morning, she is weighed down by more guilt, more sadness. Even in her dreams she is betraying Claire.

THE BLOOD ANALYSIS FROM THE PATERNITY LAB IS
waiting for Zembe when she returns from a courtesy visit to
the neighbouring precinct. She had been hoping to cajole the
station to share one of its two printers. It was a pleasant conversation, but she is coming back to work empty-handed.

She tears open the envelope and reads: the blood is
human, type B. A match to Matthews. Zembe sighs and
sinks into her seat. She wonders why she didn't pray for a
different result. This has become a secret project, one that
doesn't even find its way into her morning and evening
meditation. If she had asked Him, He might have spared her
this process, the careful search of the street where many PCF
mothers live that Zembe must now undertake, the questions
she must now ask.

Zembe takes out a map and pinpoints Florence's house.
It is on a street without many women active in the movement.
But behind Florence's house, the street that butts against her's
is more interesting. Mandla has a sister and a brother who
have medium-sized houses closer to this nice area of Phiri.
Both of them live half a block from Florence. Zembe knows
this because Mira's family are in constant confrontation with

the sister about their adjoining yards. Each spring Mira's mother watches the weeds from Mandla's sister's garden invade her carefully planted lot. She once asked Zembe to intervene, and Zembe laughed – with all the murders and thefts, she wanted a police chief to regulate the township gardens?

If Zembe opens the grid search, extends it to the block behind Florence's house, she might just stumble upon something linking Mandla to the murder.

She calls for the young female officer. "We're going back out to Florence's street. We've got to find some corroborating evidence before we can apply to DNA-test the blood found in her yard. So far we've got a blood-type match."

The woman smiles, thrilled at the first real lead in the Matthews case.

"Meet me at three o'clock with four officers. Get people off patrol duty, and tell Tosh to come in from his day off. We have to get this done immediately."

A FEW SHRUBS AND ONE PURPLE FLOWER, FLORENCE'S only living plants, defy the heat of the day. Zembe pulls up and unloads four rolls of string and a pile of wooden stakes painstakingly separated from old wood in her shed.

"We'll divide the area into square sections. None larger than the size of my desk. Each of us will then take a portion and search it carefully. Dig into the sand, look under concrete tiles and rocks. Be thorough. I want to cover this street and the one abutting the yard. Over there." Zembe points through the fence beside Florence's house.

The officers all nod their understanding and begin to divide the area. Zembe supervises from Florence's front step. She extends the search a half block in each direction on both streets. One of the younger men growls a complaint as he is ordered to attach string to the farthest house. Zembe snatches the ball away from him and sends him to the front seat of her car. He sits in the shade, sullen, like a schoolboy ordered to the corner for bad behaviour. Zembe finishes his job, completing the last square in front of a green house with a deep concrete yard and a tall fence.

They begin to work the site. Each uniformed detective crouches on the heels of his or her boots. They sift through the muck of the streets and the carefully placed dirt of the community's front yards.

The man to Zembe's left finds a handkerchief of bright red cloth with a stain on the corner and pockets it in a plastic bag from the trunk of the police buggy. A female officer discovers an abandoned running shoe and also places it in the car. There are shards of broken glass, discarded earrings, and candy necklaces, beer bottle labels and food containers. This is a waste of time. Zembe will give the officers five more minutes and then end this charade.

In a yard four houses down from Florence's and one street over, an officer yells for Zembe. Sticking out from a disturbed patch of garden soil are several ribbons of white cloth. Their ends and tips are sullied by the black dirt. Each also has a rust-coloured pattern.

"Could be blood," the officer announces triumphantly.

Zembe presses against the stiff stain on the largest swatch of cloth. She looks up and sees a familiar yard, familiar building.

Best to wait and be sure, though. The blood on this cloth could be from anywhere – a cut from a kitchen knife, a fall on the concrete stairs. Zembe packages the shreds and hands them to a courier to be sent directly to the paternity lab.

Later, she calls to make sure they arrived and begs for a quick analysis. The receptionist sounds tired of panicked requests, but agrees to pass the message on. Zembe doesn't even sit down at her desk. She takes her vest and holster and starts her rounds, desperate to keep busy while she waits for the test to return.

She intends to travel to the lok'shini. She intends to bide her time while she waits for the analysis of the cloth shreds. She intends to be patient. But after weeks of hitting one snag after another, even her pride, hanging in the balance on this one, can't deter her from following the lead. She wants to wait, but wonders if that is because the reality of the evidence in front of her is hard to handle. How could she have been so blind?

THE STREET BEHIND FLORENCE'S LOOKS PEACEFUL again without the police grid and the mess of young officers combing every inch. Zembe drives to Mira's house. Zembe feels for her gun as she raps at the door. There is no answer. She knocks harder, steps back, and tiptoes through the yard to peer in a front window. Through the bars protecting the glass, she sees a living room in disarray, blanket on the couch, dishes by the sink. But the house certainly seems empty. *Whoever was here ran out in a rush*, Zembe thinks to herself. She vows to keep the house under surveillance in the hope that Mira might return later that night. Part of her, she acknowledges, doubts very much that he will be coming back anytime soon.

She heads back to the police buggy. The windows of all the other houses on the street are lit up. Little eyes peer out towards the door of Mira's house. The whole township will hear of Zembe's visit by morning. She will be the enemy of every mama for harassing one of their leaders.

After the short drive to her side of town she hides the buggy in her garage and walks past her own haphazard collection of shrubs and rocks on the front walk. Entering her house, she feels very lonely.

SEVENTEEN

MORNING IN THE DESERT IS A QUIET AFFAIR. A FEW insects rub their legs together in a feeble attempt to rouse the world. Roosters sound sunrise, but they are so far apart, only their neighbours notice.

When Nomsulwa opens her eyes, she realizes that she has tangled the sheets into a nest around her legs. It is still cold in the room and her skin is pricked with goosebumps where it is exposed. She covers up and turns over.

"What happened to your father?" Claire asks as soon as Nomsulwa opens her eyes for longer than a few seconds. "You said he was dead. What happened?"

It takes a moment before Nomsulwa sits up on the bed. She looks over at Claire, still lying down, but impossibly awake for this early in the morning.

"Didn't you sleep at all?"

"Yes. I just stopped sleeping early." Claire shifts so she is leaning on one elbow. "What did happen? With your father, I mean."

"He was an activist. A leader of the resistance during Apartheid. He was killed by the government. Many were. My father wasn't around much. He needed to be out there, doing things. I'm pretty sure we were the last thing he had on his mind, my mother and me."

"But you must have admired him, what he was fighting for. He was part of a revolution." Claire is sitting up now so she is face to face with Nomsulwa.

"I admired him. I know that what he did is important. I just wish it had been someone else doing it. Because having someone to admire is not the same as having a father, you know?"

"I want my father back. Every day. But I also need to know that he had an impact, other than on my life and my mother's life." Claire lies back down.

"Why? Why not worry about your impact? My father didn't teach me how to be an activist."

"But still, you followed in his footsteps. My father's part of me. What he did is part of me. It's not just family history – something to pass on to my children – it's like it's in my skin, part of who I am."

"I didn't become an activist who takes off and leaves a wife and kid at home to fend for themselves."

"Well then you're a better version." Nomsulwa feels a pang of remorse and shakes her head.

"Maybe *you* are someone different from your father altogether. Maybe you are not the same person at all. I think you could just be Claire."

"Maybe." Claire seems saddened by the thought.

Nomsulwa stands up, checks her cellphone, and gets her toothbrush from her bag.

"Want to get breakfast?"

"I'll be there in a minute." Claire puts her arms behind her head, stares at the ceiling.

"Okay. I'll save a fat cake for you."

"Thanks."

Before Nomsulwa leaves she turns and adds, "I understand how what they do, our fathers, are part of us. You just don't seem to feel like he's in you at all. Instead you are trying to find him out here. I'm just not sure you're going to."

"It takes time, that's all." Claire says with a sure voice. But Nomsulwa can tell that she's not feeling quite as solid about her quest as she once was.

After changing into shorts and a T-shirt, Nomsulwa descends into the main room, now empty. Breakfast, a little amasi and cornmeal, fruit and fat cakes with jam, sits on the table. She sees Kwanele on the porch and goes out.

"You're up early." She touches his shoulder and then joins him on the steps.

"Always. You know that."

"Yes. An annoying habit. Listen, any chance you'd be able to take Claire to the water filtration site while I prepare for the meeting today?"

"You think that's smart?"

"Just give her the tour, no mention of the company, okay?"

"I'm not sure I'm up for that."

"I'm asking you for this favour, please? Just be careful with her. Make sure nothing gets out."

"Fine. No mention of cholera, Amanzi, or the water men." Kwanele's sarcasm is irritating, as if she hasn't been struggling with the same thing. Nomsulwa doesn't answer. Instead, she opens the screen door and walks to the breakfast table. She takes a seat, pours the thick amasi on her mealies, and drops a few pieces of fruit into her bowl. Claire comes downstairs and looks over the breakfast spread. Kwanele sweeps in with a smile and puts a long arm over her shoulders.

243

"Want to come to the water plant with me this morning?"

Claire doesn't answer but looks at Nomsulwa.

"Fine with me. I have a little preparation for a community meeting later."

"Meeting? I'd like to come." Claire perks up.

Kwanele looks at Nomsulwa with raised eyebrows.

"It's going to be pretty boring. Just a strategy meeting."

"I won't find it boring. I promise." Claire answers right away, starting to smile.

"Okay." Nomsulwa curses herself inwardly for giving in so easily. Having Claire at the meeting is a bad idea.

"So we'll catch you in an hour or so?" Kwanele says grimly. They start to walk away from the table. Claire reaches out before she leaves and takes a fat cake for the road.

"Well, have a good tour." Nomsulwa hopes her voice is imbued with a warning for Kwanele. As they walk away, Neil comes downstairs and begins opening the windows in the main room.

"Why don't we move outside?" he asks her lightly.

"You going to be able to carry breakfast with that bulky guitar strapped on your back?"

"I do everything with this baby on my back," Neil jokes.

"Sure you do," Nomsulwa answers, bringing her bowl out with her.

They sit. Nomsulwa takes slow bites. Neil downs a fat cake in two and then places his guitar on his lap. He strums as he talks. The surface of the wood is scratched with a cross-hatch pattern that, though it is from years of playing, looks deliberate. There is evidence of the original stain, a deep cherry, but mostly the sickly yellow of the underbelly shows through. Neil loves his guitar. He cradles it in his armpit, resting his chin on the dip in the waist when he's deep in thought. At times, she has caught him lightly kissing the upper surface, an unconscious reaction like lips to skin.

Neil gives Nomsulwa a crooked-toothed smile.

"So, sis, tell me the news from your end."

"There's not enough to tell, comrade. Not enough." Nomsulwa shakes her head sadly. She won't open up about Mira's accusation that she is too wrapped up in a white girl to concentrate on the movement she began. "We had a strong start, but things are moving slowly. There's been a split. The same old split."

"Tell me more." Neil always speaks with such formal encouragement. Nomsulwa loves this.

"Some mamas want to keep marching, train people to dismantle the water meters like the electricity boxes. They object to the direct action we've done, digging up the pipes and stuff. Ag, man. Those meters are tough. I can barely figure out how to break open the old models without causing the tamper alarm to go off."

Neil thinks about this for a second.

"I was at a conference the other week at the big centre north of the city. In a suit and tie. They never questioned who I was representing. They served me cookies and tea. I spoke with some representatives there to sell their products to the government. They gave me brochures about the new meters, the ones Amanzi is recommending to the government. It's only going to get harder. You can't even pry behind the screens of these new ones. The alarm goes off immediately and notifies the nearest company office."

Nomsulwa laughs incredulously. "You mean they intend to send a repairman every time someone fiddles with the thing? Ychoo. Unbelievable!" Nomsulwa adds flatly, "Or turn off the water and leave it at that."

"Talk to me about the white girl. Is she a comrade?"

"I'm afraid not."

"You should educate her, send her back to collect money from abroad. Most of the big NGOs here get money from America."

"I know, Neil, but she's from Canada. Anyway, she wouldn't be interested."

"Why not?"

"She just wouldn't."

"Oh." Neil drops the subject. Strums a few big chords and then retires to light finger-picking.

"Are you going to play for me tonight?"

"Of course. I always do."

He rests his head on the guitar. Nomsulwa scans the town in the distance for Claire and Kwanele. Where are they now?

"I think the mamas are right," he says.

"What?"

"We have to keep protesting. It worked before. It may work again."

"Yeah, right." Nomsulwa doesn't need to hide her disdain for the civil society route around her friend, which is more than she can say about her comrades at home.

"Also, arrests are expensive."

"Yebo. Ngiyazi." *I know.*

"And it keeps international interest strong. Last thing we want to look like is a bunch of crazy Africans. Don't want to be like Zimbabwe. We need that support."

"Sure, bru, whatever." Nomsulwa uses Neil's line. He always catches Nomsulwa off guard with his preference for civil action over civil disobedience. As if he wilfully ignores the success of campaigns that are violent, where people refuse to pay their bills and chase company reps off their land.

"Why did you say the girl wouldn't help us, again?"

Nomsulwa sighs. "I didn't. The white girl's father works for Amanzi, well, did, before he died."

"Oh." He plays again, the beginning of a song Nomsulwa thinks she recognizes. "Makes her an unlikely companion for you, doesn't it?"

"Leave it, Neil. I had to. Officer's orders. The company's working hard to keep the girl's nose out of the investigation. I owed a cop one."

"Got it." Neil strums a full chord so that the highest string twangs a little later than everything else. He doesn't press Nomsulwa. He doesn't ask her why she's making deals with the police. She feels thankful for this. He helps her ignore her problems a little longer.

"Want some tea?" Neil is already on his feet.

"We should get out of here soon. It's almost time for the clinic to open."

"We?"

"Oh, you're too old for meetings?"

"Ach, I'm too faint of heart to see you lead them."

"Heh, get us some tea and then I'll go. Alone. I'll go rouse us some mamas alone."

"Sure thing, sis."

Now that it is almost time to head over to the clinic, Nomsulwa is getting that flutter of nervousness that comes with each presentation, and today the thought of Claire being there amplifies her nerves. She wants to make sure she has everything in order. Her cellphone buzzes in her back pocket. It's a missed call from Mira. She takes advantage of the minutes alone and dials into her voicemail.

There are three new messages. The first is from Zembe, quick and breathless: "I heard you were out of town and you took the Matthews girl with you! She leaves soon. Bring her back. Now. Call –" Nomsulwa ends the message and erases it before Zembe finishes. She doesn't want to hear orders about returning Claire to the city. The second message is from Dadoo, his droning voice with little hiccups that mimic the bobbing of his head: "Ms. Sithu, I was wondering if you could leave a message indicating when you intend to bring Mr. Matthews's daughter back to the city. She is scheduled to return to Canada in three days." Nomsulwa waits for the third message, which begins as Neil walks in carrying a tray with teacups, milk, and sugar.

"Nomsulwa, it's Mira. Please call me back. I need help. The police were snooping around my house. I think they found something. I couldn't see what, but they looked too excited. Look, please, call me back. I've gotten out of Phiri. I need to meet you. Call me."

Nomsulwa hears the click of Mira's phone faintly in her ear, puts her phone down, and tries to smile at Neil, who looks quizzically at her.

"Ngiyabonga, bru."

"You should get going. I'll just run in and get the T-shirts for you to hand out."

Neil turns around and Nomsulwa brings the phone up to her ear again, as if Mira's desperate voice would still be there. She has to find a way to meet him, talk some sense into him. How could he run away from the police? In her mind Mira is a boy again. He stands on the corner behind Nomsulwa's mother's store scratching at the scab on his elbow from the last time he ran too close to the brick wall of the community centre. She takes the little boy by the hand and leads him back to her mother's yard; she cleans the scab and puts a makeshift bandage over the elbow.

"I will marry you." Mira pouts.

"You can't, dumbo, we are cousins."

"Then you have to be with me forever."

"What about my husband?"

"He can live in the shed in the back."

"With the chickens!" Nomsulwa and Mira laugh, stamping their feet against the yard's dirt.

Before leaving the compound, Nomsulwa dials Mira's cellphone. It goes straight to voicemail. She leaves a message, orders him to meet her in the town outside the compound early the next morning. She has to convince him to get back to the city before anyone finds out why he ran.

ON THE WALK TO THE CLINIC, NOMSULWA WINDS through the far side of the township where the water treatment plant is. It's not spying, she tells herself, if she happens to stumble upon Claire and Kwanele finishing their tour. But the place is deserted, and it's not until Nomsulwa gets closer to the clinic that she sees Kwanele and Claire deep in conversation, leaning against a wall, laughing and nodding.

The clinic is a small house, white walls stained red like everything else. It is on the edge of the town – sensibly away from the general population – but Nomsulwa senses that Kwanele didn't call the meeting here by accident. When there is an outbreak, people move to the nearest outpost of safety. The clinic still boils their water, distributing what it can. It has some food. And more is on the way as the next round of government assistance arrives in Victoria.

Kwanele sees Nomsulwa first and touches Claire's arm so she'll turn around. Claire waves.

They walk up behind a throng of women milling about the cordoned-off space. There are over fifty of them there, some carrying children, some dragging men behind them, a handful of reluctant participants. The crowd is talking; a low murmur of exclamations greets Nomsulwa's small crew. Compared to the sea of red at her own meetings, this collection – a smattering of colour, small numbers – is not inspiring. But every meeting is an opportunity, and Nomsulwa remembers when her own organization had only a few grumbling members.

At the front of the crowd is a chair. Kwanele leaves Claire and walks towards it. He clambers on top and claps his hands.

"Sanibonani. Sanibonani!" he shouts.

The crowd orders itself a little. People turn to face the front. Nomsulwa walks over to stand beside Kwanele. She feels shorter with the height of the chair between them. She motions reluctantly for Claire to find a spot in the audience. Claire walks timidly over to the side where an old woman stands with her grandson and stops directly behind them. The old woman notices the white girl, but does not say anything, only nods at her, and Nomsulwa feels grateful for her kindness.

"Sanibonani!" Kwanele shouts again.

"Sawubona bhuti," the crowd answers, not in unison, but like a wave running in circles around the room.

"Ninjani?" Kwanele doesn't command a room like Mira, unable to extract booming responses from small crowds.

"Siyaphila," the women answer Kwanele, more in sync now.

"Nam, ngiyaphila." Kwanele launches in. "Thank you for coming today. I know many of you stepped out of the line for the clinic and I want you to know that I appreciate that. But we are here to figure out a way to eliminate the clinic altogether. We are here to bring the water back."

The women yip and whistle. There are no walls to catch the sound, but the roof makes their calls echo slightly, or feel closer, as though the women are all huddled in a circle and not spread out under a glorified tent. Nomsulwa can see Claire is still, watching the growing energy of the crowd around her. She looks wary.

"uNomsulwa, from the Phiri Community Forum, is here to tell you about our plan. Let's welcome her." Kwanele motions to his side, then steps down and starts to sing, "Somlandela," an old song with a slow pace. The old women in the front of the room sing with their eyes closed and their voices straining, and soon everyone has joined in. Nomsulwa knows the words and sings along as well. At the end of the second verse, she is standing on the chair belting out the chorus, carried away by the emotion of the song, watching Claire start to sway in time to the music. Nomsulwa smiles at her and then immediately regrets it. She needs to get through the meeting quickly and get Claire out unscathed. The less comfortable she feels, the faster she'll leave. Nomsulwa motions for the women to quiet down and begins to speak.

"Sanibonani!" Nomsulwa shouts. She goes through the same motions as Kwanele. At the end of it, she waves her arm and yells. She owes it to these women to encourage them in their fight.

"Phansi Amanzi Phansi!"

The women respond: "Phansi!" Not a booming response, but they are warming up. The singing has encouraged their voices and now Nomsulwa can feel the energy rise to her. The Zulu accents cover the sound of the word Amanzi and Nomsulwa is relieved to see Claire seems to have no idea what the crowd around her is yelling about.

"Amandla!" Nomsulwa pushes her fist in the air.

"Awethu!" the women respond.

Then she begins in rapid Zulu.

"For months, your community has been struggling to find clean water. You have been saving for a little dribble from the tap when it is your right to have enough water all the time, for washing, for cooking, for drinking. It is not sufficient. Then you went to the river, because you had no choice, and you became sick from the water in the river. Now, your taps are dry, your river is poisoned, your families are ill, and we have had enough!"

The women yip again. They start to holler into the air. Nomsulwa can feel the explosion of a people without an

252
–

outlet. Kwanele, so good at soft words, trusting conversations, has not provided his community with a place to yell. They are furious, and their fury fuels the cries. Loud now. Claire looks at Nomsulwa with big eyes, scared, but also, Nomsulwa hopes, a little impressed, a little understanding of what all the anger is about.

A few of the men move to the front of the room and begin to toyi toyi, singing at the top of their lungs the harsh words:

Nyamazane
Hey wena, Mbeki awunangqondo
Hayi hayi

They jump from one leg to the other, pumping up and down in unison. On the outskirts of the small crowd, women join in. The boy standing with his grandmother starts to jump as well. He looks at Claire and encourages her to try. She watches, tries to jump in time as if to be polite, and the boy begins to sing again, guttural and angry. Claire stops moving. She is paralyzed by the noise and the movement. Her hair is falling out of her ponytail and her face is flushed.

Nomsulwa whistles. The toyi toyi ends. She speaks, in Zulu, in a more sombre voice.

"We have money from eGoli to set up our own water system. One that Amanzi can't control. We will all have to help raise the water treatment plant like you built your houses, together. But an engineer from the city will be here to supervise, and Kwanele will make sure we have the materials we need."

A woman yells from the front, "Will our taps run then?"

"No," Nomsulwa answers. "This is not a solution. It is a temporary fix. Amanzi controls the taps and the pipes that lead to your houses. We can give you a place to get safe water, in the meantime." She doesn't look in Claire's direction.

254

"Let's take the pipes from them. What is to stop us?" an older man yells out. He is leaning on a chair, surrounded by his family.

The crowd likes his suggestion. They take up the chanting, this time in English. The old man leads them. "Down Amanzi, Amanzi Down! Away Amanzi, Amanzi Away." The crowd toyi toyis, crouching when their voices get soft and then springing up when their voices grow. Their words string together, unintelligible, Nomsulwa prays.

But then, the old man starts a new chant.

"Kill the Water Men, the Water Men, the Water Men."

"Kill the Water Men, the Water Men, the Water Men."

The crowd pulses, the young people swerve in and out around one another, twisting as they narrowly miss their neighbours, holding their hands to the side or in front clasped together like a gun. The cry rises, louder than seems possible for the small number of people.

Nomsulwa sees Claire freeze. The accents don't mask the lyrics. Nomsulwa sees she has registered the words. She sees her face turn redder, a harsh red as if the blood is no longer covered by fair skin. Before she has a chance to react,

Kwanele sweeps past her. He takes Claire by the hand and leads her out of the clinic into the sun.

Nomsulwa, eager now to end the meeting, moves away from the still-dancing children and stands on the chair again. She quiets the crowd.

"It is dangerous to dig up the pipes. Police will come and investigate, and we can't afford to take that risk. We will use the money we have to build a treatment centre. It will be a farther walk than the river, but the water will be safe. Over time, if it works, we can raise the money to install a permanent distribution system."

Nomsulwa keeps talking, keeps explaining the plan she and Kwanele organized when she arrived. She talks about how much money there is, how there will need to be another influx of cash in a few months if they are going to complete the project. She emphasizes the fact that the cholera deaths will end if the people go to the plant rather than the river to get their water. Many of the older women think the dehydration is contagious. Nomsulwa assures them it is not.

She is speaking as quickly as she can. But her mind keeps slipping back to Claire, her reaction when she first realized the focus for the anger and frustration of the people around her.

"WHERE'S CLAIRE?" NOMSULWA DOESN'T GREET Kwanele when, short of breath from running, she gets back to the compound.

"She went upstairs."

"I shouldn't have brought her."

255

"You thought it would be good for her?"

"I just –"

"You didn't think. I know. That girl takes the reason out of you. The meeting went well. The girl will recover. Anyway, it's about time the water men saw the damage they cause."

"She's not a water man," Nomsulwa snaps. Kwanele raises an eyebrow, but Nomsulwa can't stop herself. "She's a girl whose father was just taken."

"Water man or not, it was only a meeting. She'll get over it. Though maybe you should take her back to the city. Not sure she's too fond of the desert people any more."

Nomsulwa thinks of Mira's panicked voice. She can't leave yet.

"Tomorrow, first thing."

"Suit yourself. Whatever you want to do."

Nomsulwa remembers the day her father died. The news that he had opened a parcel in his bunker. *How could anyone hate one man so much?* was all Nomsulwa could think then. Enough hate that they would build a bomb, place it in a small box, and leave it in a house where anyone could pick it up. He was just one man.

CLAIRE IS SLEEPING WHEN NOMSULWA MAKES IT to the room. Nomsulwa doesn't try to wake her for dinner; she sits with the group, picks at the beef stew and pap, but eats with no enthusiasm. Neil plays a song, "Malaika," Nomsulwa's favourite, but she doesn't sing along. When the strumming is finished, she says a quiet goodnight and heads upstairs.

Claire is still immobile, but her breathing is less regular. Before making her own attempt at sleep, Nomsulwa tells her, "We'll leave first thing in the morning, okay?"

Claire mutters, "Good." Her voice is thick and rough. Then she tugs the sheets up higher, obscuring the delicate rise of her bare shoulder in the soft light.

NOMSULWA HAS VIOLENT DREAMS. SHE WAKES UP with a start and has to deliberately open her clenched fists. It is the middle of the night, the time when everything is finally quiet and the moon is close to setting. The bedroom is still lit sparsely by the silvering light. She turns to check on Claire and sees only an empty bed with the covers tossed against the far wall.

She must be in the bathroom, Nomsulwa thinks. She waits for ten minutes and then begins to worry. She gets out of bed, covers her bare arms with a sweatshirt, and walks out into the silent hall. There are no lights, and it is darker away from the windows. No sounds echo through the centre, no soft padding of feet or clinking of glasses from the kitchen. Downstairs is empty too. The dishes from dinner are half cleaned. Some are piled, spilling discarded food over their sides, waiting for morning. Behind the long wooden dinner table, the door to the firepit out back is slightly ajar. Nomsulwa's heart sinks. She wouldn't.

On previous visits, Nomsulwa has passed out next to the old, wide fire hole that sits behind the centre. Neil, having sung her to sleep, would slump down on his guitar and the two of them would sleep off the evening's beer, waking up shaking violently from the cold. It is freezing now, the desert night snuffing out all life that dares to struggle through its shift. Nomsulwa is sure that Claire will be shivering in a corner, but she's nowhere in sight. Instead, soft tracks in the sand lead out past the fire, through the gate, and into the wide, sandy landscape.

Oh my God, Nomsulwa thinks. *Has she become suicidal?*

In the open-toed shoes Nomsulwa slipped on before leaving the room, she feels the ice-cold sand sting her feet. She hopes that Claire hasn't gone far, but each step makes her more nervous.

Although the compound still sits large behind her, Nomsulwa feels like she has walked a long way before she comes across a small figure huddled at the base of a wide acacia tree. The canopy, like an umbrella, shelters Claire's body.

She is shivering. The moonlight is disappearing, and the remaining light reflects from her pale, exposed skin.

"Jesus, Claire. What are you doing?"

Claire doesn't answer.

"It's not safe out here. We keep the fence closed for a reason. There are hyenas and snakes, and the bloody cold will kill you first." Nomsulwa takes off her sweatshirt and wraps it around Claire. Then she tries to force her to stand. Claire resists actively and yanks herself away from Nomsulwa.

"It's freezing. Please. Let's go back."

"They are wrong. They are wrong about him!" Claire says to the wide expanse in front of her.

"Okay. Sure." Nomsulwa holds out her hand. "Be reasonable. We have to go back."

"No!" Claire turns to Nomsulwa. "You didn't know him. You didn't know what he was like. He would have done something to help them if he'd been able to. If he'd understood . . ."

Nomsulwa stands, fixed, feeling as if the goosebumps on her skin might literally tear off from her body. Claire trails off. Nomsulwa reaches down once more. This time, Claire rises to her feet.

"Come back, Claire. It's dangerous. I'm sorry this upset you. I really am." Nomsulwa reaches out to wrap Claire in her arms. She wants to hold her tight enough that the apology has no choice but to make its way in. "Come here. I'm so sorry." Nomsulwa repeats the apology like a mantra.

259

NOMSULWA WAKENS BEFORE THE SUNRISE, FEELING the lack of sleep in every muscle. Mira is waiting to see her. She has to talk to him before Claire wakes up.

Nomsulwa leaves her bed silently. The room is still dark. If it weren't for the cacophony of birds outside the window, there would be no indication that morning was close. She pulls jeans on over her boxer shorts and slides a bra on under her shirt. There is no time to find new clothes. She needs to leave fast if she's going to catch Mira. Claire, after last night, will sleep through her absence. She has to.

The car starts noisily. Nomsulwa checks behind her to make sure that no lights have flicked on. She drives carefully, taking the corners with her foot half on the brake. Her hands are shaking. She doesn't turn on the radio or roll down the window. The car fills with the grumble of the engine and the sound of her heart in her ears.

When she can no longer see the compound in the rearview mirror, Nomsulwa dials Mira on her phone. He picks up immediately and tells her that he is twenty minutes out.

"Meet me at the store, the spaza near the church. I'll be there in five minutes."

"Why don't I just come to the compound?" Mira sounds exhausted, ready to lie down and sleep and forget for a moment that he is on the run.

"We don't want to bring them in on this. It's our problem, and the others will only ask questions that complicate things. You must keep this secret. You haven't told anyone, right?"

Mira grunts in the affirmative and hangs up.

Nomsulwa parks her car near the edge of town behind a gas station and walks the rest of the way towards the church. Out here things start slowly. Unlike in Phiri, people are still asleep when the first light rises over the edge of the small sand dunes. She is alone and unseen as she waits.

Mira takes thirty more minutes to arrive.

"Where have you been?" Nomsulwa yells at the window of Pim's car before he has a chance to open the door.

Mira opens the door and squints up at her. "I had to stop and get gas. It's fucking expensive out here."

"I've wasted most of the time I have waiting for you. Claire will notice if I'm gone too long. You should have stopped on the way back."

"Fuck the white bitch. What are we going to do?!"

Mira pants when he speaks, his tall body bent over the wheel. Nomsulwa crouches down to be level with the car's seat and puts a hand on his shoulder. She kneads his neck. His bent backbone threatens her own resolve. She can't have him fall apart on her.

"What did they find?"

"I don't know. How could I know? The point is that they found *something*. At my house."

"We can't plan if we don't know what they are working with." Nomsulwa points out the obvious, hoping this will trigger Mira's memory. What could possibly be in his house?

"Stop asking impossible questions and help me!" Mira raises his voice. Nomsulwa tries to calm him down.

"Look, you didn't do it. You didn't kill him. She can't prove you did something you didn't. Suka la uyisiphuku-phuku. She's going to know you ran. She's going to think it *was* you."

Mira is looking at Nomsulwa as though she is a stranger. "She can still throw me in jail. She can still put me away for the water man." He grabs her arm, squeezing the skin so hard it rises between his fingers like bread dough. Nomsulwa shakes herself free from his grasp. He stands up and pushes towards her, his breath hot on her face. "I was there."

"This is what we're going to do. You will go back to Phiri. You will get word to the police that you had a family emergency. Have that bastard you always smoke with tell his contact in the department. Then you'll go home and sit tight until this all blows over."

"Ukhuluma ngani, sisi? *What are you talking about?* This isn't a plan." Mira spins on his heels and runs his hand over his head, taking in every crevice with his fingers. He looks to the sky as if this might be a good moment to start praying. "I can't go to Sun City. I'll die. I'll die in there. You have to get me out of this."

262

Nomsulwa yanks him back towards her. "What you need to do is lie low. Is everything set for the pipe purchase?"

"Yes, yes, we only have to meet them at the farm to complete the sale. I'm supposed to call once I'm there."

"You can't be the one to go anymore. Go to the community centre, a place where you will be easily spotted. Do some work. Pretend to do some work. Do something that seems inconspicuous. Get one of your boys to go to the farm for you. We shouldn't be anywhere near those pipes when they're bought."

"But I can't –"

"Do as I say, Mira. Go back. I'll be there in the afternoon. I'll meet you at the office. I have to go. Claire is waiting. Do as I say, Mira. Promise me."

He nods and returns to looking to the sun for salvation.

Nomsulwa steps around to the front of the spaza. She knows that her cousin is still standing in the spot behind the store. Still glancing around, ready to be arrested at any moment, ready to be hauled off to the pit where so many of their friends ended up. For doing less. They ended up there for doing less.

NOMSULWA EXPECTED TO BE BACK BEFORE CLAIRE woke up. She was counting on it. After last night, she can't let the girl be unsupervised. She might run off into the desert again, this time for good. Nomsulwa needs to focus her energies on returning her to the city, depositing her on a plane bound for Canada, and forgetting they ever met.

263

The part of Nomsulwa that missed Claire, even that morning on the drive to meet Mira, the part of her that bristled when he called her a white bitch, that part takes over when she enters the compound. Zembe and Dadoo made it clear that they are ready to get rid of her. But Nomsulwa's not sure she's ready to let her go.

"Where were you this morning?"

"I had a meeting. We needed to find some people before they started work."

"You didn't tell me you had another meeting."

"It was just small. I wanted to let you sleep."

Claire doesn't look convinced. "Sure, right. Thanks."

"Are you ready to leave?"

"I just need to get my stuff."

"Well, I'm packed so . . . whenever you're done."

"We can go. Of course."

Nomsulwa opens the door. Neil is sitting at the breakfast table eating a steaming bowl of pap. She has no energy to keep up the charade. She is undone by Mira, completely blown open. It feels dangerous.

"For breakfast?" Nomsulwa greets him, trying a smile.

"Always. You off?"

"Yeah, she kind of wants to escape after yesterday."

"I get that. Shame though. You know, we could have done a lot of work if you'd have stayed a few more days."

"I know, I know." As Nomsulwa starts up the stairs, Kwanele appears above her. He is wearing nothing but a pair of rumpled shorts, and his face is creased from sleep.

"Where is she?" he mumbles.

"Good morning," Nomsulwa answers, avoiding his eyes. She is sure it is all over her, the silent film of Mira and the knife. She is terrified that her friends, that Claire, can see the awful image in her eyes.

"Is she all right?"

"She wants to head out. She's on the porch."

"We ran them off successfully," Neil calls from the kitchen.

Kwanele nods. He turns, continues down the stairs, and Nomsulwa hears the door slam.

ONCE THEY ARE IN THE CAR, NOMSULWA TRIES TO concentrate on driving, but she is feeling light-headed. She didn't eat and can't eat. The minutes creep by, each passing vehicle a surprise as it swerves around them. This is dangerous. Claire is noticing the erratic driving, growing more and more nervous. Suddenly a large minibus careens across their path, the horn sounds out.

Nomsulwa touches the brakes, which cuts the car to the right. Claire gasps. Nomsulwa grips the steering wheel, yanking their car back on course.

"What are you doing?!" Claire exclaims, fury in her voice.

"Sorry, that bus came out of nowhere," Nomsulwa mumbles, her own heart beating too quickly.

"I'd rather get home in one piece if you don't mind." Claire crosses her arms in front of her chest. Nomsulwa recognizes the signs of an outburst waiting to happen.

"Sorry."

"Why do you keep saying that? It's like a tic, sorry, sorry, sorry." Claire's voice gets faster and higher.

"I know you're angry –" Nomsulwa tries to engage calmly.

"Angry? No. I should have known," Claire almost yells. Then she pauses, purposefully shuts her mouth, and stares out the window.

Nomsulwa feels the pain in Claire's reaction. "I know I messed up, okay? I didn't mean for you to see the protest. It was supposed to be a meeting, a small gathering, that's all."

Claire whips around, more irate than before. "I thought you were my friend. I thought you were someone I could trust. I felt *safe* with you. You told me that we were there to see my father's water project, where he stayed, what he did while he was there. But you lied to me so you could drag me out to the middle of nowhere and humiliate me in front of . . . everyone." Claire's voice drops at the end. She looks down.

"I'm so –" Nomsulwa stops herself before she says, "sorry." She wishes she understood how to make Claire feel better.

"Look, just forget it. I came to find out who my father was. . . ."

Nomsulwa doesn't know how to respond. She feels the weight of the morning, the weight of the week and the week before that. She imagines moving backwards, to before the water men. She, now, is not sure how she thought she could have kept the truth from Claire, and maybe a large part of her didn't want to. She has this urge to share with the girl next to her every tiny piece of her life, the township at lunchtime, her office bustling with mamas painting banners and signs, the thrill of a meeting where a community vows to come together and change their own future. It was selfish, the assumption that she could get close to Claire without it costing anything.

"Alvin called. He said that your flight home is booked for the day after tomorrow."

"Yeah, I know." Claire seems shut.

"You must be ready to get back home."

"For what? What am I bringing back with me? I didn't find out anything new, I didn't find . . . I found nothing here. I don't know why I came." Claire turns to look at Nomsulwa driving, stares at her tense muscles and feeble attempt to focus on the road, which, despite her willing it not to, becomes busier, the tall landscape of Joburg emerging in the distance. Nomsulwa prepares herself to say goodbye to Claire.

"We're here." Nomsulwa says after she has pulled up to the hotel, cut the car's engine, and waved off the assistance of the man at the door.

"Thanks." Claire sits there, so still and quiet, staring at her own hands.

"Do you want me to take you to the airport?" Nomsulwa asks, putting on a brave face.

"No. The hotel arranges transport."

Nomsulwa feels herself shrink in the car. "Do you want some company for the rest of the day?" She manages one last attempt.

"No." Claire looks unsure, then stolid again. She sticks to her answer.

"Okay."

"You've done enough already." Claire looks directly at Nomsulwa. Her eyes are still full of anger and, behind that, hurt. She looks like she might cry and holds herself stiffly like it's the last thing she is going to let herself do.

"Goodbye." Nomsulwa says, hoping she will think of something more to keep Claire in the car. But Claire is already opening the door. She tugs her bag from the back seat, looks in one last time, and leaves.

NINETEEN

Ten in the morning and Mira is nowhere to
be found. Zembe knows that Sipho will be pleased when
he reads the report from her patrol: no sign of him for over
a day and a half. A suspect on the run looks better than a
man who volunteers to cooperate. He'll have something
to tell the community when they curse him for accusing
their leader. Mira ran. What innocent man would run?

She sits still, waiting for the office to fill with the day's
reports. Every man who enters the door and is not Mira
confirms Zembe's fears further. Now all she needs is a piece
of evidence that places Mira with Matthews. Some explanation for how the white man ended up in the township, how
the tsotsis lured him out of his hotel. She thinks about the
blonde bartender's struggle with the loud drunk man at the
bar. What if Mira used a girl to get Matthews out of the safety
of the Central Sun?

Zembe stops by the gas station on her way to
the water office. She has to update Dadoo, a moment she
is dreading. But on her way she wants to explore one last
angle. She pokes her head in, and the four men are sitting

in the exact same formation as at her last visit. The slurp of warm Coke through straws and the crunch of shells under Zembe's heels are the only sounds.

"Sawubona, bhuti," Zembe greets the ringleader.

"Ah yes, Ms. Afrika. Any luck finding our Diepkloof thief?"

"No, but I did hear that he had a nasty run-in with a set of tires."

"Yes, I heard the same thing. He's lucky to be walking around again." The men all grin, pause in their sipping.

"Very lucky, I'm sure. I'm not here to check up on you, I want to cash in my favour."

"I hope it is within my reach."

"If I give you a date, can you find out all the comings and goings of taxis from the Central Sun after midnight?"

"Is it a weekend?"

"No, a Tuesday night."

"Not a common time to travel on a weeknight. There might not be anything." The man frowns, genuinely concerned that he might be forced to investigate and still not satisfy his debt to the police.

"A white man, North American, he would have been the passenger. He might have been with a black girl. They left the hotel late, we think they left late. Just check into it for me and we'll consider the favour satisfied."

"I will try."

"I knew you would come through for me."

"Wait until I find something. I cannot guarantee

anything until I speak to my drivers," the man says to Zembe's back as she leaves.

ZEMBE PRAYS THE ENTIRE WAY TO AMANZI'S OFFICES that Dadoo is away from his desk, at a treatment plant, on a site visit, anything that will allow her just to leave a message and be able to tell Sipho that the water men are getting the personal service they demand from the police force. She can leave the file containing the blood analysis with the pinched secretary and then start the long drive back home.

Except Dadoo is most certainly in his office. In fact, he's in the atrium at the front when the elevator doors open. He turns with a look of surprise when he sees Zembe and smiles that quick, fake smile.

"Ms. Afrika. To what do we owe the pleasure?"

"Mr. Dadoo. I was just stopping by to drop off our latest update on the investigation," Zembe answers tightly.

"Excellent. We can talk in my office."

Zembe knows that Dadoo already has the information she's about to give him. He is gleeful precisely because the evidence points towards the community. Thankfully Dadoo doesn't know about the strips of cloth in Mira's garden.

Once in the office, she opens the file on Dadoo's desk. She starts to take out the blood analysis and points to the third paragraph, where the paternity lab identifies the blood in Florence's yard as a match to Matthews's blood type in the coroner's file.

271

Dadoo comes over, sits down in his chair, and interrupts Zembe after only the first sentence.

"Ms. Afrika, if I am to understand correctly, a bunch of thugs are responsible for this murder."

"Well –"

"And one of the leaders of the PCF has gang affiliations. To the 28s? Are we surprised that they are somehow linked?" Dadoo snorts. "Not bloody likely. I knew they were behind it from the beginning."

"The evidence is not conclusive yet," Zembe says but feels defeated. Dadoo leans back and links his fat fingers together. He rocks in his office chair, smiling.

"But," he begins, and pauses for effect. "Now that we are quite sure who is responsible, we can put this all to bed."

Zembe hates Dadoo and his hands so carefully placed and his little smile, more genuine than anything he's displayed before. Mira might be a killer, he certainly has the edge you need for that kind of business. But he is also the boy who held Nomsulwa while she wailed in his arms. And Dadoo is a monster, strangling the people Zembe swore to protect, excused from the role because of circumstance and the suit he wears. She resents him with every ounce of herself.

Dadoo stops rocking and moves closer, elbows resting on his desk.

"Our charge, I hear, is out of town." Dadoo shifts gears.

"Yes. She's been taken to tour the water project in Victoria."

"Are you sure that was wise?"

"It kept her busy, which was what you requested." Zembe covers her own annoyance at Claire's trip, pretending to have orchestrated the entire thing. She can't show any lack of control in front of Dadoo.

"Her flight is scheduled to depart in two days and I think we need to tell her about our latest development if we are going to make sure she's on that plane."

"You want me to solve the case by tomorrow?" Zembe scoffs.

"We know who it was. Tell her it's done. We can tie up loose ends after."

"The investigation is still very much underway. We don't know how, or why . . ." She trails off. She's not sure if she's being thorough or if she is reluctant to close the case. The fallout is going to be devastating. She could tell Dadoo her real worry, that Claire is with Nomsulwa, and letting either know how close they are to arresting Mira is too dangerous, for Zembe and for the company.

"I'm sure you will think of a way to wrap it up nicely for her," Dadoo says.

Zembe begins to protest again.

"I will call tomorrow." Dadoo gives her no chance to interject further before standing up and holding out his hand. Zembe takes it lightly and then exits quickly.

ZEMBE TAKES A PICTURE OF MIRA FROM THE FILE. It's an old photo, one she dug up when she first found the blood in Mira's yard. He looks the same though: slight frame, slight face, without his height you could think him no older than sixteen. There is none of the hardness in this picture that Zembe feels when she is with him. It is the kind of picture a mother would carry with her.

This time, she calls the hotel first to make sure Josef, the bartender, is working. The manager says that he doesn't come in until the evening shift, but he can ask him to be at the hotel within the hour if it is urgent.

"It is," Zembe assures him. And the manager is all too happy to assist, hoping, Zembe assumes, to end the investigation once and for all. She gathers the file together. Checks in with the few officers milling around the building, and then gets into her car and drives downtown.

Josef, unlike Misha, is confident and speaks with a British accent, or at least he fakes one very well. He is handsome, tall and broad, and his arms strain against the collared black shirt he wears with an easy pair of jeans. He carries himself like a man who has always known he is attractive. He has also likely always worn sharply pressed shirts, from his fancy private school to university. Zembe guesses University of Cape Town, with that accent.

Josef talks to Zembe in a conspiratorial manner about the goings-on in the hotel. He tells her about business deals in the back corners, he jokes about the drugs he sees patrons snort in the hotel bar bathroom. She listens, nodding, then prompts him to remember the night Matthews was at his bar and he begins a story.

"Those Americans get wasted, but that guy was a quiet drunk, like a shadow, ychoo. Then when the Indian guy started laying into him. That was bloody hilarious. I couldn't laugh, mind you. But the American swaying and the Indian man yelling. It was a scene. I was glad to see him leave."

"The American?" Zembe focuses in closer.

"No, the Indian."

"Did you see the American with anyone else? A girl, perhaps?"

"You mean a girl, like a *girl*?" Josef smirks. "There are lots of those, slipping in and out on the weekend. Doorman starts to ignore the riff-raff when it gets late enough, especially on a weeknight. Even the really black girls are greeted at the door like guests, tough-looking girls, girls that would *never* get in otherwise."

"And that night." Zembe tried not to lose her patience.

"That night was slow. There was one girl. Could have been one of those types of girls. A little round." Josef mimes squeezing a body in front of him. Zembe does her best to ignore it. "Cute, you know, because she was light-skinned. But not dressed the part."

"Did she talk to the American?" Zembe gets excited. This was where he could have been lured outside.

"I don't think so. But either way, I saw her at the bar after the American had left. That I remember."

"Did she order a beer?"

"What? I don't know what she was drinking. But she was looking at me, you know, like she knew what she wanted.

275

It was a weeknight, otherwise I might have taken her . . ." he trails off. "But whatever. A Tuesday isn't going to be one of those nights. Girls like that happen all the time. Just last night, a hot Indian girl was asking me about scotch. As if she drank scotch. She was just trying to make conversation. Didn't give a shit about scotch, but did about me. Bet she didn't even drink."

276

Zembe is thankful that her job is limited to the township. That she rarely has to indulge creeps like this one in fancy downtown offices. Because in these hotels, absolutely nothing has changed. She smiles an Apartheid-era smile and tries to pull Josef back to her line of questioning.

"What about . . ." Zembe pauses, lets Josef's description slide. She focuses on what is important, fingers the picture of Mira, not sure if she wants to know the answer. "What about this man?" She slides the picture over to the bartender. Josef takes it, tips it back to get a better look.

"This guy? Looks like a kid." He bites his lip. "Nah. Not that night, for sure. Don't think I've seen him before. That said, who knows?" He hands the photo back. Zembe's not sure if she's more relieved or confused.

"Do you remember what time Mr. Matthews left the bar?"

"No. I mean, it was certainly before closing. I turned around and he was gone. No big deal, really, must have gotten tired of swimming in his own head and headed upstairs."

"And no one else was left in the bar?"

"Look, there were people *there*. I mean, it's a hotel bar at night, there are always the travellers, the businessmen who can't sleep alone, the women lonely and looking for a friend to pass the time with. But I didn't see anyone suspicious. Certainly none of those *girls*, and no young guys looking to score or settle a score." Josef smiles at his wordplay. Zembe sighs, closes the file, and stands.

"Thanks for your time."

She exits the hotel. She can't arrest a man when she has no evidence linking him to the victim. She has run out of ideas. There is nothing to prove Mira and Matthews met, nothing to suggest Mira started the night's events in motion. The blood evidence just isn't enough.

TWENTY

278
–
In her car on the highway, Nomsulwa imagines Claire in her hotel room waiting for the day to pass so she can escape back home. She is packing her clothing, shaking out desert dust, prepared to leave this all behind. She runs over yesterday's events in her head, each time hoping that her imaginary self will step in, take Claire away from the meeting, freeze her, content and inspired, walking with Nomsulwa through Victoria at the end of their township tour. Make it up to her, as if that would be possible.

Nomsulwa remembers her father, stumbling across him in the middle of Phiri during a week when he was not staying at home. His arm was around a boy not much older than her. She remembers him talking in low tones, holding the boy with what seemed like love and encouragement, writing on a piece of paper as though to explain something complicated, and exuding patience when the boy needed help in understanding. The difference in attention, in tenderness and care between that man in front of her and the father she knew, was striking. She couldn't help thinking that if she had somehow been more like that boy, body all angles, face out of proportion and skin bumpy with puberty, she would have deserved a father who stayed.

Nomsulwa thinks about loss and her father. What she couldn't ask for and how it is the same now.

When she arrives at the Phiri police station, Zembe is in her office. She looks like she just arrived, her hair blown out of place by the wind and her jacket still on.

"So you decided to return from your little trip, I see," Zembe says, as she moves around some papers on her desk. "Where is the Matthews girl?"

"She's at her hotel. I brought her back, just as you asked." Nomsulwa sits down. She sets her face in a serious expression. "The girl, Claire, is actually the reason I came by."

"I'm listening."

"I want something. For me. Well, actually for Claire."

"Go on."

"I want her father's ring. Before you say no, the girl has come all this way. She's got nothing to go home with. You haven't found the murderer. Giving her the ring is the least we can do." Nomsulwa waits for a response, holding her breath, hoping she didn't give away how much she needs this.

"You talk to me as if I'm keeping the poor girl's things out of spite. I sympathize. I do. I'm not unaware of what it feels like to lose someone, none of us are. But I can't take evidence, let alone a valuable ring that was found on the body, and give it away."

"Evidence is lost or stolen all the time."

"What if we need to try the man who did this? What if we need to prove it wasn't part of a robbery? The ring would have relevance in that trial."

"Don't give me that. You and I both know that any man accused of killing a water man will go straight to jail for life."

"I don't need you explaining the court system to me."

"I know you don't. So please, let me take the ring back with me."

"It's not possible."

"What if I exchange something for it? I'll work for you for as long as you need."

Zembe stands up and moves to sit on the edge of her desk, very close to Nomsulwa. "You want to exchange, do something for me? There is one thing you have that I need."

Nomsulwa realizes what Zembe is referring to.

"No."

"This is not my choice. Things have progressed. I can no longer explain my inability to recover those pipes. I made sure you were safely away from the stolen goods before we went searching for them. But now I need those pipes. My job is at stake here."

"Those pipes are going to be sold to pay for water treatment. They are going to literally save hundreds of lives."

"I understand this."

"You can't ask for them."

"I know." Zembe doesn't move. She takes a deep breath. "But I am asking. You won't make it to the market with those things. Mira will be caught and delivered to this station before the first sale is made. I can't continue to be silent, or save you. It's now out of my hands. If you give the information now, it will be better for all of us."

Nomsulwa takes this in, wanting to see the logic in Zembe's analysis. But she knows they have a buyer, a secret meeting location where no market tourists will catch sight of the transaction. Mira has worked out every detail.

"So it's your skin you're saving." Nomsulwa pauses, tries to control her urge to lash out. Nomsulwa imagines herself writing down the location of the field where Mira has buried the pipes, sees her cousin's face when he finds out the pipes are missing. Then she imagines him discovered, arrested. It seems as inevitable as Zembe pretends it is. The anger leaves, replaced by nothing. She feels as if she is being carried, against her will, without the ability to fight back.

"I'm saving you, too," Zembe responds.

"You have to give me time to make sure Mira is long gone," Nomsulwa says, her voice dull.

"Of course."

"And the runners, from the market, I don't want them there either."

"You choose the timing."

Nomsulwa thinks it through. She hopes Mira will do as she says and not go, but if he does he will be there this afternoon and the runners tonight. That gives the police a two hour window in the late evening. If she is careful to account for her whereabouts for the afternoon, neither group will suspect her as the tipoff. The runners will be angry but assume that the dig was reported by local residents and busted by the police. Mira will . . . Nomsulwa stops herself there. She can't think about Mira.

"Seven this evening. Before it gets dark."

"The address?"

Nomsulwa takes the pen Zembe hands her. "You'll leave Mira out of it?" Nomsulwa looks up, pen poised over the paper.

Zembe nods. Nomsulwa holds the pen lightly as she writes down the address, as if pressing gently will make it less real.

"One more thing," Zembe says as Nomsulwa shoves the address across the desk. "It's about Mira."

"You just promised he'd be left out of this." Nomsulwa is exasperated and overwhelmed. She's not sure how much longer she can keep this up.

"It's not about the pipes. We found pieces of cloth with the water man's blood buried in his front garden." Zembe announces it without ceremony and then pauses.

Nomsulwa wills herself not to react with anything but surprise. Holding her breath, holding it all in, she runs through all the ways Mira could have let this happen. He could have tried to clean up, could have gotten blood on his clothes. But he wouldn't be stupid enough to leave evidence in front of his own house, would he? She tries to imagine him, panicked, left with the responsibility for a murder he didn't commit. Who knows what mistakes he might have made?

"Someone is framing him," Nomsulwa says. "He didn't kill any water man. I would know if he'd done that."

"We have blood evidence linking him to the murder. And he certainly has the motive and connections."

"What has this got to do with me?" Nomsulwa's voice gets higher.

"So you will be careful. I want to keep you out of this."

"I am careful. And Mira had nothing to do with it. Am I free to go?" Nomsulwa is empty, everything spent.

"The ring." Zembe offers. Nomsulwa nods. Zembe gets up from her desk. She leaves the office, shutting Nomsulwa in.

The walls close. Nomsulwa fights the urge to dash out of the building into the open air. She tries to calm her breathing. When Zembe returns, she is carrying a small plastic bag. In it is Claire's father's ring. She places it on the desk. "I will call when the pipes are secured."

Nomsulwa grabs the ring and stuffs it in her pocket. She stands up.

"Don't. Don't call. I'd rather not know."

Zembe doesn't say anything more. She lets Nomsulwa walk out.

TWENTY-ONE

284
–

ZEMBE BEGINS TO PREPARE FOR THE PIPE RECOVERY.
The water man is far from her mind for the first time in
weeks and his absence makes her feel lighter, more sure of
each decision. She is beginning to dial Sipho when an
officer knocks, enters, and hands over a small stack of messages. Zembe dismisses her and then glances at the top
piece of paper:

> From: Taxi Rand Zone 3
> To: Zembe Afrika
> Message: No drivers remember an American travelling
> to or from the hotel that night. Only found one town-
> ship taxi that had been at Central Sun. Driver saw a car
> arrive and leave the hotel quickly, after midnight. Driver
> a man. Passenger a woman, black, hair in dreads or
> twists. No address or name.

Zembe thinks about the hair rings found on the body.
She thinks about Josef's description of the woman at the
bar. Light skinned. Then she pictures Mira. His bald head,

the way he stumbles, can't seem to get anything right, needs someone to tell him what to do and how to do it. She rereads the note and she knows.

TWENTY-TWO

NOMSULWA WAITS UNTIL SHE IS SAFELY OUTSIDE OF Phiri before she rips open the sealed police evidence bag. She lets the ring rest on the car seat beside her, too nervous to touch it just yet. Her driving is erratic, attention split between the road and the object beside her. It is like the water man's ring has a life of its own.

When she parks at the hotel she takes the ring, slips it in her pocket, and hurries through the lobby and into the elevator without being spotted by the front-desk staff. She travels up to Claire's floor and knocks on the door of her room.

Claire swings open the door and steps back, obviously surprised to see Nomsulwa again. Before she has a chance to say anything, Nomsulwa steps in, looks at the carefully folded piles of clothes on the floor next to the open suitcase, and then sits on the edge of the bed.

"What are you doing here?" Claire asks.

"You know nothing about me. Not really," Nomsulwa says.

"Look, I'm trying to see my way clear to leaving. I can't –"

"Maybe there are things you should know," Nomsulwa interrupts. "About me. About *my* father." Nomsulwa leans forward, holding her hands out in front of her, inviting

Claire to sit. "I won't take long, and then you can finish packing." Claire does as she's asked. She let's the door close and sits across from Nomsulwa.

Nomsulwa accepts this as permission. She takes a deep breath and begins the only story she can tell.

I WAS TEN THE FIRST TIME MY FATHER POINTED A gun at my mother. He was home from a campaign, that's what they called them, but I know now they were in hiding, planning to blow up industry targets, learning how to make bombs that were stable enough to transport. He had wandered in late the night before, gotten undressed, left his gun on the living-room table, and slept on the couch. I saw him first, woke him, and made him tea. I sat across from him, watching him sip it, letting him relax in the quiet room.

She took her time getting ready, as if to let my father know that we weren't waiting for him. His return was just another Saturday event. When she did enter, she was dressed simply, a forced smile pasted on her face. Even that disappeared when she saw the gun. She grabbed it, furious. She accused him of wanting me dead, of not caring if his own child lived or died. Why else would he bring a gun into this house, after he knew she had forbidden it.

At the word "forbid," my father lunged at my mother. No woman was going to tell him what to do. He wrestled the gun from her hand, breaking her finger, I imagine now, though she made very little noise when it happened. He cocked the gun, holding it in front of her, desperate to silence her no

287
–

matter what it took. But my mother kept insulting him. Her voice calmed. The tone got quiet. She didn't take her eyes off the gun. She told him that he wasn't welcome in her house, that there wasn't a place for him any more if he refused to take responsibility for the upkeep of his child, for my safety.

He was shaking with anger, finger on the trigger. I thought he was going to kill her, knew he was capable of it. But instead, as if giving us a gift, he uncocked the gun, slid it into his pants pocket, grabbed his jacket, and walked out.

My mother collapsed. She was crying. I went to help her with her hurt finger, but it was clear to me that her tears were more about his leaving than the pain in her hand. She brushed me away. I was glad to leave. I followed my father's path out the door.

I was mesmerized by him, couldn't see anything beyond his face and wanted nothing but the smell of leather that followed him everywhere. The few moments in which he was genuinely kind, when he helped me learn to pitch a cricket ball or tie my shoes, were all in Technicolor. Glorious. My mother was like a faded picture compared to him. Leaving her wasn't just easy. I had no choice.

He walked ahead of me and I liked it that way, knew that it was dangerous to get too close when he was in a mood like this. But eventually he stopped and waited for me to catch up, then went on more slowly so I was in step. When we were close to the town, he bent down and smoothed my braids.

He told me he loved me. And my mother too, if only she wouldn't make things so hard all the time. He told me he was leaving. And I asked him to come home soon, knowing that I had no effect on him.

Then he walked across the street, leaving me behind. He wasn't going yet. He wasn't due to leave until that night at least; they always travelled by night. But he was done with me. He found a friend at the grocery across the street, lit a cigarette. I stood watching him. He never once looked in my direction.

I don't know how long I was there for. But after at least an hour, my cousin came, sent by my mother, to see if I was okay. He was always trolling the streets for good games. Without him, my childhood would have been nothing but cleaning with my mother and schoolwork. I didn't want to take my eyes off my father, but Mira dragged me away from where I stood. He brought me to a nearby alley where his friends were hanging out.

These kids were tough. The oldest had a gun he carried with him everywhere, though I'd never seen him use it. In the alley, there were bullets strewn on the ground and the boys were sorting through them in a group. I knelt down to join, fascinated, until I was the only one left playing in the sand.

It wasn't until the oldest boy pointed the gun he had at me that I knew what I had to do.

I asked for the gun, and Mira encouraged the boy to hand it over. They went on playing, scuffling behind me, as I walked to the edge of the alley, right where the shadow's cover ended. I found a bullet in the sand, loaded the gun, and clicked the chamber. I knew how to handle the heavy thing as if by instinct, had seen too many people load guns too many times – my father just one of them. I knew he was standing close, across the street to the left. I raised the gun. He was there. I could feel him. Chatting and pulling on a cigarette, wasting time until he could leave for good.

I trained the gun on a dog across the way. I should have chosen a wall, a signpost, but something about the dog, about picking something living. I just knew it would matter to him. It would show him that I had real courage. I clicked the trigger twice, felt the empty response of the gun, clicked the trigger again and was surprised as the kickback bolted through my arm. The boys ran to where I was, but the dog barely moved. He was hit and fading. He looked behind him, turned to see the source of the pain. Then his head fell to the dust.

I didn't worry about the dog. I felt powerful, justified. All I could think about was finding my father, hoping beyond hope that he had seen what I had done. I was sure he would be proud. Sure he would march over and sweep me up in his arms and carry me to the house a hero. See my daughter, just like me, a fighter like me.

But he did not.

He looked at me, holding the gun in my hand still. He looked at the dog. He stamped out the end of his cigarette, nodded goodbye to his friend, and, as if none of us existed, he walked away.

His expression didn't change. I was left with all the feeling, pain in my arm and chest and eyes, and I felt like collapsing under it all. If my cousin hadn't dragged me home, I'm not sure I would ever have been able to leave that spot.

"MY FATHER WAS PART OF THE MK LEADERSHIP. HE travelled in for the Sasolburg attack. He met Walter Sisulu. He was a hero. That is what people understand. And that is what everyone remembers. Everyone but my mother and me."

Claire sits very still. Her eyes are full of sympathy, which is not the feeling Nomsulwa was hoping to inspire, the relief she had tried to bring to Claire. She speaks with more urgency. "You need to understand, the people who hate your father think of him only as the water man. They don't know what a good father he was to you. They missed that part of the story."

"Does it matter?" Claire's expression hardens.

"Does it matter that my father was a man who beat his wife and kid?" Nomsulwa stops, not believing that she has said this out loud. She feels like she might cry and takes a sharp breath in to stop the tears. This is not what she had planned. The ring is in her pocket. Now is the time to give it over. But Claire's hands are on her face and Nomsulwa can't move.

"You deserved better," Claire whispers, leaning in to Nomsulwa. Pressing her cheek to Nomsulwa's, letting her face stay there, as though to become accustomed to such closeness.

"So did you," Nomsulwa responds, unable to breathe. Claire kisses Nomsulwa's face, her forehead, her cheeks.

Claire exhales audibly. In that second, the sound of Claire's breath around her, Nomsulwa imagines the water man's daughter is hers.

Then she pulls away.

Claire stands, brushing Nomsulwa's hands off her shoulders, keeping her at a distance. "How can it be? How can a place have someone like you and also have people who –" Claire stops short, takes a breath, tries to blow out the anger. It doesn't seem to work. "How can people . . . cut a man's heart out after he's already dead . . . just for fun?" Her voice breaks completely.

Nomsulwa is not thinking. She watches Claire, but her mind is still in the moment when the girl was next to her, face close. "The 28s," she says, almost by rote.

"The men who killed my father." Claire sits back down on the bed, defeated.

Nomsulwa doesn't register the information right away. The 28s. Her mind is full of Claire's hands on her face and so the gang, the knowledge of the gang and what they did, stays as a lone thought for a second. Then she remembers the shreds of cloth in Mira's front yard, the panic Mira felt in the desert. She puts them all together. It seems impossible. He couldn't have done something so barbaric.

"You deserved better." Nomsulwa gives herself one last moment of peace, resting her lips against Claire's forehead, willing Claire's shaking body to quiet. Then she stands up, forces herself to back away, slings her bag over her shoulder, and surveys the room. She takes the ring out of her pocket and places it on the edge of the bed. She turns and walks out.

She doesn't look back. If she did, she wouldn't be able to let the water man's daughter go.

NOMSULWA MAKES IT OUT INTO THE OPEN AIR. She feels lighter without the ring, without the pipes, without Claire to anchor her. Even the pain in her chest from leaving Claire is an emptiness. Relish this freedom, she thinks. Because the other part of her knows that it cannot last long. The other part, the larger part of her, realizes what has been done. What Mira did for her. How he took the knife from his family's kitchen, took a rock from the lot next door, used all this strength to open the body, break through skin and muscle and bone and remove the heart. Against her will she visualizes every second, every detail of the night. She imagines her cousin, knife in hand, arms raised over the body underneath, the flesh split apart, revealing coagulated mounds of blood and tissue. He strikes, his sweat mixing with blood in the crevice of the water man's chest.

He did this for her. Sacrificed everything for her.

Nomsulwa gets into her car. She drives the highway back to Phiri maybe for the last time. She passes her township's streets with a new appreciation, letting the personality of each corner, each store and shebeen, wash over her. She tries to soak it all in, to accept what is to come. She tries to relax as she turns the corner and pulls into the parking lot of the Phiri police station. There isn't much to lose now.

There isn't much she is giving up. At least that's what Nomsulwa tells herself when she knocks on the door to Zembe's office, walks in without an invitation, and sits down.

"I know what happened to the water man," she begins.

Zembe stands and closes the door without a word.

TWENTY-THREE

THE RAIN GOD SENT DOWN SHEETS OF WATER TO FILL THE
*riverbed. The water flowed clear, past the mothers gathering
reeds for their roofs and baskets, past the boys tossing rocks
across the dip to screaming girls trailing bright cloth. The village thanked the Rain God. They pulled large basins to the
river's edge and sank them under the water. The basins filled,
and men and women hauled the great vats up the bank and to
their homes. They drank the water freely, they mixed it with
their corn flour for bread and cakes, they poured it over their
parched bodies.*

*Men noticed the power the rain gave the great bull. They
noticed and they wanted it for themselves. So they took the water
from the river and directed it through shiny silver pipes and let
it fall from hard metal faucets into the villagers' waiting basins.
In return, the village gave the men gifts, and songs and stories
were created to honour those who had harnessed the water.*

*But soon the gifts ran out. The people's throats grew too dry
to sing. The pipes held the water fast. And the villagers died one
by one until there was no one left who remembered the night the
Rain God transformed himself into a great bull and descended
to earth on a bolt of lightning.*

No one left who remembered what the girl had sacrificed, and how, in the end, it had not been enough.

THIS IS HOW SHE REMEMBERS IT: VIVID, SHARPLY detailed. It will not fade.

Nomsulwa sinks into the sticky surface of the couch – May has not brought relief from the heat. Last night's pipe "recovery" and today's meeting and march through downtown have taken their toll and she feels the shake of exhaustion in every muscle of her body. Mira, across from her, holds Pim's hand, clutches it hard enough that Nomsulwa can see in the grip all his investment in the woman next to him. He retells, for the second time, the way he had led a toyi toyi at that day's protest. The way the group of PCF protestors had danced in front of the water cannons and the police officers' decision to step aside when they reached the City Hall.

The kettle rattles on the stove and Pim gets up to pour the water. Mira closes his eyes for a second, seeming to relish the sounds of the household. Nomsulwa watches the happy man in front of her.

They are all sipping deep-red tea when Aluta, Pim's oldest, emerges from another room, done up in makeup and tight, bright clothes. She is fifteen, but she looks younger with all the blush and eyeshadow she has put on. Pim freezes mid-sip.

"Get yourself back in your room and put on some clothes."

"I'm going out."

296
–

"Not likely."

Another girl, a friend from school, steps up behind Aluta. "We are just going to visit with some friends in the city. This is what everyone is wearing."

"You're not dressed like that," Pim accuses the friend who is wearing simple jeans and a sweatshirt.

"I'm on my way home now to change."

"All right, then. Call your mother and let me talk to her about these plans you say you have." Pim puts her hands on her hips.

297

–

"Yeah, you could do that." Aluta drags her friend through the living room. "If what you thought mattered at all."

She leaves and marches down the block. Pim rushes after, yells out to her daughter, but Aluta keeps walking, long, awkward steps in heels too high for her.

At the front door Nomsulwa puts a consoling arm around Pim's shoulders. "Don't worry. Mira will go with her to the city. He'll keep an eye on her."

Mira rolls his eyes, but Nomsulwa knows he'll go. He understands Pim won't relax until Aluta's home. He grabs his stuff and leaves, following the girls down the street.

IT IS BARELY TEN AT NIGHT WHEN NOMSULWA GETS a call from Mira telling her to come to Skybar, a club downtown. He's spent his taxi money and they're in trouble.

She doesn't pause to finish her drink. She collects her bag, straightens her pants and shirt, and nods goodbye to the shebeen owner. She gets into her car and begins the drive to the club district. The night is black, no moon, and the few street lamps seem to flicker more than usual. Nomsulwa hopes she can avoid the huge potholes and sharp breaks in the road by memory. The drive passes too slowly. She is sweating when she finally arrives.

Mira is standing outside the club holding Aluta in his arms. She stares over his shoulder, immobile. Nomsulwa approaches.

"What happened? What happened to her?"

Mira's eyes are wide. "A man, in the club, a white man, he took her into his minibus and . . ."

His voice fades out, but it doesn't matter. Nomsulwa can see the blood dried on Aluta's lip, the wrinkled fabric of her clothes.

"Where were you? Why weren't you watching her?"

"I . . . was. I turned around for a minute and . . . she was in a big group . . . it was safe."

"Where is he? What does he look like? Did she describe him?"

"The American, she says it was an American. White. Blond hair."

Nomsulwa doesn't put her hand on Aluta's shoulder to soothe her. She doesn't hug Mira or forgive him for his carelessness. She walks into the club and begins to circle the room.

In the corner, an Indian man chats up a waitress. His head is bald and he stares at the woman's breasts as he speaks. Directly to his right, a line of young coloured boys lean against the wall smoking cigarettes and eyeing the dance floor. There is a thicket of black men and young girls grinding to the music. The only white man in the bar is seated behind the gyrating throng, dishevelled and drunk. His eyes swim, lids close intermittently. His skin glows red, pulsing red in his cheeks and neck. Nomsulwa imagines the red head exploding. She walks to the corner of the room and leans against a wall, blending in with the crowd.

The Indian man comes close to her target.

"Ready to go?" he asks.

"Yes. Please."

The men wave their bills at the waitress and stumble out of the club. Nomsulwa watches, following cautiously. The men climb into a white minibus with an older man half-asleep at the wheel. Nomsulwa repeats the licence plate to herself enough times to commit it to memory and then runs back over to her cousin.

"Go now, Mira. Take her home. Here are my keys. The car is over there."

"Did you find him, Nomsulwa? Did you beat him good? Did you get him for what he did?" Mira rambles, face pressed into Aluta's hair.

"Shhh now, Mira. She's going to need her sleep. I'll handle it, I promise."

Nomsulwa leaves Mira and Aluta and starts weaving through the minibuses and limousines. Club patrons are exiting the buildings alongside the street and stumbling into their rides home. Nomsulwa spots the Indian man holding the American as he leans out the side of the moving van. He throws up into the street and the wind whisks away all traces. Nomsulwa runs to the curb and hails a taxi, one of the few unchartered rides on the strip. She orders the driver, an older man with more than one cross hanging from his rear-view mirror, to head to the hotel row in the downtown business district. He nods and cuts into the stream of traffic entering the highway, taking the same route, Nomsulwa hopes, as the white minibus. It's almost eleven. Her mind is racing, the image of Aluta with her bloody lip becomes a filter through which she sees the highway split in two and her exit for hotel row coming close on her right.

Once the tall buildings close in, the taxi slows down.

"Where to, sisi?" the driver asks.

"Just keep moving, slowly. I'll tell you when we're there." Nomsulwa scans the licence plates of the vehicles stationed in front of the hotels. Each building is more impressive than the next. Grey and huge, they flutter their flags of South Africa, England, and America.

Halfway down the block, Nomsulwa sees it. The driver is bent over, straining to pull something out of the back of his minibus. She double-checks the plate numbers, thankful that the downtown rejuvenation project came with increased enforcement of illegal taxis. A few years ago, most of the minibuses had no plates at all. The white man stumbles out, followed by the Indian. She hands the driver money and steps out of the car.

Her hands are shaking as she rolls up the black shirt she is wearing so that her midsection shows. She ruffles her twisted hair and lets it fall in front of her eyes. The top is not cut low enough to show her breasts, but it is tight, and she hopes that is sufficient. When she walks up the steps to the front entrance of the hotel, the doorman smiles at her and turns to the side, as if to say, "It's your time of night now, sweetheart. Good luck."

The lobby of the Central Sun is blistering with lights. Nomsulwa winks at the boy manning the front desk and murmurs her excuse, "Meeting a colleague for drinks." Her accent, put on to impress, makes the word lengthen to sound more like "*caawleargue.*" He nods and returns to his paperwork, too used to the girls in and out of the hotel after hours.

Nomsulwa checks the lobby first. She's only minutes behind the white man, hopes he has not yet made it to his room. The elevator bank is silent, no faint ding of doors opening on a higher floor. She worries about looking lost and so holds her shoulders back and saunters into the bar area, left of the main lobby, where tables line a mirrored, circular room. They are covered in white tablecloths hanging at precise ninety-degree angles. At each setting, a wine glass cradles an artfully folded napkin. There are quite a few patrons still scattered around the room. A couple lean into their cocktails. A group of four men sit two tables away. They argue loudly and slam the table, making the napkins jump.

Nomsulwa approaches the bar. In front of her, the Indian man is fussing over the drunk American. He tugs on his shirt almost like a child nervous about upsetting his parent.

"Piss off, Alvin, I want to have a drink."

"Are you sure that's a good idea? It's already been a long night."

"You're the one who persuaded me to go out. I was the one who wanted to go to bed!!" The white man yells this.

"We should get you up to your room. Here, I'll take you." He moves to help the American off the stool.

302

"No!" Several people at the bar look around to see what the disturbance is. But quickly the two men are drowned out by an uproar from the room behind them. The female bartender catches a knowing look from her male counterpart and saunters over to the table of men. She leans over the group, lets her breasts peek out at them, then focuses on the ringleader, mussing his hair and whispering in his ear. Eventually, he follows her out towards the elevators. The other three wear big grins but are now quiet.

"Look. Let's meet tomorrow in the office when we both feel better," the Indian man says.

"You were angry about how I handled that meeting, how I upstaged you. But we had to be tough. We *had* to tell them that the company was serious about getting the water system in the ground by the deadline. We have to meet that deadline!"

"I wasn't angry."

"Yes you were and so you punished me."

"This is insane, Peter." The Indian raises his voice. "You need to take yourself to bed."

"You're going to pay for this. Whoever put you in charge of this project is going to hear from me."

The room becomes clearer, brighter. Nomsulwa feels rage fill her. They are water men. Aluta's face becomes so many faces: the mamas who sing in her community centre, the children who dip buckets into dirty gutters next to wells no one can afford to use anymore.

"I'm done," the Indian announces before leaving the bar. Nomsulwa takes his seat quickly and turns slightly away from the American to face a man in a grey suit speaking into his cellphone. The light from the screen glows on the edges of his ear. The American takes another sip from his glass. The remaining bartender stands expectantly in front of Nomsulwa and she orders a beer.

"Drink up, sis, we're closing soon," he says as he hands her a cold bottle.

The American shifts and pushes back from the bar. He unsteadily makes his way to the far corner of the room. Nomsulwa waits a moment, then she throws down ten rand and stuffs the receipt in the pocket of her shirt.

The men's bathroom door has shut by the time Nomsulwa arrives in the dead-end alcove. She doesn't hesitate outside but walks through, under the flowery "Monsieurs" written in gold paint. There is a sharp corner, hiding the interior. She eases the door closed, giving away nothing as she slips in and around.

The American stands at a sink, water running, face and collar wet. He stares in the mirror, letting the tap empty into

303
–

the porcelain bowl. Nomsulwa walks up to the row of sinks and, taking a brass knob in each hand, turns on another faucet, and then another. The sound of running water grows and makes the American look around. He opens his mouth and blinks rapidly at the woman next to him.

He makes a move to leave. Nomsulwa blocks his path.

"You forgot to turn it off," she says.

"Wha?" The American tries to push past but almost loses his balance. He straightens and attempts to navigate around her.

"The tap." She points calmly to the first sink.

The American looks where she points, then shakes his head and pushes her hard, trying to shove her out of the way.

She lunges as soon as his hands make contact with her shirt. She catches his collar and pushes him up against the wall to their right. The edge of the sink stops his back and bends him so his face is forced to look up at his attacker. Though she is smaller than he is, he is unsteady on his feet, alcohol slowing him down.

She begins to speak softly, whispering in his ear. "You think it's okay to force little girls to lie with you you hit her you let her bleed you locked her in the car you let her bleed, you hit you think it's okay to force little girls to –" Her grip tightens around his collar. She is no longer sure if she is holding on to cloth or folds of skin. Tighter. Anger is in Nomsulwa's hands, in her legs, pushing against the man's crotch. *Water man*, Nomsulwa thinks. *Water man* is all she can think.

The man thrusts his weight back into her, lifting himself off the sink, but the floor, now slick with water, causes him to lose his footing. Nomsulwa braces herself for the fall and ducks into the thick body in her arms. She hears the clear hard sound of skull on porcelain as they drop and then sees the water man rest limp on the floor. Blood drips out of a small cut on his head. It slips out of his ear and into a small pool around them, turning the floor a delicate pink.

305

NOMSULWA STARES AT THE MAN NEXT TO HER, HER body taut and waiting for him to lunge. She watches for movement, for the fight to resume, but he remains still. Her first feeling is of relief, relief for her own escape without confrontation, without injury. He could cry out at any moment and she would be arrested and thrown in jail for years after this kind of trespass. But he doesn't call out. And soon the relief fades.

She stands up straight. A pool of water is rising around her shoes. The sound of the running water fills all the empty space around them and she starts to shake. She quickly closes the taps and tugs the man's body. She drags him as best she can into the corner stall, panting, despite the short distance and the way the man's pants slide over the wet floor when she lifts his shoulders. When she hears a knock and then the sound of the door opening, her breathing stops altogether.

"Hallo?" The bartender's voice wraps around the corner. "We're closing up now. Anyone here?" The cursory check.

There is a pause. Then the door closes again. Nomsulwa buckles, almost sitting on the body beneath her. She can't stop shaking.

Nomsulwa counts the breaths as though she is counting seconds. When she can't stand the wait any longer, she steps carefully away from the stall and sneaks a look out the bathroom door. The bar is silent. She braves a few steps farther and sees that the dining room is closed up and pitch-black. She takes her cellphone from her jacket pocket and, fingers trembling, punches in her cousin's number.

"Ku-late! *It's late!* Where are you?"

"Hurry, Mira. I've done something . . . I need help."

Nomsulwa checks the bar exit and finds the broad wooden doors closed and locked for the night. She has to find another way out.

Behind the bar she spots a dolly and wheels it to the bathroom. The body is so heavy. That is all she can think: the heaviness of death. When she was struggling with him he didn't seem as bulky. He seemed light, fragile; now it takes all her strength to lift one leg and then the other up a few inches. When his torso is half on the dolly, she begins to push him out of the bathroom. A leg catches on the door, snagging the body, threatening to push the water man off completely. She shifts the leg and rebalances her load.

There is a service door in the back of the dining room leading into a narrow alleyway behind the kitchen. She pauses, knocks on the door, hoping that Mira has arrived.

There is a faint knock back. She mutters to herself, like she's saying a prayer. Then she pushes the door open.

Rats scurry away from her feet as she drags the body into the warm night air. How can her story of what really happened be believed? How can she be forgiven? Mira begins single-handedly moving the dolly towards the car. She hears police sirens and loud yelling. Mira shakes her shoulder, bringing her back to the silence around her.

"Camon, sisi!"

She thinks she feels the body jerk, looks down, and sees a stolid face, round eyes, calm and still. *Don't look down again.*

Mira lifts the body and cradles it into the back seat of the car. Nomsulwa gets in the passenger side. Her sweat has dried to a cold cake on her chest and bare arms. She has lost the ability to think, her body acting as if controlled by something outside herself. She is cold and then too hot and then freezing again.

They drive on in silence, nothing but a taxi and a few anonymous dark cars left in the hotel district. Eventually they take the exit towards Phiri and head down the street that leads to Nomsulwa's house. When she starts to protest, Mira shushes her, assuring her that he has a plan. He takes a turn and ends up in the driveway on his family's property.

He opens the back door, drags out the body, and waits for Nomsulwa to follow. She pauses for a moment, breathes, gets her bearings.

Mira lifts the shoulders and Nomsulwa picks up the dangling feet and legs. They struggle with the weight, stumble in the shadows, careful to stay in the ditched edges of the road where the grass covers their lower torsos and their cargo.

At a T junction, Nomsulwa stops. Mira urges her on.

"Keep going, there is a hidden yard a small ways up this block. We will go there."

She nods, resigned, and continues down the road.

When they arrive, Mira leads them to the middle of the sandy plot. He gently lays down his half of the body and she does the same. She looks around her, notices that there are no windows looking out over this one corner of her township. A neighbour's washing hangs on a thin line of string above them, shielding them from the street.

"Let's get out of here," Nomsulwa whispers urgently, becoming a little more herself, returning to the role of elder and leader.

"No." Mira looks directly at her, focuses in on her like there is nothing else around him. "You have to go home and leave me here."

"What?"

"You have to go home. Clean up. Burn your clothes and leave me here. I'll handle everything else."

"What are you talking about? We need to scour the car, get rid of any evidence. Let's get out of here!" Nomsulwa tries to take Mira's arm.

He reacts by snatching her clothes and dragging her in close to his face. His eyes are sunken from exhaustion, his breath sour from sleep, he whispers very quietly, "Go. I am handling it." Nomsulwa feels suddenly afraid of the boy she loves so much. He gives her a slight shove backwards. Then stands waiting for her to obey.

Nomsulwa turns away from the body; she turns away from her cousin, forcing herself into the black night. She leaves Mira alone in the sandy yard.

TWO HOURS LATER SHE IS SITTING ON HER FRONT step. It is getting light out, and it is certainly getting cold. She is shivering, rocking back and forth, her thin clothes doing little to protect her. Mira walks towards her, a black reed swaying in the milky light. His face, when he gets close enough, is streaked with sand and drawn tight. He comes and sits beside Nomsulwa without a word.

Nomsulwa watches the sun rise. She holds her hands in the growing brightness around her, willing the warm rays to burn them clean. They get hotter, they grow dryer and less pliable, less strong and unwieldy. They become her hands again and that is, in some ways, the worst part.

THE NEXT MORNING, THE MAID CLEANS THE MEN'S washroom first. There is a pool of dirty water on the far side of the floor, under the row of sinks, that didn't make its way to the large drain in the middle of the room. She takes out the mop, soaks up the liquid, and empties it into her bucket.

Just outside the door of the farthest stall is a dried stain, pink-brown like vomit. She sprays the tile with ammonia and wipes it clean. *Another rich man who can't hold his liquor,* she thinks as she works.

By the time the early breakfast is served, the bathroom sparkles like new.

TWENTY-FOUR

ZEMBE MEETS SIPHO IN HIS OFFICE. SHE IS WEARING her good suit. She carries the file and fiddles with the thick pile of papers.

The secretary, smug the last time Zembe waited next to her desk, is now very officious, seems almost intimidated. After only a few minutes, Zembe is ushered inside.

Sipho is not alone in the room. One of the white senior officials from the meeting over three weeks earlier has beaten her here. She nods a greeting to both men and then places the file on the desk.

"We've solved the Matthews case."

"I'm listening," Sipho says, unable to keep the smile out of his eyes. Excitement emanates from the white man, too, as he reaches for the file.

"It's not as sound as I'd like. We found evidence that Matthews was lured from the hotel. He was then definitely transported into the township where he was killed and dumped."

Zembe pauses, not sure she is ready for this. But then she thinks about the girl at the hotel and in the car, hair tied back, face contorted with anger. She thinks about that same face leading marches through the government compound down-town, peering over trenches filled with company steel, ferrying fresh water to Zembe's neighbours when their water allotment has run out. She thinks about her tending to her sick mother, and to Claire Matthews. She has chosen to protect Nomsulwa, no matter the cost. She takes a deep breath.

"There were prostitutes at the bar that Matthews was at before he was killed. One in particular that Matthews took a liking to. That prostitute has ties to the 28s, to Kholizwe."

The white man slams down his hand in triumph.

Sipho is more measured in his response. He looks intently at Zembe. "I thought there was no way Kholizwe was responsible for this. Isn't that what you told me?"

"I was wrong. I jumped to conclusions too early."

"And the man from the water movement, the PCF? He was our chief suspect . . ." Sipho presses further.

"He was, but he has been cleared. There is no way he was anywhere near the hotel that night. The blood evidence was all on the route from Tiger's shebeen, where Kholizwe is based, to the dump site."

"No other eyewitnesses? Have you found the car? A prostitute left with a white man from a fancy hotel and no one saw?"

"Like I said, it's not perfect."

The white man clears his throat and looks pointedly at Sipho. "I think we can make it work."

Sipho looks skeptical, but doesn't object. He knows, as Zembe knows, that the department's desperation encourages a resolution. There's enough power behind the water company that even a thin case will almost certainly find its way successfully through the court system. The strings that no one would pull when Zembe arrested Kholizwe four years ago are at their disposal now that they have the backing of the water company.

Zembe tries to focus on this. She tries to think of the gratitude she now feels for the chance to arrest Kholizwe. She tries to forget about how she destroyed the note from the taxi company; how Nomsulwa had come to her office after the Matthews girl had left and had offered herself, told the truth. She had told Nomsulwa she was upset, to go home. They would discuss the matter in a few days, when things were more clear. But she made no record of their meeting and left all mention of Nomsulwa out of the file.

She added a page to the file instead. An affidavit from Councillor Phadi describing the woman he saw disappear with Matthews: one paragraph detailing how Matthews was seen with a well-known prostitute brought by Mandla, but who was owned by the 28s.

Zembe had sent Tosh to Phadi's house with the understanding that the entire case rested on linking a certain woman with Matthews at the hotel. She explained how close they were to getting this monster off the street. He returned with a neatly written statement confirming exactly what Zembe needed. He was eager and ready to please, his face full of success. Zembe didn't ask him how he did it. She is better off not knowing.

"Then let's arrest him." Sipho gives in and pushes his chair back. "You have a location, I presume?" he asks Zembe.

"The shebeen, Tiger's. He is at his base now."

Sipho picks up the phone and mumbles directions to his secretary. He waits a moment on hold and then begins to dictate orders into the phone.

Zembe waits. Sipho hangs up and lifts his eyes to hers.

"We'll meet four national cars on the corner two blocks from the shebeen in an hour. Legal is drawing up the warrant now. They'll need you to fax over the affidavit right away. Call one of your buggies to come as backup and make sure they know what they're up against."

Zembe nods and turns to leave. Sipho stops her.

"Wait. Leave the file here. I'll need to look through it."

Zembe does as she's told. "I assume *you'll* fax the affidavit, then?"

"Yes. Go get your men ready."

ZEMBE GROWS NERVOUS AS SHE DRIVES BACK TO THE township. She has an urge to take a detour, to enter the wide atrium of her church and prepare herself. She doesn't know what to expect and half hopes that Sipho will find an anomaly in the file and call the whole thing off. She needs a moment to collect herself, find the certainty she is used to feeling.

But she drives directly to the station. The main room is full of officers on their lunch break, laughing with one another, most seated around the main table. The older men shout, slapping each other on the back with each joke. Zembe approaches Tosh and two friends quietly eating sandwiches of French fries and ketchup in hamburger buns.

"You expect to do police work on a meal like that?"

Tosh defends his lunch. "It's good. And I haven't had any problems keeping up with my shift. None of us have."

"Then prove it. Meet me outside with a buggy."

"Where are we going?" another asks, mouth still full and outlined in a ring of red.

"Arresting Kholizwe."

All three boys stop chewing. They put their sandwiches down, wipe their hands and mouths on thin napkins.

"National gave us the go-ahead based on the affidavit?" Tosh asks, beaming with pride.

Zembe nods her head. Her officers spring into action. They bustle about the main station room collecting their holsters, badges, straightening shirts and ties. Tosh stoops to retie his boots.

Zembe watches them for a moment before closing the door to her small office. She puts her second gun in its holster and changes into the black-crested jacket of her SAPS uniform. She reties her hair away from her face and takes off her watch and jewellery. Her motions are methodical; she wills herself not to feel anxiety or doubt. She prays for the strength to remain confident and composed. Then she prays for the safety of her officers.

When they arrive at the meeting place, the national cars are already there. Zembe steps out of the buggy and meets Sipho on the dusty street corner.

"We're bringing attention to ourselves stopping this close to his location," Zembe says, before Sipho has a chance to speak.

"We're moving out now. Coming in from all directions. I want you to follow me and approach from the front."

Zembe gets back in the car and starts the engine up. They round the corner and drive down a small street, keeping the front door of Tiger's shebeen in their sights. The building looks deserted. Nothing moves, even when all five cars pull up and Sipho gets out from behind his door. He's begun to motion the left flank of national's men to move in when a single shot is launched from a window of the shebeen and hits the tire of his car. The rubber wheel lets out a slow, wheezing sound. No one moves. Zembe is the first to act.

"Tosh, go get the others and make your way around the perimeter. We need to secure the back. Sipho, keep them busy up front. Shoot high, keep them distracted, not dead."

She crouches behind her three officers and they use the cover of the police cars to break the direct line from them to the front door. The national team is positioned behind the bodies of the buggies, using the tires and the lengths of the car frames as protection. They are already returning fire. Zembe keeps low, counting on the distance between her team and the walls of Tiger's to avoid being hit while moving. The noise of gunfire is more rapid now. The sound is accented only by breaking glass and a few shouts from both the men outside of Tiger's and the men scrambling inside the shebeen.

Zembe gets to the side wall of the shebeen and looks back to see two national officers following her team. They have their guns drawn, their bodies protected by helmets and vests. Seeing their signal to fall back, Zembe motions for her own men to move aside and let them pass. Tosh and the others crouch low in the surrounding grass, ready to cover them on their entrance. She trains her gun on the lone window in the back. The national men move forward. A face appears and Zembe shoots, missing the small target but pushing the gunman back out of sight. The two lead officers push through the door, guns constantly firing.

She hears a shout from her left and sees Tosh topple, clutching his neck. She drops her gun, forgetting about the men inside. The gouge in his collarbone is small, a clean shot through the skin, but the amount of blood tells Zembe that something is seriously wrong. Tosh grips his body. He tries to sit up. He whacks Zembe's hand away as she attempts to stop the bleeding. But soon his arms become slack. Her men keep firing. Sounds of yelling and the smell of smoke surround her.

Zembe can see nothing but the boy lying there. Then she realizes that the gunfire has stopped. She screams for help and immediately four men lift Tosh and bring him out in front to the bullet-ridden police buggies. She doesn't wait to watch them load him into the back seat and drive off. She goes directly to the door of Tiger's and looks in. There are three men on the floor and at least five national officers moving debris around. Zembe doesn't recognize two of

317

–

the fallen men. They look to be in their early twenties. Both have gunshot wounds in multiple places. One of them whimpers a little. An officer bends down and takes his pulse. He calls outside.

Zembe moves towards the third body, farthest from either door. Kholizwe has only one wound, a single hole between the eyes. Shot from close range.

318
–

THE AMANZI OFFICE SENDS A LETTER OF COMMENDA-tion to Zembe. They will, no doubt, call the Matthews girl and inform her that her father's murderer was killed while resisting arrest. Zembe hopes this gives her some peace.

Sipho does not seem as thrilled with Zembe's work as the water company. Three days after the botched arrest, he shows up at Zembe's office. His black suit looks as though it weighs him down. She closes the door behind him. Sipho lays the file down in front of her.

"The case was shit."

"I didn't tell you to kill him. I was ready to play this one out in court."

"It's a good thing they had different orders. We would have lost."

"I'm burying an officer today. Did you really come all this way to berate me about a file that's closed?"

"No. I came for the funeral. And to give you this." He deposits the morning's paper on her desk.

"I have that. I picked it up on my way to work. I've seen the article about Tosh."

"That's not what I want you to look at." Sipho flips through and stops on a small story next to a black-and-white photo in the front section. Zembe leans in and begins to read.

> The Phiri Community Forum held a rally yesterday, shutting down most of downtown Johannesburg. Over five thousand women and children swarmed the steps of the Mayor's office building, blocking traffic in both directions. Their demand: a grant for the township of Victoria – recently hit with an outbreak of cholera. Nomsulwa Sithu, a spokeswoman for the PCF, told reporters that a mere 25,000 rand would be enough to save the entire community from certain death. The Mayor's office did not release a comment regarding the social unrest, but sources inside the municipal building say that negotiations are underway for temporary assistance . . .

ZEMBE STOPS READING. THE SORROW OF TOSH'S death is replaced momentarily with pride – Nomsulwa will make the water run. But Sipho is reading over her shoulder, and Zembe's feeling of success evaporates in his hot breath on her neck.

"How is it that we never connected her to the recovered pipes?" he asks with an edge to his voice.

"We had no evidence –"

"Well, that didn't stop you in the Matthews case, now did it?"

"The funeral is today. I don't have time to rehash a case that is closed. You got your pipes, deal with the witch hunt for the PCF another day."

"We're not done with her, or her gang. I'll be expecting your full cooperation on this in the future."

Sipho walks out without giving Zembe a chance to respond. She finishes reading the story, puts on her own black jacket, and prepares herself for church.

320

—

THE PASTOR AT THE BAPTIST NAZARETH CHURCH lets Tosh's father lead the service. His wife and remaining son scream their eulogy as if screaming will keep the tears at bay. The crowd of friends and officers returns the cry to the speakers. They toss the grief back and forth, reducing its size and power each time. Zembe stays tucked at the back of the room on her knees in fervent prayer, begging for forgiveness.

ACKNOWLEDGEMENTS

I learned a great deal about writing, story, and the process   323
of putting a book together from the friendship of Louise   –
Dennys, Ric Young, Ann Marie MacDonald, Alisa Palmer,
Naomi Klein, Avi Lewis, Patricia Rozema, Lesley Barber,
Paula Todd, Anne Greene, and Jane Saks.

Michael Helm, Anne Greene, Harriet Sachs, Clayton
Ruby, Louise Dennys, Karen Connelly, Karen Wookey,
Paula Todd, and Jane Saks read early drafts of this book.
Their feedback and patience was invaluable. My agent,
Jackie Kaiser, took me in and found a home for this book
against impossible odds. Grateful thanks to my editor, Lara
Hinchberger, and to Ellen Seligman and Kendra Ward, for
all their help and support.

The stories and events in this book were inspired by
research done in South Africa in 2003 and 2004. That
research, and my time there, could not have been as rich
and rewarding without the staff at Schools for International
Training, Zed McGladdery, Shane Duffy and Nomawethu
Fonya, and the people who took me in during my stay in Cape
Town and Johannesburg, Yolisa Cuku, Litha Cuku, Alutta
Cuku, Mira Cuku, Virginia Setshedi, Nomfundo Setshedi,

Relebogile Setshedi, and Tracey Fared. Many women involved in the anti-privatization movement talked to me about their experiences, including Mama Dalina, Hameeda Deedat, Linah Gcumisa, Bongani Lubisi, Zodwa Madiba, Zanele Mahamba, Elizabeth Mokgatle, Eunice Mthembu, Florence Nkwashu, Maniera Peters, Sindiswa Titi, and Nonhlanhla Vilakazi. Victor Lakay and Alvin Anthony helped shape my research. The Zulu translations in this book were completed with the help of Mpume Nkosi and Hlonipha Mokoena. Mistakes or liberties taken are entirely my own.

This project has taken many years and, so, it is the product of many years of support and love from my family and friends. My sister, Kate Ruby-Sachs, encouraged me from the beginning. My parents and grandparents, Geoffrey and Pamela Sachs, gave me the freedom and the confidence to pursue the writing pipe dream. I owe a debt of gratitude to those listed above, as well as to Jane Sachs, Andreas Agas, Georgia Sachs-Agas, Romie Sachs-Devere, Simon Sachs, Danette MacKay, Charlotte Sachs, Adrienne Sachs, Tony Sachs, Joyce Cohen, Bailey Cohen-Krichevsky, Vilma DaSilva, Rachel Sutherland, Betty Orr, Nancy Goodman, Brent Knazan, Frank Addario, Heidi Rubin, Marial Addario, Katie McKenna, Christin Baker, Deb Mell, Brian Blair, Nicole Schmidt, Jackie Pye, Liana Buccieri, Chad Kampe, Montana Burnett, Nicole Bashor, Olivia St. Clair, Nicole Naghi, Jackie Tate, Rick Salter, Liora Salter, Prerna Tomar, Jacoba Rozema-Barber, Caitlin Snow, Alex Leo, Betsy Ware-Fippinger,

Regan Doody, Jean Friedman-Rudovsky, Shireen Tawil, Christopher Kaminstein, Daniel Naymark, Joanna Lambert, Stuart McLean, Max Mishler, Ron Murphy, Ashley Peoples, Sarah Polley, Moran Sadeh, Brian Shiller, Stacy Zosky, Mandy Machin, Harvey Strosberg, Jay and Jordana Strosberg, Sharon Bedard, Jorge Soni, Ariel Lewiton-Lown, Kathleen Trotter, and my friends and colleagues at Avaaz.

Jane Saks

EMMA RUBY-SACHS's journalism has been published in *The Nation* and *The Huffington Post*. A graduate of Wesleyan University and the University of Toronto law school, Emma lived in South Africa for periods in 2003 and 2004 while studying. She has worked as a civil litigator in Windsor and Toronto and currently works with Avaaz, a progressive online organization. *The Water Man's Daughter* is her first novel. Born in Toronto, Emma lives in Chicago. Visit her website at www.emmarubysachs.com.